IRISH REIGN

IRISH REIGN

A DIAMOND RING DARK ROMANCE

THE IRISH MOB TRILOGY
BOOK 3

ALIX KEY

DIAMOND
FREEPORT PRESS

Published by Diamond Freeport Press
P.O. Box 42133, Arlington, VA 22204

ISBN 978-1-95018-474-3

Discover other titles by Alix Key at www.alixkey.com

091825ak

ALSO BY ALIX KEY

Find a complete, up-to-date list of Alix's books at www.alixkey.com.

The Kidnapped Series

Diamond Solitaire

Rough Diamond

Conflict Diamond

Priceless Diamond

The Irish Mob Trilogy

Irish Brute

Irish Vice

Irish Reign

The Boston Mob Trilogy

Her Irish Savage

Her Irish Protector

Her Irish King

The Taming the Mob Princess Trilogy

Taken Enemy

Twisted Enemy

Tamed Enemy

The Sinful Mafia Series

Sinful Mafia Santa

Sinful Mafia Deception

Sinful Mafia Seduction

Sinful Mafia Salvation

WORD OF WARNING

Irish Reign **is a dark romance.**

It contains hard-to-read scenes, graphic language, and explicit sexual content.

A complete list of potential triggers can be found at:

https://alixkey.com/books/irish-mob-trilogy/

Please don't read this book if you are sensitive to any of those triggers. But if you believe in the power of true love to bring joy and fulfillment to consenting adults, then this is the book for you.

Welcome to the Diamond Ring.

THE IRISH MOB SERIES, A RECAP

Have you read *Irish Brute* and *Irish Vice*, the first two books in the Irish Mob Series?

You can get your copies by typing

https://alixkey.com/PB4US
and
https://alixkey.com/PB5US

into your phone or computer browser.

If you don't want to read them—or if it's been a while—here's a quick summary of what happens in *Irish Brute* and *Irish Vice* (minus, of course, the spicy scenes!)

Having successfully represented Irish mob boss Braiden Kelly at a tax hearing, lawyer Samantha Mott receives a phone call from her cousin, who is being attacked by her Mafia kingpin husband, Antonio Russo. Samantha hears Russo murder her cousin in a horrific way.

Braiden drives a devastated Samantha home through a massive winter storm. The following morning, Russo insists that Samantha marry him, but Braiden intervenes, claiming he and Samantha are engaged.

Braiden and Samantha marry, although he secretly arranges for a defrocked priest to conduct the ceremony. They live at Thornfield Hall, accompanied by super-competent Fairfax (Braiden's chief of staff), mute Aiofe (Braiden's ward), and creepy Grace (Aiofe's nurse).

Samantha, still working for the tax-haven freeport, lives with strict self-imposed limits—only wearing black and white, never indulging in anything soft or feminine—to atone for something terrible she did "That Night", eleven years ago.

Braiden adds his own house rules: Samantha must never touch the door that leads to the mansion's third floor. Also, she must eat breakfast every morning, end the workday by six o'clock, and wear pretty floral skirts after hours (without panties!) Even as Samantha thrives under Braiden's imposed structure, she discovers the confusing pleasure of being punished for breaking his rules.

As Braiden and Samantha's relationship heats up, so does the gang war between Braiden and Russo. Russo attempts to blackmail Samantha with proof of what she did That Night, demanding that she give him Braiden's business contacts. Samantha resolves to face the consequences for her long-ago mistake instead of betraying her husband.

Braiden's boss in the Grand Irish Union, Kieran Ingram, forces him into humiliating peace talks with Russo. Moreover, Russo discloses Samantha's secret: While driving drunk and high, she killed three people in a hit-and-run crash.

Shaken by Russo's growing power, Braiden and Samantha turn on each other. Samantha flees Thornfield, seeking shelter in a cottage on the tax haven grounds. Miserable without each other, they become resigned to separation.

But when Braiden attends a client event at the freeport, he disrupts an attempt on Samantha's life. Disarming a hitman disguised as a waiter, Braiden kills the man (before, alas, they learn who sent the murderer).

Samantha returns to Thornfield.

The morning after a joyous reunion, they sit down to breakfast, only to discover an uninvited guest. Braiden reluctantly tells Samantha: "This is Birte Antóinín Mason. My wife."

An ashamed Braiden explains. When he married Birte in Ireland, her brother Niall was so opposed that he attacked Braiden. Niall died, and Birte went mad. Braiden brought Birte to America (along with her mute niece, Aiofe, and her crazed nurse, Grace). Birte's mental state is so fragile that he has kept her locked on the third floor for her own safety.

Appalled, Samantha moves into the pool house. (She cannot leave Thornfield because she fears whoever sent the freeport hitman.) Braiden agrees to let Birte roam the house.

Thornfield life quickly becomes even more complicated. Fiona Ingram, the sex-pot daughter of Braiden's boss, arrives to observe how he runs the Fishtown Boys. And Madden— Braiden's brother—repeatedly accuses Samantha of working for Antonio Russo.

Braiden ignores Fiona's advances and punishes Madden for his innuendos. Samantha agrees to submit sexually to Braiden, but only after she extracts a promise that he will bring in a priest to minister to Birte and Aiofe. She steadfastly refuses to sleep in the main house.

Goaded by Fiona, Braiden hosts a party for his made men. During the revelry, Fiona challenges Samantha to a dirty limerick contest. Samantha fails spectacularly and is further humiliated by Braiden reciting his own filthy poem. They only reconcile after a brutal scene of submission and domination in the pool house.

Days later, Braiden attends a business meeting in Boston. He encounters Kieran, who demands that Braiden marry Fiona by Easter.

Samantha, meanwhile, is dealing with the fallout of That Night being disclosed. The Delaware ethics board launches an inquiry to determine whether she can keep her license to practice law. A podcast broadcasts her sordid story. Paparazzi gather outside Thornfield.

Easter arrives without Braiden marrying Fiona. Kieran vows revenge. Fiona leaves Thornfield, turning to Madden for solace.

Samantha finds a threatening note from Fiona. Tired of gamesmanship, she drives to Boston for a direct confrontation. Threatened by Kieran, Samantha vows she'll bring in the FBI.

After Samantha leaves, Kieran calls Braiden and demands he execute her. Braiden confronts Samantha when she returns to Thornfield, resulting in a massive fight.

Samantha flees to Dover. Submerging herself in work, she hires a private investigator to finally learn who sent the assassin Braiden killed months earlier. She learns that Madden sent the killer. Madden has betrayed Braiden and is working directly with Russo.

Braiden, meanwhile, continues to defy Kieran, resulting inadvertently in the old man's death. Braiden sends his Warlord, Patrick Moran, to relay the bad news to Fiona (who has been badly beaten by Madden).

Samantha returns to Thornfield to warn Braiden of his brother's treachery. As she arrives, the garage explodes from a firebomb planted by Madden. Braiden orders Samantha to take Aiofe to the safe room.

Madden lurks in the safe room. Samantha only survives when Aiofe (finally!) speaks, warning her of danger. When Braiden arrives, Madden unsuccessfully tries to kill himself. Braiden tortures and kills Madden in secret so Russo does not know his pawn was exposed.

Samantha and Braiden reconcile, and Samantha agrees to

sleep in the main house. They awake, though, to a massive fire. Ordering Samantha to safety, Braiden fights to rescue Birte and Grace from the third floor.

Samantha huddles with Fairfax and Aiofe, staring into the black pit of the doorway, waiting, hoping, praying to see the man she loves…

1

SAMANTHA

I t takes so little time for a home to burn to the ground.

I'm standing outside Thornfield, looking up at the massive stone mansion as flames engulf all three floors. My throat aches—from smoke or from holding back tears or from screaming for Braiden Kelly, the man I love.

Less than five minutes ago, Braiden and I woke from sated sleep, finally reconciled after an argument we never should have had. As the smoke detector shrilled its warning, Braiden draped me in a waterlogged towel and forced me out of our bedroom, ordering me to get down the stairs and out the front door. My lips are bruised from the last kiss he gave me.

Braiden is still in that hellscape.

"Samantha!"

I whirl at the sound of my name, even as I realize the voice belongs to Alec Fairfax, the elfin man who keeps every aspect of daily life running at Thornfield. He's hurrying toward me from the back of the house. His cottage and the other homes for staff are safe from the fire, for now.

Fairfax's hand is gripped by Aiofe, Braiden's ward. The child has seen far too much violence in her eleven years. Until last night, trauma kept her mute. I could almost believe that I imagined her speaking, until she flings herself at me, burying her face in my T-shirt.

"Samantha." She echoes Fairfax, her voice almost lost in the crackle of flames. "Where's Uncle Braiden?"

Fairfax is already composing his ever-present reassuring smile. It's not until I falter, trying to tell Aiofe the truth without terrifying her, that he realizes the danger Braiden's in. "Sweet God," he murmurs, turning toward the house. "I called 911."

Before I can tell him that I did too, glass shatters onto the granite cobblestones of the driveway. More windows are bursting from the heat. Most of the rooms on the second floor are consumed by flame. Curtains have caught, and shadows look like a ghost army fighting to escape.

"All right," Fairfax says, as if this is nothing worse than a pot boiling over on his stove. "Let's move further down the drive, all of us."

We can't take refuge in the garage. *It* was firebombed earlier tonight when Braiden's traitor brother tried to lure him to his death. The firefighters must have left too soon. A few live sparks still lived among the ashes. They blew to the house and caught on the roof.

Fairfax glances down and sees my bare feet. "Mind the glass," he says.

I move, but I don't care about the glass. My eyes are on the third floor. Braiden should be there by now.

Where are you? Get out! Now!

The third floor is where Birte Mason lives—Aiofe's aunt, the woman Braiden married seven years ago. And Birte is watched over by Grace Poole.

I've been suspicious of Grace from the moment I arrived at

Thornfield. She's devoted to Birte, and to Aiofe too. But she's a drinking alcoholic who is always looking for a way to duck out of work. A couple of months ago, she allowed Birte to set fire to the door of Braiden's office, kindling it with large church candles.

Birte, with the cross she wears around her neck and the rosary she chants at dinner. Birte, who dresses like a nun.

Over the past four months, Birte has spiraled into madness. I don't know if my presence has been the trigger, or Braiden's violent life as Captain of Philadelphia's Irish mob, or all the other disasters from Birte's past.

And if Birte set that earlier fire…

Maybe the house didn't catch from a stray spark.

Maybe this was all planned.

In the relative safety of a curve in the driveway, Aiofe shifts from foot to foot. She's trying to get a better view of the burning house. "What's that smell?" she asks.

"I don't—" I start to say, but then I realize I smell it too—the sweet, pungent reek of gasoline. "Fairfax?" I ask.

His nod is grim. He hurries over to my Mercedes, the only car to survive the garage fire because it was parked on the driveway. Fairfax kneels beside it, then comes back with a length of garden hose. "This was in the tank," he says. "Someone siphoned off the petrol."

Jesus. No wonder the fire is burning so strong.

Braiden, what's taking so long?

"Samantha?" Aiofe asks. I wonder how many questions she has pent up inside after seven years of silence. "What's that paper?"

"What paper?" I ask. But following her gaze, I realize I'm still holding the document I found on the floor of the bedroom I share with Braiden, just before the smoke detector went off. Someone slipped it under the door while we slept.

It looks official. It's printed on heavy bond. There are illustrations around the border—a church at the bottom, scrollwork filled with shamrocks and harps at the top. The text is printed with heavy black letters that look like a monk wrote them in the Middle Ages. Three signatures run across the bottom.

A single word is stamped across the document in crimson letters: Annulled. And someone has scribbled through Birte's name, using blood-red crayon.

"It's a legal document," I tell Aiofe. "From the church in Ireland. It says your Uncle Braiden never married Aunt Birte."

"But he did," she says. "I was there."

She *was* there. She was present at the church when her father tried to kill Braiden. When her father killed her brother by accident. When her father turned his knife on himself.

I don't know how to explain that Braiden's marriage to Birte was never consummated. I have no idea what Aiofe knows about sex. She turned eleven earlier this month, but most of the time she acts like a child half her age.

I suspect that if Grace Poole hasn't taught her about her body, no one has. Grace Poole, who is somewhere on the third floor of the house.

Braiden, get out of there!

Even as I look back at the fire, I put together a story to explain what has happened. I don't know that it's true. I only hope I'll get to prove it, once Braiden comes out the front door, carrying Birte, guiding Grace.

Here's the tale that makes sense: Braiden received the signed, sealed paper sometime in the past week. I don't know when the annulment arrived. I didn't even know he'd applied for one. I was away from Thornfield, nursing wounds from the cruel things he and I said to each other in a heated fight.

But Birte found the document. And when she did, something snapped inside her fragile mind. This time, she wasn't satisfied with lighting just a few candles. This time, she came to my car, siphoned gas, and set fire to the entire house.

"Samantha?" Aiofe asks. "Didn't Uncle Braiden marry Aunt Birte?"

"It's complicated."

"But Father Regis says—"

Fairfax interrupts. "We can ask Father about it later."

I shoot him a look of gratitude. But Aiofe isn't through with her impossible questions. I almost regret that tonight is the night she finally chose to speak. "You didn't answer my question. Where is Uncle Braiden?"

I swallow hard. "He's inside the house. He's getting Aunt Birte and Grace."

"And Uncle Madden? Uncle Madden's hurt. Is he still in there? Is someone helping him?"

Fairfax and I share another glance over Aiofe's head. Madden was trying to overthrow his brother, trying to steal the Philadelphia mob from Braiden.

Aiofe saw Madden shoot himself in the face, a suicide attempt gone awry. She didn't see Braiden torture his traitorous brother. She doesn't know Braiden executed Madden for what he did. She doesn't know Madden's body lies somewhere in the furnace of the second floor.

Once again Fairfax saves the day. "I hear sirens. Don't you?"

Before I can strain to hear them over the crackling flames, Aiofe shouts, "Aunt Birte! There! On the roof!"

I follow Aiofe's pointing finger.

And she's right. Somehow, Birte has made her way onto the parapet that runs at the foot of the gabled roof.

She's standing on top of the stone barrier, feet steady and firm. Her white gown billows in the air currents from the fire. Even at this distance, I can see the heavy gold cross she keeps around her neck. Birte's bright red curls frame her face. Her eyes look black from here, but I know they're the color of summer grass.

"Aunt Birte!" Aiofe hollers from the driveway. "Aunt Birte!"

I can't believe Birte hears her, not at this distance, not over the flames. But the woman on the roof tilts her head at an angle. A ravishing smile floods her face, as if she's listening to a chorus of angels. She clutches her cross with both hands. She nods once.

And she steps off the parapet.

We can't hear her hit the ground, not with all the other noise. But Aiofe screams, her throat tearing like cheap cotton. Fairfax and I grab her at the same time, keeping her from running across the shattered glass to the broken, bleeding body.

Aiofe fights us. She bites. She scratches. She keens like a wolf, head back, mouth open.

Birte doesn't move. Birte will never move again.

But shadows flicker inside the gaping front door. For a moment, I think it's just a trick of the fire. But then I see broad shoulders and long legs. A bare chest and jet-black trousers. Dark hair and the planes of a face I know almost as well as my own.

Braiden.

He staggers across the driveway, drawn like a cursed sailor to Aiofe's siren song. He doesn't glance at Birte, doesn't seem to notice any of the destruction around him.

"She's dead!" Aiofe shouts. "Aunt Birte's dead!"

Braiden pulls her to his chest. Sobbing and shaking, she lets him hold her. He spreads one hand across the back of her head, muttering something in Irish.

His hands and face are covered in soot. His bare skin is scattered with bright red burns. The scar on his forearm, reminder of the school shooting he survived when he was half Aiofe's age, looks dark and angry.

"Samantha?" he calls, peering into the night and I close the distance between us.

"Thank God you made it out," I say, more whisper than actual speech.

His other arm brings me into the circle, and I feel his hand on the nape of my neck. The annulment is crushed between us, but I don't care. I could stand here until the end of time; I never want to move.

I realize I'm still wearing my collar, the emerald necklace he gave me when I accepted him as my Dom. His fingers brush the locked clasp, and I'm so grateful he's alive that my knees threaten to buckle.

The first firetruck appears on the winding drive. Fairfax moves to greet it, prepared to help in any way.

With Aiofe still between us, I make myself ask Braiden one question, even though I already know the answer. "Grace?"

He shakes his head, a single terse move.

Grace Poole won't steal his liquor ever again. She won't be drunk before noon. She won't leave the door to the third floor open, letting Birte slip free.

I lean my head against his shoulder. "You tried," I say.

The firefighters are shouting orders behind us. They've discovered Birte. Someone crouches beside her, taking her nonexistent pulse. Teams of men drag hoses into place, but there won't be much of Thornfield for them to save.

Braiden tightens his grip on my neck, pulling me even closer. His lips find my ear. I *feel* him speak, more than hear him. "Help me, Samantha," he says. "I can't see a thing. I'm blind."

2

BRAIDEN

"This'll help with the pain," Doc Kelleher says, pouring a vat of sulfuric acid into my eyes, first the left, then the right.

I manage not to kick him in the bollocks, but the twin daggers of agony shove me into my thickest Irish accent. "Jaysus, man! What are ya doin' t' me?"

"Blink a few times."

I'm blinking like he's just blown the entire Sahara Desert into my face. Thank Mary, Jesus, and all the saints that Doc insisted on treating me in the private bedroom of the Rittenhouse's Presidential Suite. The last thing my men need is to see their Captain crying like a little girl. If any of our enemies gets wind of how badly injured I am...

But Kelleher's right, as always. The worst of the searing pain I've felt for the past twelve hours is eased by the drops he's just given me. Now it only feels like I've scrubbed my eyes with bleach.

"You can take these every four hours," he says, folding a bottle of eye drops into my hand. My vision is so cloudy I can't make out our fingers between us. "I'm leaving another bottle on the night stand. Those go in every morning and every evening for a week. With corneal flash burns, you're at high risk for infection."

"Twice a day. Right."

"Plenty of patients take oxy for the pain. Want me to leave some?"

"I'm good." I've got access to all the opiates a man could ever need. But I won't be taking them, not when the Fishtown Boys need me at my best.

"There's no reason to suff—"

"How long until I can see?" I cut him off. He should understand. In my line of business, weakness kills.

I get the vague impression that he's shaking his head. "If you rest? And wear dark glasses? Seventy-two hours."

"And when I do neither?"

He sighs. "An extra day or two. Corneas heal quickly."

"So I'll be better by week-end." I cough a little as I say it. My throat feels like it did when ten-year-old Madden and I stole two packs of Da's Marlboros and dared each other to see who could smoke them fastest.

Madden... Fucking shitehawk.

"Rest will help that cough too. Prop yourself on pillows if you have trouble breathing." He closes his heavy bag with a grunt. "Call me if your eyes get worse. Or if you decide you want the pain meds."

"Seamus will see you out," I tell him, climbing to my feet. I can hear my quartermaster talking in the next room, his voice low and steady. "And could you send Samantha in?"

"As your doctor, I strongly advise you to avoid sexual relations for the next forty-eight hours."

I grimace. "Send her in, please."

I'd like nothing more than to give Samantha a ride, searing

eye pain or not. But we have something more important to discuss.

She closes the door behind her. I can't see her fingers on the knob, but I know precisely how she moves. I can picture her checking the latch with one quick tug, making sure we won't be interrupted. "What did the doctor say?" she asks.

"I can only be saved by regular blowjobs, every hour on the hour."

"Braiden—" She sighs in mock exasperation. At least, I hope it's mock.

In any case, her sigh has told me exactly where she's standing. I get a hand around the back of her neck, same as I did outside the burning Thornfield.

Despite doctor's orders, I regret having given her the key to her collar. If she still wore her emerald, I could order her to her knees.

Instead, I tug her over to the side of the bed. We sit, chaste as missionaries, as I ask, "How's Aiofe?"

"She's sleeping in the other suite. Seamus' wife is with her."

"How much does she know?"

"She saw Birte fall."

I wince as the old scar on my forearm begins to throb, the itching burn I've lived with for nearly thirty years. Before I can dig at it with my nails, Samantha says, "It's not your fault."

"I tried to get up to the third floor. The entire staircase was on fire. Half the steps had already burned away."

"It's not your fault," she repeats. "You had no way of predicting Birte would do that."

Seven years of guilt feels like a load of iron ore across my shoulders. "I wish I knew what set her off last night."

"Oh my God..." Samantha breathes. "You didn't see..."

"What?" And when she hesitates: "What didn't I see, *piscín*?"

My pet name for her—*kitten*—breaks down her defenses. "Your annulment. Birte put it under the bedroom door while we were sleeping."

I left the document in my office. Birte must have crept out of her attic room during the night. She must have found the official paper on my desk.

I don't know if the stabbing pain I feel is from my eyes or my smoke-ravaged throat or if it's pure guilt. I made a mess of Birte's life for years. I should have found a way to set her free sooner than I did. I should have brought in the doctors she needed, her and Aiofe both.

"It's not your fault," Samantha says a third time.

It'll be donkey's years before I believe her. But mourning my mistakes now won't help those still living. I make a conscious effort to sound like I'm Captain of the Fishtown Boys. "Where's Fairfax? We need some basic supplies if we're going to be at the Rittenhouse for a while."

"He's being his usual efficient self. Clothes for you and Aiofe will be delivered by six o'clock this evening. He's having my things sent over from the pool house, along with some of his own from his cottage."

The pool house… After everything that happened last night —Samantha coming home to warn me about Madden, the confrontation in the safe room, Samantha consenting to wear my collar, the fire—after all of that, I'd somehow forgotten Samantha was still living in exile in the pool house. When she wasn't hiding in Delaware. When we weren't feuding.

She says, "Fairfax is having groceries delivered too. I reminded him we have nowhere to cook, but he insists on bringing in some of Aiofe's favorites."

I make a mental note to give him a bonus, the next time I can actually see the screen on my phone. I regret the thousands in cash I had in my office safe. I suspect all of it was incinerated last night.

Samantha leans forward and brushes a kiss against my cheek. "You need to rest."

"I need to see my men. And they need to see me."

"They can see you after you take a nap."

"They need to know nothing's changed, just because of a house fire."

"You could have died in there."

"I didn't."

"You could have—" A hiccup breaks whatever she's trying to say.

Even with my shite vision and pain that grows sharper with every beat of my heart, I find the waterfall of her straight, black hair. I wrap my fist around it, using it as a lever to tilt her mouth to the perfect angle.

"I didn't," I whisper against her lips. She resists for a moment when I kiss her, as if there's more of an argument to be had. But finally she sighs and lets me in. Eyes closed, so it doesn't matter if I'm blind, I deepen the kiss.

Every inch of me aches. My eyes are stabbing knives directly into my brain. My lungs feel like they're packed with sand. I don't have the breath to hold the kiss as long as I want, and when I break off, I'm gasping.

But my cock doesn't know any of that.

"*Mo chailín maith*," I breathe into her mouth. *My good girl.*

She pulls away. "No," she whispers, her forehead against mine. "You need to sleep."

I catch her hand, intending to set her fingers against my trousers, to let her know how much I need *this*. But when she rejects me, slipping away again, I lower myself to asking, "Am I hideous, Samantha?"

She laughs. "You always were, you know." She kisses the back of my hand. "Seriously," she says. "Rest."

I want to protest. I want to tell her if she won't have me, I'll go out to my men. *They* need me. Instead, I find myself yawning hard enough to dislocate my jaw.

Samantha slips away. "I'll come back soon."

I let her go, fairly certain I have no choice.

I'm almost asleep when my phone rings. I fumble for it on the nightstand, knocking over the bottle of eyedrops Kelleher left behind. When I finally get the damn thing in my hand, I can't make out the letters on the screen. I answer just before the call goes to voicemail, snapping, "Kelly."

"Boss." It's Patrick, my Warlord. It's been less than twenty-four hours since I sent my chief enforcer to Fiona Ingram.

Because that's the other crisis brewing. Fiona's father died last night. Kieran Ingram was the head of the mob in Boston. But more than that, Ingram was the general of the whole Grand Irish Union, all of us captains throughout the United States.

The bastard wanted me to kill Samantha, supposedly because of a shite threat she made. Really, he wanted me to prove my loyalty to the Union. When I refused to follow orders, a raging Ingram coughed up a rotten lung and died. Now his followers want me to pay.

Last night, I knew Kieran was dead before Fiona did. She called to say she'd made the mistake of her life, thinking my brother was the kind of man she could build an empire with. She had the black eye and busted lip to prove it.

Madden was a feckin' bully his entire life. But Fiona never deserved what he did to her.

I sent Patrick to break the news about her father when I couldn't go myself. When I had Madden to manage.

Closing my eyes now, I hear Patrick say, "Condolences, Boss."

I don't know how much he's heard—about Birte, about my eyes, about Thornfield. But I choose to believe he's talking about stone and mortar, because that's easier than the rest. "We'll knock it down and start over," I say. "For now we're at the Rittenhouse, Presidential Suite. Liam'll get you a key."

"About that, Boss... Herself is... Madden did a lot of damage."

My fist folds in the sheets. I don't have any regrets about how my brother died. But I'm starting to wish I tortured him for longer before that final blow. "How bad is it?" I finally ask.

"She shouldn't be alone right now. Not with her da gone and things gone arseways up in Boston."

Fiona once told me her da meant for her to take his place when he died. But those Boston boyos are old school. They'll never let a woman be in charge. Not without a fierce battle, one I'm not sure Fiona can win.

I've known Patrick Moran my entire life. He was my father's Warlord before he was mine. So I hear all the things he isn't saying, all the secrets hiding behind his spoken words.

"You're taking her up to Boston, then," I say.

"If you'll let me, Boss."

Jesus Christ. Another Fishtown Boy, fallen to Fiona Ingram's feckin' magic. If she could bottle what she has, she'd take over the world, one horndog eejit at a time.

Patrick's my *Warlord*. I need him here more than ever.

But it's not a bad idea for me to place a man in Boston. To find out how serious those jackeens are about revenge. To have someone on the ground if things go seriously pear-shaped with Ingram's clan.

"Go ahead," I tell him. "But don't let me be surprised by anything going on up there."

"You won't be, Boss."

I trust him. He's my best man.

He even knows to wait a respectful moment before he says, "Speaking of surprises... I'll be taking Fiona round to collect her things before we leave. Any idea if Madden'll be there to give us trouble?"

Any chance you murdered your cunt of a brother last night?

That's the question Patrick knows better than to ask out loud.

Before I carved Madden into dog food, the gobshite confessed to working with my archenemy, Philadelphia's Mafia capo, Antonio Russo. The goombah prick has been squeezing my territory for the last two months—plus, he has a history of threatening Samantha.

It's time to do some housecleaning, mob-war style, but I don't have a lot of weapons I can leverage. Not with my operations in disarray, my income seriously down, and my home destroyed. But maybe—just possibly—I can use the fact that no one knows Madden is dead.

I might send a false report to Russo. I might…

Shite, I don't know. My eyes hurt too much for me to think.

But I'm not admitting to anyone that I killed Madden. Not yet. Not while that fact might still be a tactical advantage. So I say: "He was at the house last night. Blew the garage to smithereens. But no one caught him on the grounds. The boys couldn't find him."

That's the truth.

Just not all of it.

I picture Patrick's dark eyes narrowed, the silver in his hair catching the light as he nods. "I'll let you know if we see him then."

"You do that," I say, as if I believe it's an honest possibility.

"If you need help while I'm gone, you could do worse than asking Rory O'Hare."

Rory. Patrick's second. "Thanks," I tell him. And then with a reluctance I won't admit out loud: "Save travels."

I end the call and fumble the phone back to the nightstand. I should go out to the living room. I should tell Seamus to bring in Rory. I should check with Fairfax, see if the fire inspector has made a preliminary report yet, find out if the fire was hot enough to destroy my brother's body.

But my eyes are still closed against the pain. And my lungs are still refusing to take a full breath. And the pillows on this bed are so soft…

I fall asleep holding on to Samantha's promise that she'll be back soon.

3

SAMANTHA

~

I hate the Rittenhouse.

It's the most luxurious hotel in Philadelphia. They keep a file on Braiden. They know to make his bed European style, without a top sheet. They stock Jameson in his mini bar. And they deliver five newspapers every morning: *The Philadelphia Enquirer*, *The Wall Street Journal*, *The New York Times*, *The Washington Post*, and *The Irish Times*.

The suites are finely appointed. The room service meals are some of the best I've ever eaten. The staff is expertly trained, and I've never made a request they couldn't meet.

But the Rittenhouse is where Braiden and Russo met to hammer out their territorial dispute, back in February. It's where Fiona Ingram first played her hand, trying to squash Braiden beneath the Grand Irish Union's heel. It's where Madden publicly accused me of being Russo's whore.

And it's where Antonio Russo revealed my darkest secret to the world. He told Braiden, the Delaware bar, and every reporter he could reach about That Night. About the biggest mistake I ever made. About the single wrong I can never atone for: Driving drunk on a winding mountain road, resulting in the deaths of three innocent people.

So it's no wonder I despise being trapped in this golden cage.

When I sit down for coffee in the living room of the Presidential Suite, I shouldn't be surprised to discover I'm front-page news in my hometown newspaper. After all, Braiden and Russo are evergreen subjects for articles. Locals follow stories about organized crime as avidly as they track the Eagles and the 76ers, the Phillies and the Flyers.

Paparazzi have been trailing me since Russo announced how two of my cousins and an unnamed vagrant died in a mountainside ditch. I've become the subject of this season's Mousetrap podcast, a true-crime series that details every mistake I've ever made. Just last week, the *Enquirer* ran a huge exposé about me, telling the world about my connections to the Mafia and the Mob, about my fight to keep my license to practice law.

And the Philadelphia paper is back for more this morning. Apparently, the *Enquirer* sent a reporter out to Thornfield. While the view through the gate was obscured, there was enough steaming wreckage from the fire to make the estate look like a combat zone.

"Struggling Lawyer Loses All in Suspicious House Fire," blares the headline.

The article is a masterpiece in innuendo, recycling last week's hatchet job. Every single statement is factually true. I can't begin to make a claim for libel or defamation. Among other facts, the article states:

My father was a lieutenant for Don Antonio Russo.

I witnessed my parents' death in a car explosion when I was ten, and I was taken in by an aunt and uncle with close ties to the Mafia.

After killing three people while driving drunk, I fled to New York, where I assumed a new name.

I am currently under investigation for those three deaths, and the Delaware bar is holding an ethics proceeding to determine the status of my license to practice law.

I work for a tax haven that caters to sometimes-shady billionaires.

I married Braiden Kelly, Captain of Philadelphia's Irish mob.

A woman and her full-time caretaker perished in a fire at Braiden's mob compound on Monday night.

I did not immediately answer reporters' questions about this story.

I try to sip the dark roast coffee delivered by room service when they brought the morning newspapers. Ordinarily, caffeine is a jolt to my system, anchoring me for a long day of work. This morning, though, the coffee sludges through my veins like frozen motor oil, slowing every synapse in my brain.

Braiden is savoring his tea, brewed as dark as his own reputation. The liquid in his cup glints like midnight in the sunglasses he's wearing as a reluctant concession to Dr. Kelleher, as long as we're in the privacy of our suite. "What?" he asks, when I set aside the paper.

"Nothing."

"I'll call in Fairfax and have him read to me."

Braiden Kelly does not make idle threats. So I tell him: "It's an article about me. In *The Enquirer*. Tying me to the fire."

"Who else has the story?"

I don't want to know. But I don't have that luxury, not anymore. Not with my career hanging in the balance.

So I page through the other papers, reporting to Braiden as I go. *The Washington Post* treats me like an entertainment piece; the article in its Style section notes my preference for Balenciaga suits and Louboutin shoes. *The Journal* and *The Times* pick up the business angle, mentioning my employer,

Diamond Freeport. They note Braiden's Kelly Construction, detailing some of the major contracts he's had in the past few years.

"*The Irish Times* is silent," I tell Braiden. "For now. Satisfied?"

His eyebrows rise above the frames of his sunglasses. He's still recovering from physical injuries and emotional exhaustion. But that doesn't erase the fact that he's my Dom, and he expects me to treat him with respect.

Before he can make that point, my phone rings. It's yet another new cell—my third in as many months—sent overnight from the freeport. Life with Braiden is rough on my electronics.

When I see the caller's name, I answer quickly. "Sonja," I say, trying not to feel like a little girl called before the principal at school.

Sonja Heller is the attorney representing me in my Delaware ethics hearing, the one that will decide whether I get to keep practicing law. She looks like Taylor Swift and she sounds like Judge Judy. She's as tough as tungsten, and junkyard dogs flee in terror when she walks past their chain-link fences.

"What the actual fuck," Sonja says, in a voice loud enough for Braiden to hear, even though she's not on speaker.

I remember that I'm a lawyer too. "I didn't ask for that sort of coverage."

"Lie low, I told you. Keep your name out of the press. Don't feed the goddamn publicity machine."

"Do you think I *wanted* my home burned to the ground?"

Only two days ago, I was hiding out in a string of Dover hotels, avoiding that so-called home because I couldn't face the things Braiden and I had said to each other. But I don't have to explain my change of heart to Sonja.

She wouldn't understand. She doesn't have a heart of her own. Proof in point: She says, "I *think* you should have called me, the instant you got someplace safe."

"I had a few other things on my mind. Do I need to repeat? My *home* burned to the ground. People I love were injured."

"Which only makes me wonder how you feel about the people who died."

"That isn't what I—"

"I shouldn't have to remind you that the Delaware bar is deciding whether you committed a crime of moral turpitude on that mountaintop, eleven years ago. They want to know if your drunken killing of three people makes you unfit to practice law. The last thing they need to read on the front page of the Philadelphia paper is your connection to two more corpses."

Three.

Madden was in that house.

And he was tortured before he died.

But I tell Sonja, "If you have a way to keep reporters from publishing their stories, I'm all ears. But if you're only calling to give me a hard time about circumstances that were absolutely, completely, one hundred percent beyond my control, then I'll hang up, and we can both go back to getting work done for the day."

She softens a little. "I'm your lawyer. You should have called me."

I concede the point. "I was going to. After I got to the freeport today."

"We need to make an official statement. I'll clear an hour this morning. Can you be here by eleven?"

"Eleven," I agree.

"How is Braiden?" she asks, extending the olive branch just a little farther.

"He'll be fine." I wait just a beat, then add, "Thank you for asking."

"I'll see you at eleven."

When I hang up, Braiden says in a conversational tone, "Over my dead body."

"What?"

"There is no way in bloody hell that you're driving down to Dover today."

"You heard her. We need to make an official response."

"You've got a phone. A computer, too. Call down to the front desk and reserve a meeting room. You can talk as long as you'd like anywhere at the Rittenhouse, so long as four of my men remain on guard while you do it."

He's deadly serious. And his restrictions etch into my skin like acid.

"Braiden," I say. And then for the first time, because I want him to listen: "Love," I call him. "I work in Dover, Delaware. Sonja Heller is my attorney in Dover, Delaware."

"Don't talk to me like I'm two years old."

"Then don't act like you are!" I regret my tone the instant I see his jaw set. After taking a deep breath, I try again. "Madden is gone. He can't hurt me. Ingram is dead. He can't test your loyalty anymore, and he can't order anyone else to tip your hand."

"There's Russo," Braiden says.

"Who was relying on Madden to know what the Fishtown Boys are doing. This has to be the *safest* time to go, as far as Russo is concerned. His crew must be in total disarray."

I've lived my entire life surrounded by criminals. I know I'm right.

Braiden pinches his lower lip. I wish I could see his eyes behind those glasses. From the tight lines on his forehead, I can tell he's still in a lot of pain.

"Please," I say. "When we get to the end of all this, I need to know I did everything I could to save my license."

I hear what I don't say—that I'm nearly convinced I'll lose at the hearing. That I can't see a path clear to continuing the job I love.

And even if I somehow win the ethics case, there's also a criminal investigation going on. Detective Tarrant on the Philadelphia police force is digging into That Night so prosecutors can decide whether they'll charge me with murder.

Braiden finally sighs in resignation. "Liam will drive you."

"Of course," I say.

"You'll go to Sonja's office and return directly here."

I'd rather go on to my office at the freeport and spend the rest of the day working productively there. But I decide not to push it. "Okay."

"Give me your phone."

"Why?"

He just holds out his hand. And because he's already given in so much, I type in my password and hand over my device.

He holds it so close to his face he barely has room to touch his fingers to the screen. I try to read what he's doing in the reflection of his black-pool sunglasses, but I can't follow the display. He hands the phone back with the app still open; he's making zero effort to disguise what he's done.

"You're *tracking* me?" I ask in disbelief, refusing to take the damn thing.

"I'm making sure you're safe."

I think about refusing. I've never given anyone access to the stalker apps other people take for granted. My years of living under an assumed name made me far too cautious.

But I suspect Braiden already has a way of tracking Liam. The only real surprise is that he didn't insist on monitoring me months ago.

"Fine," I finally say.

I hold out my hand for my phone, but his vision hasn't improved enough to see that far. I have to take it from his fingers. And that small action, more than anything else, makes me forgive his invasion of my privacy.

He's hurting.

He's worried.

He's the most over-protective S.O.B. I've ever met in my life.

"I'll be back by 2:30," I say. "Which you'll know by staring at your own damn phone."

His feral grin almost makes me glad I've given him a victory.

4

BRAIDEN

~

Samantha's trip to Dover proceeds without any problems. She's back to the Rittenhouse suite at 2:29, precisely one minute before her promised return, which makes me wonder how long she loitered in the lobby before coming upstairs. She's followed the rules, though, so I have no right to complain.

"I'll be working in the bedroom," she tells me.

I understand she's chastising me for keeping her from her freeport office. If we weren't surrounded by half a dozen of my Fishtown Boys, I'd make her pay for the insubordination. Both of us could use the release.

But we *are* surrounded by my men, all of whom are suddenly busy, studying their phones or the paper maps we've spread out on the table.

Plus, my eyes still ache like the bleeding wounds of Christ.

And I need to *see* my sub if I'm going to discipline her properly.

"Fairfax is serving dinner at six," I tell her pointedly. I want both of us to believe I still make the rules.

She doesn't reply.

I wait until she's closed the bedroom door before I lock myself in the jacks off the living room. I run water in the sink, because luxury hotels don't provide the sort of soundproofing I used to enjoy at Thornfield. Two days living here at the Ritten-house, and the lack of privacy is already driving me mad.

Wrestling my phone out of my pocket, I'm pleased to discover I can keep it a full handspan from my nose as I tap the screen. That's progress.

Liam Murphy answers on the first ring: "Boss?"

"I have a project for you."

"Sure thing, Boss." If he's hoping I'm about to send him back out with Samantha, he's smart enough to keep his voice neutral.

Which is the only reason I tell him, "I want my brother's car."

I've spent the better part of the day thinking about this.

Chances are, the McLaren is in plain sight, somewhere in Philadelphia. Madden planted it somewhere before he sneaked onto Thornfield land, armed with a pipe bomb to take out my garage. My brother was stubborn and impulsive and he never met a rule he wouldn't break for the sheer hell of it. But he'd make sure to leave himself a clear alibi, all the same.

I want the car picked up, because I don't want anyone asking uncomfortable questions about Madden's whereabouts. I don't want people wondering why a car worth half a million dollars is sitting somewhere, unattended.

The Fishtown Boys are used to the back and forth between Madden and me. There's not a man on my crew who would question my boosting my brother's car. And once I get the McLaren locked behind Thornfield's gate, I'm pretty sure no one will think to ask when Madden's taking it back.

"Boss?" Liam asks. He's not arguing. Not telling me it's a

shite assignment. Not saying it's impossible. But he honestly seems not to understand.

"Madden's McLaren. I want it parked at Thornfield by midnight." And just in case he's thinking of cutting corners and boosting it off some street somewhere: "With the keys."

"Do you know where it is?" He's good. There's not a hint of grievance in his voice.

"Track it down."

"You've got it, Boss," Liam says.

And the confidence in his voice actually makes me believe he'll get the job done.

Liam Murphy is as good as his word. He returns to the Rittenhouse at a quarter to midnight. My eyes are aching—tired as well as burned—when Seamus opens the door to the suite. But I can see the glitter of the keys when Liam drops them in my hand. He passes me his phone, too, with a picture of the ugliest acid-green car I've ever seen in my life, safe on the driveway in front of Thornfield's burned-out ruins.

I can't tell if my watering eyes are due to my scorched corneas or the color Madden chose for his substitute cock.

"Did you have to kill him to get it?" I ask casually.

Seamus knows the truth; he saw every last thing I did to my brother in the Thornfield infirmary. But the men still poring over screens and documents—the ones building barriers against Russo and whatever Boston sends our way—they don't know how handy I am with forceps and a scalpel.

Liam shakes his head. "I paid for some time with two of Mimi's girls. The ones she gave Madden when he did the milk run last week."

Plenty of people know Madden collected my accounts four days ago—everyone who handed over an envelope. But Fiona Ingram is the only person who knows Madden stole my money.

Everyone else thinks he was just a loyal soldier, playing the game as it's always been played.

This is the first I've heard of Madden taking a ride as he collected the money that should have been mine. I think of Fiona's broken, bleeding face. I wonder how long Madden made her wait while he had his fun with Mimi's girls.

I wave Liam over to the bar Fairfax outfitted at the far end of the living room. Blinking hard, I pour him a few fingers of Jameson, waving away his thanks as I ask, "What did the girls have to say?"

"Madden threw some cash around before he left. Said he'd make it back at Darragh's executive game."

Darragh McCarthy runs my high rollers game out at the Avalon, the last three days of every month. It's exclusive enough that everyone—even my second-in-command—has to wait for a seat at the table, sometimes for weeks.

The attraction isn't just Darragh's top-shelf booze and the New York call girls he brings down for the night. It's the no-limit betting.

And Madden was there as often as Darragh let him darken the doorstep.

"So you traced the fecker to the Avalon."

"He booked a suite, Monday through today."

Of course he did. To a casual onlooker, that suite proved Madden was at the Avalon for three days straight. He had a place to take a shower, maybe grab half an hour's kip between hands.

Darragh's game is strictly confidential. Every man at the table is sworn to secrecy about who attends. Any player who gabs outside of the room will never be invited back.

But I'm willing to bet Darragh will tell *me* that Madden got there early and lost big on his first few hands. Maybe Darragh gave him a bottle of the Macallan 25, just to make sure *I* didn't have any beef with how the game was run. Darragh will assume my brother stumbled back to his room, slept off his shite luck at the table, and spent the rest of his time nursing an unholy hangover.

I can tell a different story. I don't have proof, but I know it's true. I can feel it in my bones.

Madden took a cab home, paying cash, so there'd be no record. He beat the shite out of Fiona. And then he took another cab to a little side street, two blocks from Thornfield. He opened a triple-locked gate that leads to a water overflow pipe, one that only he and I knew about. He crawled through the muck, like we both did as kids. And all the while, he planned how he'd get rid of me, how he'd hand the Fishtown Boys to Russo and settle in to the golden life of a Mafia capo.

Fucking traitor.

For public consumption, I'm still working the angle that I have no idea where my brother might be. "So Madden was still at the Avalon?" I ask Liam.

He shrugs. "His car was. The valet left it in the front circle, with all the other supercars."

That's what hotels do—show off big-spending guests to all the jackeens stopping by for the night. It makes everyone feel important. Plus, it guarantees no minimum-wage attendant will ruin a custom paint job on tight corners in a garage.

Liam says, "I waited for the valet to take his smoking break. Talked to him outside the employee entrance."

"Risky, that."

Liam shrugs. "I made sure he was the one facing security cameras. Plus, I wore a baseball hat. Hoodie. Jeans. Coppers won't have much to go on."

"Until your man sits down with one of those sketch artists."

A rude sound lets me know what Liam thinks of Philadelphia' finest. "I was ready to go as high as ten thousand for the keys. But the eejit only asked for a grand."

I shake my head. "Almost makes you feel sorry for the man."

"I hit him hard enough to make it look real. A real pistol-whipping. He might even keep his job."

"Not likely. Not after hotel security put one and one together."

Another shrug. "He can argue a stranger took the car. I didn't show him the gun when we talked by the door. And I wore a ski mask when I strapped him. A gray sweatshirt too, one of those souvenir jobs: 'Property of the Philadelphia Eagles.' I even changed my trainers."

"Did you have any trouble getting the car back to Thornfield?"

He shakes his head. "I drove like my grandmother, on her way to Sunday Mass. Billy Walsh let me in at the front gate. There're cones all around the house, and crime-scene tape around Sam's Mercedes. I parked the McLaren at the far end of the drive, took a pic, and covered it with a tarp."

Christ. I forgot about Samantha's car.

Someone—the chief fire inspector—is sure to have questions about a new vehicle appearing on the property. But that same someone's going to have a lot more questions about Madden's body, once it shows up in the ruins. I'll deal with that when I have to.

"So what are you out, all told?" I ask Liam.

He shakes his head. "Consider it my gift to you, Boss."

He's paid for two whores. Bought off the Avalon's eejit valet. I'm certain he trashed both outfits he wore, and he got rid of the gun too. The night's cost him a few grand, even without the valet charging him top dollar.

But he gained something more than a joyride in an acid-green McLaren.

He's proven once again that he's a man I can trust.

I think about that neon nightmare of a vehicle. Maybe when all of this is done, I'll have the car done up in a respectable color —red or black or even the papaya orange they use for their Formula 1 team.

Maybe I'll need to sink it in the Schuylkill.

But for now, I can leave it as is. As far as anyone knows,

Madden is whoring around, maybe following up on yet another dream gig that'll make him a feckin' billionaire.

I half-wish Fiona had made her bruised face public, so I could use it as an excuse for my cowardly brother lying low. But she's chosen to protect her privacy, and I owe her that much, after all that's gone between us.

Someone will come sniffing around for Madden eventually. And when that happens, I figure the McLaren will give me options. I can lie about my shitehawk of a brother for eons.

At least until people forget they care about a two-bit, lying, back-stabbing cunt who should have been walked off a pier years ago.

5

SAMANTHA

It takes a week for Braiden's eyes to heal. The day that Dr. Kelleher clears him for driving, he grabs the keys to a new Jeep he's had delivered to the Rittenhouse. He disappears for hours. I expect him to come back in a better mood, but he's only more stressed for having skipped a day at work.

The next morning, I wake to cold sheets on his side of the bed. Sighing, I wrap myself in one of the Rittenhouse's luxurious terrycloth robes. Fairfax has breakfast waiting in the suite across the hall.

A Thornfield breakfast was a thing of glory—fried eggs, sautéed mushrooms and grilled tomatoes, heaps of bacon and sausages, and bowls of hash. Thick hand-sliced toast was served with butter, marmalade, and multiple types of jam. Yogurt was ladled by the gallon, surrounded by berries, honey, and fresh-toasted muesli.

Here at the hotel, Fairfax compensates by ordering half a dozen breakfast platters. It's not the same, of course. Nothing is.

I help myself to crème brûlée French toast with vanilla whipped cream. When Fairfax comes in with a fresh carafe of coffee, I gesture at my plate. "You could do better than this with a hot plate and a camp stove."

"It's kind of you to say so." He hovers after filling my cup, fretting over the silver-domed plates on the sideboard.

"Pull up a chair," I finally offer, but I'm astonished when he does. I can't remember sharing a single meal with Fairfax at Thornfield. He and Grace always ate in the kitchen.

He plucks a croissant from a basket but sets it on his plate uneaten. He picks up a teacup, then returns it to its saucer. He reaches out and shifts the sugar bowl a quarter inch to the right.

"Miss Samantha," he finally brings himself to say.

"Sam," I remind him gently. That's what he's called me since Braiden brought me home.

"Sam," he says, clearing his throat and studying the silver-ware. Finally, he looks me in the eye. "This isn't working."

My first instinct is to reassure him. He's managed miracles, adapting the Rittenhouse for all of us. He commandeers meals from room service like an admiral controlling a fleet on the high seas. He reviews our closets on a daily basis, sending clothes to the hotel laundry and retrieving perfectly pressed garments. He has fresh flowers delivered from a local florist every three days.

But that's not what he means. So I agree with him. "It's not."

"I'm worried about Aiofe." He keeps his voice low; she's just behind the bedroom door.

Guilt shoves something cold and sharp between my ribs. "I haven't paid as much attention to her as I should have." I've been focused on Braiden's recovery, and on Sonja's plans for my hearing, and on work, because I can't let things fall apart at the freeport.

He waves off my confession. "She's a lamb. Does exactly as she's told. Doesn't complain about a thing."

"So the problem is…"

"She *should* be complaining. She should be acting out. She lost Miss Birte and Grace."

Those women—flawed as they were—were the closest thing to family Aiofe ever knew. "If you think a nanny would help…"

"She's too old for a nanny. Maybe an au pair, to be a companion after she finishes schoolwork for the day."

"You know Braiden will approve the expense."

"It's not money!" Fairfax must hear the sharpness in his voice, because he repeats himself in a much quieter tone. Then he says, "It's safety. Security. She needs more routine than following me about all day."

"We never should have told her tutor she was taking a break. Call John Bell and get him back here tomorrow."

Fairfax frowns. "I already tried. He's backpacking in the Andes. His first vacation in seven years, and he can't be reached."

"All right. Aiofe needs a companion. She needs classes. What else?"

He glances at the bedroom door, as if he fears Aiofe might be spying on us. "She has nightmares," he says, his voice nearly a whisper. "More nights than not, she wakes herself screaming."

"Why haven't you said something before?" I don't mean it to sound like an accusation, but I know it does. The thought of that poor child, haunted even while she sleeps…

He hunches his shoulders, and I'm reminded that life has been hard for everyone since the fire. "With Mister Braiden struck blind? With you handling those nasty reporters?"

"We all want what's best for Aiofe."

"What's best for Aiofe is living in a normal house. Sleeping in a normal bed. In a room decorated for a normal girl. All of this is too much, too large, too overwhelming. And…" He winds down his tirade.

But I push. "And what?"

"And she should see a doctor. Not Kelleher. There's nothing

wrong with her body. But she's survived a lot of trauma. She should speak with someone who understands."

I've been saying the same thing to Braiden since I met the child. I thought Birte should get therapy too. If she had, maybe we'd all still be living at Thornfield.

"I'll see what I can do," I tell Fairfax.

"Thank you." He pauses, as if he's about to say more, but he settles for topping off my coffee again, pouring from the carafe. "Thank you," he says once more, and this time he sounds decisive. Leaving his croissant behind, he heads into the bedroom, where I hear him cajoling Aiofe into drawing him a picture.

Aiofe needs structure.

Aiofe needs rules.

Life at Thornfield was filled with them. At the most basic level, breakfast was mandatory. Everyone gathered in the dining room every single morning; there was none of this drifting by for a bite here, a meal there.

I blush, thinking about the rules *I* lived by: No work after six o'clock. No black and white clothes after business ended for the day. No trousers either, only skirts. No panties.

I fought those rules every step of the way. But there's a hollow inside of me that longs for the return of that slice of normal, everyday life.

And I know exactly how to make that happen.

6

BRAIDEN

The valet takes the keys to my Jeep and hands me a claim check. The doorman greets me by name: "Good evening, Mr. Kelly." The front desk clerk offers the same greeting, as does the concierge. A bellhop steps out of the elevator as I approach, and he holds the door for me, automatically reaching inside to press the button for my floor.

Other men get off on this kind of attention. They want to be fawned over. Told they've got the biggest dick.

I just want the peace and quiet of living in my own home. And I spent the last three hours hearing all the ways that isn't going to happen, not anytime soon.

I wasn't surprised by any of the details. Not when Philadelphia Fire Commissioner Warren K. Chesterton insisted on meeting in the back room of a manky restaurant on the furthest edge of the city's northern suburbs. It turned out Chesterton's daughter owned the place. She was the guilty party for the menu's unholy fusion of Hungarian and Japanese cuisine.

Given the antacids Chesterton downed like popcorn, he's not a fan of the food either. But he was more than happy that we had the back room to ourselves. That privacy gave him a chance to open the briefcase I brought him. He had the nerve to count the bundled bills, as if I've failed to honor my payoffs in the past.

Maybe someone else has been cheating the commissioner.

Or maybe he didn't trust a man who's come to bribe him twice in less than a year. Fair play to him, he didn't mention the tiled room in the basement at The Hare and Harp, the downtown bar where I used to conduct my business. He didn't say a thing about the over-size drain that survived Antonio Russo's arson, or the charred metal tools that hinted at the room's true purpose.

The same way he didn't comment on an extra skeleton in the ashes at Thornfield.

He just texted a number to my personal phone. A very large number—four times what I paid for the Hare.

Feckin' vulture. Another grab like that, and I'll be forced to remind him he works in a dangerous business. Men die at fire scenes all the time. Even commissioners.

So, by the time I get back to the Rittenhouse, I'm feeling assaulted by foods that should have never shared the same kitchen, ravaged by a greedy man who'll have my bollocks in a vise if I so much as light a candle for the next ten years, and worn to a nub by the worst rush-hour traffic I've ever seen in the City of Brotherly Love. It's half past eight, and I should have been here by six.

No amount of arse-kissing from hotel staff will change that.

At least the living room is empty when I get to the suite. After a week of shoring up every possible gap in our security, I've sent all the Boys home for a long weekend. Nothing short of all-out war with Russo—or Boston—will make me call them in before Monday.

Stripping the knot in my tie, I head into the bedroom.

Samantha is pacing near the table in the corner. She's wearing one of her suits, all black of course, with a white top that plunges dangerously close to an unprofessional V. Her feet are cased in heels that telegraph a message straight to my cock, and that's before I catch a glimpse of their scarlet soles. She's pinned up her hair with a single pencil, and from the way tendrils curl against her neck, she's worn it that way for at least an hour or two.

"I don't care, Mary," she says into her phone. "Things are too busy right now. I'll go over the Dubois contract tonight, and we can wrap up that regulatory review for Cole Wolf tomorrow. But I'll need you in the office all day Saturday. Better plan on Sunday too."

She notices me studying her, and she holds up a finger, telling me she'll only be a minute. Apparently her assistant, Mary Rivers, has another complication.

"Well, have a courier deliver the documents tonight. Tell Rider we can talk at seven tomorrow. Before his other meeting." She sighs in exasperation, shifting through the papers stacked on the table. "If I can make do with just coffee, he can too."

Mary must have a problem with that plan as well. Samantha listens, a frown twisting her lips. "I know you can't say it that way. But we can't clone ourselves, and he's being unreasonable." With her free hand, she rubs her temple, as if a headache pounds there. "Okay. Send me the draft. I'll read it tonight. After Dubois' contract. It should only take an—"

I've heard enough.

It's easy enough to pluck Samantha's phone from her hand. I don't bother greeting Mary; we've spoken often enough. "Change of plans," I say. "Samantha has a family emergency. Clear her schedule till Monday. She won't be taking any calls."

My fingers falls on the red button before either Samantha or Mary can protest.

The look Samantha gives me is pure outrage. "You have no right—"

"I have every right, *piscín*. We have an agreement, you and I."

She looks around the hotel room, gesturing as if I've lost my mind. "We're not at Thornfield," she says.

"Did I ever say my rules were limited to Thornfield?"

"*House* rules," she says.

"This is our house now."

I watch her line up arguments. I won't be surprised to hear that she's memorized the entire Pennsylvania Code, or at least the sections that apply to the hotel industry. Fully intending to distract her, I pluck the pencil from her hair. As long black curtains fall around her shoulders, I step back to study her furious face.

"What time is it, *piscín*?"

"I'm not your *piscín*. Not here. Not now."

"You're always my *piscín*." I catch her wrist, so those kitten claws can't reach my eyes. "What time is it?" I repeat.

She cranes her neck to look past me, to the clock on the nightstand. "8:52."

"And when does your work-day end?"

She's sullen, but she answers. "Six."

"So you owe me two hours and fifty-two minutes."

"You weren't even—"

"And that's ten more, for talking back."

"There's no rule that says—"

"Twenty."

She opens her mouth. Closes it. Glares at me with murderous intent.

The truth is, I'm short on tools to make my *piscín* comply. Floggers, paddles, canes, gags—they've all burned to ash at Thornfield. The bed here doesn't help much—there's no place to tie her up.

But playing with Samantha has always been more about her mind than my toys.

I sit on the edge of the bed. "Strip," I say.

She glances at the open bedroom door. "Anyone can just walk in here."

"That's thirty extra minutes. Please. Keep complaining."

"Braiden, be reasonable."

"*Strip*," I say. It's the first time I've used my Captain's voice in days. And Christ, it feels good.

She steps out of her shoes. She shrugs off her jacket, draping it over the back of one of the chairs by her papers. She shimmies out of her trousers and pulls her top over her head until she's standing in front of me, wearing nothing but white cotton panties and a featureless bra.

Other women wear lace and silk. Other women long to be pampered.

But my *piscín* has rules for herself. She thinks she needs to be punished for the mistakes she made in her past. She doesn't deserve soft things. She doesn't deserve color.

She's wrong. She deserves all those things and more. One day, I'll make her believe that.

Until then, I'll give her the punishment she craves.

"You're not naked," I remind her.

She looks toward the door again. "This is a *hotel*," she says, as if I might not be familiar with the concept. "There are *maids*. Turn-down service. Not to mention the fact that half the Fishtown Boys have keys to the room."

It's my job to make her forget all that.

My fingers close around her wrist, pulling her onto my lap. I've given her spankings before. That was the first lesson I ever taught my *piscín*. But I've never actually put her over my knee. I've never felt her fight for balance, squawking in embarrassment as my open-handed blow forces her belly against my swelling hard-on.

"Say *red*, and I'll stop," I promise.

She bites her lip, but she nods an acceptance to keep us safe.

Which means I can tug her panties over her hips. I can work the clasps on her bra with one hand, freeing her tits to dangle beside my knee. I can rub my palm over the warm, smooth skin of her arse, and then I can order, "Count."

When I start, I'm not certain how many times I'll spank her. But the first imprint of my hand flushes red, sending such a rush of blood to my cock that I have to catch my breath.

She's so beautiful, spread across my lap. Her pale skin looks like milk against my charcoal trousers. The mark of my hand stands out like spilled wine.

I nearly lost this sight forever. One more minute in the fire, five, ten... I don't know how long I had before the damage to my corneas would have become permanent.

My hand is dark against her flesh. Rough. And when I spank her again, she moans like she's already on the verge of coming.

The scent of her blooms beneath my hand—a whiff of soap and shampoo from her morning shower, the punch of sweat as her body braces for another blow, and the sweet, salty tang of her cunt heating beneath me.

"Tell me you want this, *piscín*."

She's proud, though. Even after all these months, she still thinks it's wrong to test her body's strength. She bites her lip and closes her eyes, ignoring my command.

Of course she pays for her silence. Again. And again. A dozen times more.

"Tell me, *piscín*. Say it. Say the words out loud."

"Yes!" she finally shouts. "Goddammit, yes! You win. You always win. I want you to spank me."

But she wins too. Because I roll her onto the bed. I ignore her hiss as her well-tanned arse rubs against the comforter. I kneel in front of her, and I spread her legs, and I bury my face in her soaking snatch, fucking her with my tongue until she howls.

After I make her come, I bite the inside of her thigh, sucking hard so she'll have my mark for days. She grabs my hair as I eat her out a second time, and she pulls hard enough to make my eyes water. I don't stop until she breaks again, chanting my name like a prayer, squeezing my head between her trembling thighs.

I ease her knees off my shoulders and sit back on my heels, wiping my mouth with the back of my hand. When I think she can hear me, I ask, "Where's your collar, *piscín?*"

I know she wore it from the fire. She needed the key from my pocket to set her free.

"I— It's in the safe."

I go to the closet. "What's the combination?"

She shakes her head, as if she doesn't understand the question. But she says, "Zero, one, one, zero."

Beneath her lawyer grit, my *piscín* is sentimental. That's the date we stood in front of the altar at St. Columba's.

I collect the collar from the safe and fasten it around her neck as she sits on the edge of the bed.

"I don't..." she says. "But why..." And then she's focused enough to say, "You already spanked me."

"And now I'm going to do something more."

"I don't know how much more I can handle."

"How much more I can handle, *sir*," I prompt her.

The reminder makes her open her mouth to protest. But I plant a finger on the emerald, pressing it into her throat. She swallows hard and says, "Sir."

I stare at her for just long enough to make her squirm. And then I say, "Make me a drink."

"What?"

I wrap her hair around my fist. "Make me a drink, *piscín*. And don't make me repeat any more orders."

"Wh— What do you want to drink?" And then she remembers. "Sir?"

"Jameson. Neat."

She has to go into the living room. To be in full view of the door. For just a moment, I think I've found her limit. I think she'll stop me—*red*.

But she nods. She stands. And she crosses to the well-stocked bar and pours me a generous whiskey. Four fingers. Neat.

I sip before I sit on the couch, knees spread wide. I want her skin against mine. I want to pull her onto my lap, to feel her wet heat against my thigh.

But more than that, I want to test her. I want her to follow the rules. And in this place, in this room, it will be infinitely harder for her to do that if I keep on all my clothes.

I snap and point to the carpet between my feet. "On your knees, *piscín.*"

I don't know when I learned to read Samantha Kelly like a book. I don't need to see her scowl to know she hates the symbolism of what I've just commanded. And I don't need to hear her quickened breath to know she wants to do it.

She kneels.

I lean back on the couch and spread my arms wide. I nod toward the tent in my trousers, the hard-on she's delivered. "Suck my cock."

Her eyes narrow. She's done it before, taking as much plea-sure as she gave. But I've never pushed our roles so far, never forced the visual that I'm her Dom and she is very much my sub.

"Don't make me ask again, *piscín.*"

"You didn't ask," she mutters. But just before I grab her chin, she ducks her head and whispers, "Sir."

Her fingers shake—maybe with anger, maybe with excite-ment. She works my belt buckle, leaving the ends loose beside my fly. She turns the button. She slides the zipper and eases my cock free. And when her lips close over me, I groan like I'm breaking in two.

I've set a dangerous game for both of us. I'm closer to the edge than I imagined. The third time I hit the back of her throat, I clutch my glass of whiskey so tight, I expect it to shat-ter, but I find the will to order, "Stop!"

She freezes with her tongue still pressed against my bollocks.

Gritting my teeth, I pull free, and for one dark second, I think I let her go too far. But I take deep breaths, and I tighten every muscle in my abs, and I hold onto the Jameson like it's the last flask in a desert.

When I'm back under control, I say, "Stand."

"I don't un— Did I do something wrong?"

I push myself to my feet, which means she has to stand, or be edged into the coffee table. I hitch my pants up to my hips and close my fingers over her biceps, purposely gripping hard.

"Let's go," I say.

And I walk her to the corner of the room. To the pair of windows that meet in a single line of glass, rising from knee to ceiling. To the view of Philadelphia, spread out beneath us, the nearest building blocks away.

"Hands on the windows," I order.

She's covering herself, right arm across her tits, left fingers fanned across her crotch. The door behind us is no longer her greatest fear. She's forgotten about maids and turn-down service and wayward Fishtown Boys. I'm telling her to show herself to the entire city.

"*Piscín*," I prompt, my voice a dangerous rumble.

She takes a step forward. I can see her body reflected in the glass, her face torn between shame and desire. This is what I would have lost, if my eyes had never healed. This is what I would have dreamed about forever.

She braces herself with a full breath. She closes her eyes.

She can stop me. She controls this.

She takes another step and plants her hands on the glass.

I move behind her, pressing my cock between her legs until she shifts to let me in.

Her cunt is soaked, exposing the lie that she doesn't want to be here. I penetrate her slowly, feeling the flutter as she melts around me. I spread one hand across her taut belly, holding her tight.

"Look at us," I tell her. When she resists, I pull her closer, forcing her to straighten her arms. "Open your eyes, *piscín*. See what you're doing. What you're letting me do."

She does it. She opens her eyes. She stares at our image in the glass, our reflection bright from all the lights behind us, her naked body framed by my clothed one.

I grab her hips and start to pump.

The fact that she came twice in the bedroom means nothing. She's primed by the heat of her well-spanked arse. She's riding the terror-thrill of exposure. She's arching her neck, stiffening her thighs, and when I shift one hand to find her clit, she breaks around me like a crystal cup.

Her fingers spread wide on the windows. She presses her tits against the glass. She pushes her arse against me, and I manage one more stroke before I'm shattering too, plowing deep, pulsing hard, pressing my cheek into her spine.

It takes a few minutes before I'm steady enough to lift my weight from her back. She sways as I slip out of her, a tiny wordless cry escaping her lips. I hitch up my trousers and then I half-guide, half-carry her over to the couch.

I don't have chocolate. I don't have arnica gel for the marks I've left on her body. I don't have a fully stocked kitchen with food to restore her after all she's given me, given us.

But I can cradle her body against mine. I can stroke the hair from her face. I can finger the emerald at her throat and tell her she's magnificent, she's my treasure, she's *mo chailín maith*.

And when I carry her to bed and kiss the lace of scars above her temple, I can whisper, "House rules. Breakfast tomorrow."

And I can wonder at her knowing smile, at the look of total satisfaction as she falls asleep inside the iron curve of my arm.

It's not until I'm falling asleep myself that I realize my *piscín* has topped from the bottom again. She manipulated me like the expert attorney she is. She goaded me into enforcing the rules she knows by heart.

I'll make her pay.

But for now, I can't regret a single thing she's done.

7

SAMANTHA

We all eat breakfast together in the second suite on Friday morning—Braiden and Aiofe and me. Fairfax hovers like a new mother as he sets room service dishes on the table. I'm as hungry as a long-haul trucker, and I ache in places where I didn't even know I had muscles. My ass is so tender I wince every time I shift position on the stiff hotel chair.

"Are you okay?" Aiofe asks, a frown puckering the space between her eyebrows.

"I'm fine," I assure her.

"You look like you're sitting on tacks," she says.

I catch Braiden preening, like he's done something admirable. "There's something tacky going on," I tell Aiofe. "But I'm fine."

It was easier to keep our sex life private when Aiofe stayed in her own silent world. She looks confused by my reply, but I cut off further questions by asking what she's going to do for the day.

"I don't know," she says. "Watch TV. Maybe take a nap."

"What if we get out of the hotel? Want to go to the Liberty Bell?" I loved my school visits to the landmark when I was her age.

"No one's going to the Liberty Bell," Braiden says.

"How about Independence Hall then?" I ask, as if I don't understand Braiden's objection.

"Forget about it," he says before Aiofe can reply.

"The Franklin Institute?" I challenge him. "Or the art museum? Or maybe we could go to the aquarium."

"Go to your room," Braiden tells Aiofe, who is watching us avidly.

"I'm still eating breakfast," she protests.

"Fairfax!" Braiden calls, even though he's standing just six feet away.

Fairfax swoops in to collect Aiofe's plate and her glass of milk. "Come along, sweetheart. Let the grown-ups fight."

"We aren't fighting!" I call after them, as Fairfax closes the bedroom door.

"Stop," Braiden says, his voice low and gritty.

"I'm not wearing my collar now," I point out.

"You're not taking Aiofe out of this hotel."

"Then what's *your* plan?"

"My plan?"

"Will you keep her under lock and key forever?"

"You, of all people, know it's not safe out there."

I set my knife and fork across the edge of my plate. "Of all people?" I ask, with deadly precision.

He leans back in his chair. "You want me to spell it out? All right. One. Kieran Ingram put a price on your head. Two. Madden did his level best to take you out. Three. Antonio Russo is stirring again. He boosted one of my trucks last night, a full load of electronics. Left a good man knocked out by the side of the road."

I didn't know about Russo. But I'm ready to fight back on

the other two points. "Kieran Ingram's dead. Who's in charge of Boston now?"

His mouth twists like he smells something foul. "No one. Not yet."

"And who's running the Grand Irish Union?"

"Don't push me, woman."

I don't back down. "Who's running the Union?"

"No one. Not until the captains gather for a vote."

"So Ingram's clan and the Union are in chaos. They're fighting for their own territory, finding their own boss. No one has the resources to come down here from Boston. Not now."

"You can't be certain of that. My job is to keep you safe."

"No," I tell him, and I make my voice gentle because I need him to hear me. I need him to understand. "Your job is to run the Fishtown Boys. And you can't do that if you let ghosts run you."

He's not ready to give in yet. "Madden—"

"We both know Madden isn't a threat anymore." I glance at the bedroom door. Aiofe already knows too much about her uncle's last hour on earth. I don't want to give her more fuel for nightmares.

"He was working with Russo."

"How many men do you have watching Russo, at this very moment?"

Braiden looks away.

"Two?" I push. "Four? A dozen?"

"I have men watching Russo," he concedes.

"And how many men could you assign to guard us, if Aiofe and I went to the Liberty Bell?"

"There is no reason on earth why the two of you need to see a giant cracked bell."

"You're wrong," I tell him. "There's every reason. Aiofe needs help. She's talking, and that's a miracle. But she lost Birte. She lost Grace. She even lost her tutor. She has nightmares—

just ask Fairfax. She needs something—some structure, some rules."

He snorts.

"Dammit, Braiden, don't do that. You got *your* rules back last night. Are you going to say you don't feel better this morning?"

He opens his mouth. Closes it. Fiddles with the handle of his teacup.

I push my advantage while I can. "And while we're talking about Aiofe... You let her see Father Regis, and he helped, for a while at least. But she needs more now. She needs to test that voice of hers. She needs to use her words. Get her a real doctor, Braiden. If you truly believe your job is to keep her safe, get her someone to talk to."

"Jesus, Mary, and Joseph," he complains, pushing back from the table. I let him go.

Aiofe and I don't get to the Liberty Bell, or Independence Hall, or the Franklin Institute, the art museum, or the aquarium. But at four o'clock in the afternoon, my phone buzzes with a message. There are three names listed, with phone numbers and links to websites.

BRAIDEN

Choose one and call for an appointment. Pay what it takes to get her seen next week.

8

BRAIDEN

After her weekend of enforced leisure, Samantha moves fast on making the appointment for Aiofe. She shifts her own schedule so she can be there for the girl. I put Rory O'Hare in charge of their security. He's the man Patrick said I could rely on.

Because, despite my most pointed phone calls, my Warlord is showing no sign of coming home from Boston any time soon. He's too good a man to break by giving a direct order. Not when I can't be sure he'll take it.

But O'Hare brings me his plan before Samantha and Aiofe leave the hotel. He's got one man in a car in front of my girls and one man in a car behind. Liam Murphy will drive Samantha and Aiofe with O'Hare riding literal shotgun, a weapon in his hands from door to door, courtesy of Pennsylvania's open carry laws.

It's a good approach, the sort of thing I'd plan myself. I sign off on it.

When they get back, O'Hare reports directly to me, in the Presidential Suite. He says no one followed them there or back, and I believe him. He's able to recite the make and model of every car that entered the therapist's parking lot while Aiofe and Samantha were inside.

Samantha reports in too. "I wasn't allowed to sit in on the session," she says.

"So how do you know it worked?"

"Therapy doesn't *work*, not like that. It'll take a few visits at least. After a month or two, we can ask Aiofe if she wants to continue."

I shake my head. "No Kelly has ever needed a head shrinker."

"And look how well your family handles trauma." She doesn't look at my scarred arm. She doesn't need to.

"Fine," I say. "We'll talk to her in a month."

"But there are some changes we need to make in the meantime."

"What sort of changes?" I ask warily.

For the first time since walking into the suite, Samantha looks uncomfortable. "We should have a funeral for Birte. And for Grace Poole too."

"The fire's still under investigation," I say.

"And it might be for months. Aiofe needs closure now."

"Do you honestly think she's strong enough to face a crowd of people?"

"There won't be a crowd. Just the family and a priest. You can tolerate a legitimate priest conducting the service, can't you?"

That's a dig about our wedding. A taste like quinine paints my throat. "Go ahead," I concede. "Schedule it at St. Columba's."

Samantha nods, as if she's crossed an item off a long list. "I want to enroll Aiofe in summer school."

"You're out of your feckin' mind."

"She's already gone three weeks without classes. And I'm not sure how much she learned before she was talking. I spoke to Fairfax today, and he thinks John Bell might stay in Patagonia. Aiofe needs to be reading at grade level."

How the hell does Fairfax know what John Bell is planning? But I argue: "She reads every night before she goes to sleep."

"Half of those are picture books. Grace Poole was her primary caretaker, and that woman was barely literate."

"Grace Poole—" I start to defend myself.

"Plus," Samantha rolls over my objection. "Grace spoke to her in Irish half the time."

"There's nothing wrong with Irish."

"Of course there isn't. But you want Aiofe to succeed here. In the States."

Samantha knows exactly where to find my soft bits. Of course I want Aiofe to succeed. I owe that much to her, after all that happened in Ireland.

But I protest, "You cannot drop that innocent child into a public school. You can't tell her to sink or swim, and all her troubles be damned."

Samantha looks wounded. "Of course not. But a parochial school would be perfect. I'll talk to the priest at St. Columba's. See what he recommends."

"What's next on your list?" I ask sourly.

"We need a house."

I laugh. "We have a house."

"How long before we can move back into Thornfield?" she asks. "If the fire department clears us tomorrow and you pour in every last resource from Kelly Construction?"

I answer grudgingly. "A year."

"And you honestly intend for us to stay in this hotel for those twelve months?"

I look around. "There are worse kips in the world."

Samantha has her facts drawn up like she's arguing before the Supreme Court. "Aiofe's a child. She needs a child's bedroom. A playroom. A kitchen where she can learn to make cookies."

"Fairfax can get her up to speed once we're back in Thornfield," I say dryly.

"How much longer do you think Fairfax will stick around? Ordering room service is a little below his pay grade, isn't it?"

"Alec Fairfax is the most loyal man I know."

She changes tack. "You and I need some privacy."

"That wasn't a problem Thursday night."

She blushes, but she doesn't give in. "That was a mistake."

"You don't believe that for a moment."

"Okay. It wasn't a mistake. But it won't happen again. If there were pictures, even one… I'm about to face a hearing on whether I'm fit to practice law. All it takes is one board member to say what I let you do to me is perverted. Immoral. Sick." Her chin starts to quiver, but she doesn't stop. "Don't do it, Braiden. Don't make me choose between my career and you."

The eejits who will hear her case have their own secrets. Everyone does. And I'm not opposed to manufacturing a little evidence, to planting it either, if that's what it takes for Samantha to keep her license.

But that's not what she wants to hear. Not today. So I sigh and say, "Tell Fairfax to look around for something on the open market."

"Something to rent?"

I shake my head. "Not with the security we need."

I see her start the calculations—closing costs, agents' fees, insurance, and all the rest. And that's not counting the fact that I was down a quarter of a billion dollars after Russo boosted my container full of cocaine. That my territory was cut at a summit in this very hotel. That I'm bleeding money to Warren K. Chesterton and I've paid every one of my loyal Fishtown Boys a bonus, even though my income's in the jacks.

But it's not her job to worry about any of that; it's mine. If Samantha thinks we need a house, I'll get her one. I protect my family. So I remind her, same as I'm reminding myself: "I'm a billionaire. I can buy myself a house."

She knows about my money. We met at a feckin' tax haven.

"Anything else?" I ask, eyebrows raised.

She shakes her head, awed into silence for once. "I'd say thank you, but that doesn't seem to be enough."

I shrug.

Her eyes brighten, as if she's just had a brilliant idea. "I could wear my collar—"

"Not tonight."

"Fairfax can keep an eye on Aiofe—"

"No."

She sits back, confused. "Did I do something wrong?"

"Aside from making me think Thursday night was my idea?"

"It was!"

I just stare at her, focusing on her throat, where my emerald would rest if she wasn't such a strong-willed sub.

"You decided what we did," she amends.

I still don't answer.

"We both needed it! Didn't you feel better after we…"

How sweet. She doesn't know which words to choose. I decide to toss her a lifeline. "Sure, I felt better after fucking you blind. And I want nothing more than to put you on your knees again."

"Then why not—"

"Because you're my sub, *piscín*. You need to learn a lesson. You do not top from below. And I'm Dom enough to teach that to you."

Her old defiance rides high. "So you're never putting me in my collar again?"

"I'll put you in your collar when *I* decide it's time. Until then, you can think about what it means to truly submit."

She opens her mouth. Closes it. And I leave the room before I can change my mind.

I'm in for a week of cold showers. Maybe more, if Samantha stays as stubborn as I know she can be.

9

SAMANTHA

I hope Braiden will relent on his no-sex rule after he spends a long day studying real estate listings, but he doesn't. I think he might change his mind after another day spent reviewing Fishtown security with his acting Warlord, but I'm wrong. I do my best to get under his skin when I get ready for bed—strutting across the room in my high heels as I return my skirt to the closet, stretching for the covers as I climb into bed, shifting closer and closer as I find a comfortable position amid the ocean of white-cased pillows…

He mutters under his breath. But he doesn't reach for me. Not even when he wakes with a wicked case of morning wood.

Frustrated, I consider leaving the hotel and heading across town for my morning meeting, but I'd rather convince Braiden I'm playing by his rules. So I phone my lawyer, Teddy Newland, and I ask him to come to the Rittenhouse. I secure us a meeting room downstairs. Teddy has done enough work for the mob that he doesn't even blink at the four men standing guard.

Or maybe he doesn't notice them.

Teddy could be someone's kindly grandfather, the type of man who's always prepared with a peppermint in his pocket and a pat on the head. His fringe of gray hair makes him resemble a gentle old monk. His eyeglasses slip down his nose so frequently I wonder how much he can actually see out of the smudged lenses. A stain darkens the crimson of his Harvard tie, blurring the word *veritas*—truth—on its miniature shield.

Teddy looks like a long-retired absent-minded professor. But he sounds like one of the sharpest legal minds I've ever encountered.

"Detective Hiram Tarrant is an old-school cop," Teddy says. "If we look at the testimony he's delivered in trials over the past five years…"

Teddy pulls up an elaborate spreadsheet on his computer. The document is filled with cross-referenced information—judges' names, criminal counts, number of witnesses, even the number of exhibits filed by the prosecution in each case. Teddy walks me through the data, doing me the honor of treating me like a fellow professional. He never talks down to me, but he makes sure I understand the gravity of the situation.

He concludes: "So Tarrant is a bulldog. He doesn't get bored, and he doesn't get sloppy. He'll put in the extra hours to get the job done."

I nod slowly. As a taxpayer, I should be grateful for the man's dedication. As a likely criminal defendant, I'm sickened. "And what that means for my case is…"

Teddy pushes his glasses back up the bridge of his nose. "There's good news and bad news."

I can't imagine anything good about the situation Teddy's just laid out. But I humor him. "And the good news is?"

"The statute of limitations has expired on a lot of counts the prosecutor might consider. Leaving the scene of an accident… Duty to render aid… Aggravated assault or insurance fraud or intimidation of witnesses... Those all washed out after five years."

I already know what he's going to say next, so I cut to the chase: "And the bad news is there's no statute of limitations on murder."

"Or manslaughter. Or vehicular homicide."

I let the words hang in the air for a full minute before I ask, "So what do we do?"

Teddy pushes his glasses again. "Unfortunately, at this point, there isn't a lot we *can* do. Detective Tarrant has to finish his investigation. After he's gathered all of his evidence, he'll pass it to a prosecutor. The prosecutor will decide whether to proceed with a criminal case against you."

There isn't a prosecutor in Pennsylvania who won't jump at the chance to drag me into court. Not after the paparazzi have been agitating for months. Not after what I did.

"That's it?" I ask. "We just wait?"

Again with the glasses. Teddy peers at me through the smudges, his watery blue eyes kind. "We *could* hire our own investigator. We can track what Tarrant does. Follow the physical evidence he comes up with. Study the same facts, talk to the same witnesses."

"And the advantage of that?"

He tilts his head just a little, projecting a soft, quiet sympathy. "We won't be surprised. We can begin to build our defense. Figure out the story *we* want to tell at trial."

There'll be a trial. Neither of us doubts that.

I take a moment, but I nod. "Go ahead, then. Let's get as much information as we can."

He clears his throat softly. "There's something else."

I wait through the pushing up of the glasses. Through another throat-clearing. Through a distracted thumbing of the stain on his tie. "Something else?" I finally urge.

"We can do some research on Tarrant himself. Find out

about the detective's personal life. See if there's anything that might...discredit him on the stand. Nothing's come up in the research we've already done—" He gestures at his spreadsheet. "But a proper investigation might find..."

He puts the slightest emphasis on the word *proper*, just enough for me to realize he means exactly the opposite. An *improper* investigation might come up with something worthy of blackmail. An even *more* improper investigation might actually plant misleading evidence, something to discredit the stalwart Detective Tarrant.

Braiden can do that. In fact, he's probably done things like that dozens of times before. Hell, he can probably send one of his men to convince Hiram Tarrant it's not worth investigating me for one more day, one more hour, one more minute. He could get rid of Tarrant altogether.

No.

Some bridges stretch too far. I killed three people That Night. I won't compound my crime now.

"Thank you," I tell Teddy. "I don't think that's a good use of our resources. Not now. And not down the line."

From his slow nod, I know I've made myself understood.

"But let's shadow Detective Tarrant. Let's keep an eye on what he finds. Let's avoid any surprises."

"I'll take care of it," Teddy says.

There's more—a discussion about staffing and how things slow down in summer and how my case isn't likely to move forward before early fall, barring any major change in circumstances.

That means barring the ethics board finding me unfit to practice law. Teddy doesn't say the words out loud. It's like he's superstitious, like he doesn't want to risk bringing down the same fate on himself. But we both understand precisely what he means.

Finally, he stands. He dusts his hands down the front of his suit. He locks his briefcase with careful, precise motions.

I see him to the door of the conference room, and his hand is dry as he shakes mine. "I wish you all the luck in the world, Ms. Kelly," he says.

I'm going to need it.

10

BRAIDEN

Saturday morning, I pull into the Dover airfield, driving straight to a private hangar at the far end of the compound. My Jeep looks like a second-class citizen among the luxury vehicles of the other members of the Diamond Ring, but the freeport's other billionaires don't seem to notice.

After years of working with Trap Prince, I know better than to shake his hand. He'll do it; he's not a feckin' animal. But after, he always looks like he's plunged his fingers into a bowl of raw tripe. So we settle for friendly nods, and he gestures for me to climb the steps into his private jet.

Half the Ring is already on board. We've all followed the dress code on the invitation that arrived by email—collared shirt, no jeans, no shorts. Arsene Dubois has a smear of sunscreen on his nose, but no one else has mentioned it, so I keep my gob shut.

"Anyone know where we're going?" Carl Braxton asks, barely looking up from his phone. I wonder if he's closing some illegal arms deal even as we wait on the tarmac. He has customers in every time zone on the planet.

"I tried to hack the flight plan, but I couldn't get in," Cole Wolf says.

"That's a first." Gage Rider is sipping a Bloody Mary that looks to be nine parts vodka.

Wolf shrugs. "I'm the one who upgraded Prince's system. I should have left a back door."

I'm willing to bet he's done just that; he's only playing hard-to-get because he wants to be one of the guys.

Steve Torrington flashes a smile that's served the insurance executive well for a lifetime. "You're going about this all wrong, boys. Just offer the pilot a good enough tip, and you'll get our destination in no time."

"Try that with my pilot," Trap Prince says from the door. "And you'll find out what it's like to fly in the motherfucking cargo hold."

We laugh, because Prince pretends it's a joke. But no one tries to storm the cockpit with bribes. Instead, we take our seats when the pretty flight attendant asks us to. We put on our seatbelts like we're all proper choir boys.

I find myself next to Sawyer Best, which suits me fine. The man knows the value of silence—he built his career as a military interrogator—but he's happy to talk shop if anyone has questions about how to run a private army.

I'm not looking for soldiers. But Best has other skills I might need. I wait until he puts down his glass of fresh-squeezed orange juice. It's early in the day for the twenty-year-old bourbon he prefers.

As we reach cruising altitude, I ask, "You do consulting work on physical security, don't you?" The Diamond Ring is all about cutting through unnecessary shite.

"What do you have in mind?" The man is locked up tighter than a bank vault. Which is excellent for my purposes.

"I'm thinking of buying a house. Something near Philly, for my family. Temporary, for a year or two."

"New construction?"

"If you tell me that's better."

"New homes already have networks built in, for surveillance, for computer security. They've all got windows like department stores on Fifth Avenue, but you can replace those with bulletproof glass."

"And old homes?"

"Some of them are built like forts. They're more likely to have property, a place where you can build a proper gatehouse, install perimeter protection, that sort of thing. Of course, some of them are money pits that can't anchor a deadbolt."

"I'll probably go new. I'm moving fast."

"Sam wants out of the Rittenhouse?"

Of course he knows Samantha. She's his lawyer too, at least for all his freeport deals. But I still have to fight the urge to shove his juice glass down his feckin' throat at his presuming to know what Samantha wants.

Instead, I shrug, as if my promise to leave the hotel isn't important. "She wants bigger closets."

Best gives me a look that says he doesn't buy my lie for a second. But he says, "I've got a man. He can look over any place you're thinking about buying, give you a run down on the security pros and cons. He can supervise whatever work you decide to put into the place."

"I'll be in touch."

We spend the rest of the flight talking about meaningless shite—hockey playoffs where his Washington Capitals annihilated my Philadelphia Flyers, the Fed's idiotic waffling on interest rates, Elon's latest rocket to blow up on the launch pad. We're just two billionaires enjoying a day off, and neither one of us has ever dreamed of breaking a law in our lives.

I've kept an eye on the window the whole time we've been in the air. We've traveled south from Dover, with the sun on our left. Two hours after take-off, we're touching down at a tiny airstrip—there isn't even a control tower. A sign on the one building in sight announces we've arrived at Daniel Field.

Six luxury town cars wait by the runway, trunks open. We approach like kids on Christmas morning. I'm not surprised that Gage Rider finds his prize first.

The former hockey player whoops as he lifts a leather bag out of the trunk. It looks heavy, which makes sense, because it holds fourteen golf clubs along with—as Rider quickly displays —balls, tees, gloves, towels, and a miniature first aid kit.

"Gentlemen," Trap Prince says, with a gloating smile. "Welcome to Augusta National."

He deserves the gloat. The club is famously closed to the public. The Masters was played here just weeks ago, every blade of grass manicured to perfection for the days-long televised orgy. There are just three hundred members, and they're only allowed on the course from October to May. Each member is allowed to invite four friends for a single round of golf each year.

There are twelve of us in the Diamond Ring. That means Prince found three Augusta members to invite us in as guests. *Bought* three members, more likely.

By the time we arrive at the first tee, boasting is in high gear. I've spent some time on golf courses—more, before I took over the Fishtown Boys from Da. But my fourteen handicap is nothing compared to Rider's four.

Prince divides us into foursomes and reminds us we're responsible for making good on our own bets. Dubois immediately starts in with his group, calling for Dots, his betting game of choice. He sounds like an eejit, going on about barkies and pinnies and poleys.

Cole Wolf looks at Torrington, Weber, and me and suggests, "Hundred grand a hole?" We shake on it, and Weber tees off.

Torrington takes the first hole. Wolf and Weber tie the second, carrying over the bet. A gust of wind makes me lucky on the third.

I wait until we're walking to the fourth tee before I ask Wolf, "Say you were wiring a new house to block electronic surveillance."

"New to you? Or new construction?"

I've learned my lesson from Best. "Both."

Wolf nods. He's not big on wasting words.

I've been a lot more concerned about the feds getting into my business than I have been about other crime bosses hacking their way in. But by the ninth hole, Wolf has convinced me I've been looking at it all wrong. Criminals like me are *always* a concern.

"So, how many guys like you are out there?" I ask Wolf. "Who else would Russo hire?"

"There's no one like me," Wolf says, as we watch Torrington drop one onto the green. "But three, maybe four pretend to do what I can."

"You've got a man? Someone in Philly who can do the work once I've found a place?"

Wolf shakes his head. "I don't play well with others. You hire Wolf Hall, you hire me."

He'll cost a fortune. And Declan, my clan's long-time computer expert, won't be thrilled. But it'll be worth it, if I'm certain the new place is secure. We shake on it and Wolf steps up to the tee.

Prince knew what he was doing, dividing us into groups of four by nearly equal skill. We trade off holes on the back nine. I manage to birdie fifteen, but I'm out three hundred grand at the end of the day.

Ordinarily, I wouldn't think twice about the loss. But as they say, one hundred grand here, one hundred there, soon we're talking about real money. I tell myself it's only cash flow. I've still got a grip on my finances.

Prince picks up the first round of drinks in the clubhouse. I take my time, working my way across the room to where Connor Boyle is watching the other members of the Ring. He holds his massive shoulders perfectly still. Only his eyes move, as if he's weighing danger.

I touch my Jameson to his Guinness. "Good day on the links?"

"Dubois's a right eejit, when it comes to betting."

Boyle's accent is thicker than mine. I don't know the full story, but his da kept him in the kennel for years, a rank enforcer instead of on his clan's council, where his last name should have put him. He's got scars on his knuckles to prove he did his job, and rumor says he still carries his butterfly knife, pistol, and garrote wherever he goes.

He became king of New York around the same time I took over Philly, but we've never been exactly friends. Not enemies either—Boyle keeps his own counsel.

But I ask him: "What do you hear from Boston?"

He shrugs, a mountain threatening a landslide. "There've been ructions since Ingram's girl got home."

"Who's been fighting?" I want to know if his sources match mine.

Another shift of those shoulders. "Rumor says the girl's staking a claim. Her uncle too, her da's Clan Chief. And Ingram's Warlord's weighing in."

"Jaysus." I hear myself slip into his brogue.

He pins me with a flat gaze. "I expect your Warlord's told you the same."

Fair play to him. He knows Patrick is at Fiona's side.

In reality, my so-called Warlord has only texted a couple of times. Herself's still rough, Patrick says. Ring if I need him home. He can be at my side in hours.

On the homefront, Rory O'Hare is working his old boss out of a job. And keeping a man up in Boston means I'll know if—when?—Ingram's crew remember they want my blood. So I haven't ordered Patrick home. Yet.

I salute Boyle with my glass, twitching my lips like I don't care what happens north of the New Jersey state line. "Boston's far from Philadelphia," I say.

Boyle nods, as if those words are profound. "Far from New York, too."

As long as we're still talking, I give another push. "But the Union covers all."

By tradition, a new general is only named one hundred days after the death of an old one. That's over three months for a questing man to gather votes. No one has yet knocked on my door for support. But Boyle says, "I hear Reardon's getting restless."

"Out in Chicago? I'd expect him to let the First Four handle this."

Chicago's a wean, compared to the East Coast dynasties— Boston, New York, Philadelphia, and Baltimore. The Union general has always come from one of the old families.

"Boston's a holy show right now," Boyle says. "I'm still proving a second son can do the job. You've got that goombah prick breathin' up yer arsehole, so you don't have a chance in hell. Reardon must think he has a chance against Baltimore. New Orleans and San Francisco will fall in line."

It's the longest speech I've ever heard Boyle make.

And it's the first I've heard that I don't have a chance in hell.

Until this moment, I can honestly say I haven't thought once about taking a run at General. Between Thornfield burning, Madden dying, and Russo plotting... Boyle's right. I've a lot on my plate.

But as the silence stretches out between us, I let myself imagine life without a general grabbing ten percent of everything I earn. How it would feel to be my own man, free and clear at the top of the Union...

And suddenly the idea of bending a knee to Mickey Reardon makes my Jameson taste like piss.

If Boyle's realized I'm thinking too much, he doesn't give a sign. Instead, he looks across the clubhouse, where Prince is calling us all over to the bar. We cross the room together.

Prince has prizes for the day's outing. Rider lodged the lowest score, no surprise. Best told the filthiest story on the back nine. Torrington landed the most business. Everyone laughs, and the winners stand us another few rounds.

Now that I've thought about trying for General, I can't stop tallying my chances. Sure, money's tight right now. But the Fish-town Boys are more profitable today than they were when I took over from Da. The other clans'll see the value in that. Or they will, once my cash flow is adjusted.

The best thing I could do to raise my chances? Get rid of Antonio Fucking Russo for good. Destroy Philadelphia's Mafia once and for all. The Union couldn't ignore that.

And while I'm at it, I can cure cancer. And generate world peace. After all, I've got almost three months before the captains vote.

I'm not going to reach a decision about running today. So I might as well relax and enjoy the top shelf booze. I just played the most exclusive golf course in the world. Samantha's waiting for me at home. I'm certain she's fretting that I'll never put her back in her collar, which limits my options for tonight but will pay off well down the road.

I'm good at playing the long game. Always have been. So I order another whiskey. And I laugh at someone's bad joke. And I tell myself Boyle's flat-out wrong when he says I don't have a chance in hell.

11

SAMANTHA

~

The funeral is held on a rainy Wednesday afternoon. Braiden decides that one service will serve for both Birte and Grace. They lived together on the third floor of Thornfield. It only seems right they should be remembered together now.

We mourners only fill one pew in St. Columba's. Braiden and Fairfax wear jet black suits. I don't own a dress that's black. My work clothes are all tailored pants and blazers, and my skirts are all riots of flowers. I decide it's more respectful to wear trousers, like the men.

Aiofe wears a simple black frock with one row of ruffles above her knee. Her hair is pulled back with a matching ribbon. Her face looks as pale as the milk tea Braiden pours for her every morning. Her eyes are red from crying, her nose chapped from blowing.

Rory O'Hare and three of his enforcers occupy the bench behind us. I'm not sure any one of them could have picked the first Mrs. Kelly out of a police-mandated line-up, but the men are there as protection. They wear black and keep their mouths shut. No one could ask for more.

That's it. No one else remembers Birte or Grace.

Braiden could have ordered Fishtown Boys to occupy more pews. He could have gone overboard completely and required wives and children to fill the church. But in the end, he decided to tell no more lies about the girl he married in Ireland, about the nursemaid he brought to the States.

Father Regis conducts the mass. He met both women, so he manages to say something personal in his short homily. He remembers Birte's piano playing and her simple devotion to her faith. He mentions Grace's attentiveness to Birte.

After the final prayers for the dead, Father Regis stops in front of our pew. He rests a hand on poor Aiofe's head and prays out loud that God will comfort her. If he condemns my dry eyes and Braiden's and Fairfax's, he doesn't say a word.

Father Regis heads back to the vestry. O'Hare and his men fill the aisle, a black-clad wall between us and the outside world. We four mourners follow behind, quiet shadows beneath the dark stained glass.

Antonio Russo is waiting on the front steps of the church, immaculate as ever in Armani. Three of his goons stand behind him, their brightly colored casual shirts obscene in the spring sunshine.

Braiden shoulders past a bristling Rory O'Hare. "What the fuck are you doing here?" he growls.

Russo's eyes open wide in pretended surprise. "I believe you once told me that Mother Church keeps an open door."

"You're not inside the door," Braiden points out. "You're lurking on the steps."

"*Lurk* is such an unpleasant word."

"What do you want, Russo?"

"I came to offer condolences to my sweet Giovanna."

Braiden's shoulders seem to swell beneath his jacket. "She doesn't need your lies."

Russo turns to me. "Is that the way of these Irish dogs, Giovanna? They will not let you seek the comfort of your people?"

It's bait, and I know it, but I can't keep from biting back. "I don't need your comfort, Russo."

He looks hurt. "There was a time when you called me Antonio."

I called him *Don* Antonio. But that was before he murdered my cousin. Before he threatened to lock me into a marriage I never desired.

"How did you even know we'd be here?" I ask, not giving him the satisfaction of calling him anything.

"I was saddened, of course, when I read about your tragedy. On the front page of the paper, no less. I paid—generously—for a mass to be said in Birte Kelly's name. So Father Regis was only too willing to tell me when a funeral was scheduled."

I shouldn't be so shocked to hear the Catholic Church was bribed. Before I manage an answer, Braiden tosses an order over his shoulder. "Rory. Get Aiofe to the car."

But Russo intercepts O'Hare before he gets the child clear. The Mafia capo kneels on the top stone step, plucking the seam of his virgin wool slacks. At Aiofe's eye level, he says, "I am sorry you have lost your auntie."

Aiofe looks to Braiden for reassurance, but whatever she sees there makes her more afraid. She tries to ease behind O'Hare, hiding her face against him.

"Leave the girl alone," Braiden says, his voice deadly still. But he can't spill the blood he wants to shed. Not here, in broad daylight. Not in front of Aiofe, who has already seen too much blood on church steps.

Russo reaches out and wraps one of Aiofe's curls around his finger. "Such pretty hair," he says. "Like your auntie, I hear."

Braiden's hands knots into fists. I want to slap the sneer from Russo's face. But neither of us does a thing because Aiofe's already terrified.

"Do not cry, *principessa*," Russo says. "You can visit the grave of your auntie. You can ask her to watch over you. There is only a small chance that grave will be unsafe."

"Rory!" Braiden barks, his Captain's voice off its leash.

O'Hare scoops Aiofe up like she's a pile of laundry. The side of his hand crashes hard on Russo's wrist, forcing Aiofe's hair out of the intruder's grasp. O'Hare's long legs manage the steps two at a time, and he shifts Aiofe's head to his shoulder as he carries her to the replacement Bentley that arrived only this morning. Fairfax hurries after with one apologetic glance, as if he knows he can be of no concrete assistance with Russo on the prowl.

Russo's men gather close behind him. He shakes his wrist, channeling all his hatred into a glare at Braiden.

"Don't waste your time," Braiden says. "Birte will be buried in her family plot, in County Cork."

This is the first I've heard of the plan. But under the circumstances, I approve.

Russo turns his bullying to me. "Will Kelly send you away as easily, Giovanna? After he tires of your *figa*?"

Braiden bulls forward. "Say one more word to my wife—"

"But that is the problem, is it not? My Giovanna is not your wife. Not after you strong-armed your so-called priest to do your wedding."

For one blind moment, I think Father Brennan has betrayed us. I wonder how Russo threatened him. I wonder how long Father Brennan held out before he caved.

But then I realize Russo has never spoken with the defrocked priest. He learned the truth from someone even closer to Braiden.

Braiden draws the same conclusion. "Don't believe everything my brother tells you." He remembers to use the present tense, because no one else on these steps knows Madden is dead.

"Your brother?" Russo sounds politely confused.

"Do you suck Madden's cock?" Braiden demands. "Or only let him fuck your guinea arse?"

Russo's men surge forward, all three moving as one. Russo, though, holds up a commanding hand. He clicks his tongue, tsking with a mournful look at me. "Poor Giovanna. Does he kiss you with that mouth? After saying such things on the steps of a church?"

I clutch Braiden's arm, because nothing good will come of trading more insults. "Come on," I urge him. "Aiofe needs us."

"Do not be in such a rush, Giovanna. When I heard you would be at church today, I invited some friends to join us."

"Let's *go*," I say to Braiden, because there's no one in the world Russo could have invited that I want to see.

But before we can move toward the Bentley, half a dozen cars pull up to the curb in front of St. Columba's. People tumble out the doors, most brandishing phones. A satellite truck parks across the street as someone shoves a microphone into my face.

"Samantha!" people shout. "Sam! Look this way! Turn here!"

And then the questions start.

"How long did you and Braiden plan your fake marriage?"

"No comment," I say, just the way Sonja trained me.

"Was your fake marriage a tax dodge?"

"No comment," I say.

"Was Birte Kelly pushed?"

"What the actual fuck?" I can't keep myself from shouting.

Of course they jump all over that. Suddenly, everyone has questions about Birte—when Braiden and I locked her in a basement, how long she was our sex slave, how much of her fortune we stole. There aren't enough "no comments" in the universe to answer the absurdities.

The instant we were swarmed, Russo stepped away. Now, he stands at the base of the steps, ignored by the media circus howling for my blood. I don't know how many of the questions spring from the paparazzi's imagination, and how many he planted before he arrived to torture us.

"Smile, Sam," someone shouts. "Let's see that killer grin."

Braiden finally gets his arm around me, and I huddle next to his side like I'm taking refuge from a rainstorm. O'Hare's men close behind us, and we belatedly make our way to the car.

I end up in the back seat of the Bentley; Braiden takes the front. Aiofe is sandwiched between Fairfax and me. She buries her face in my blouse as O'Hare starts the slow process of navigating through the crowd without crushing anyone.

I cover Aiofe's head with my hands, doing my best to shield her. Phones are slapped against the car windows, and shouted questions vibrate through the glass.

"You're fine," I tell Aiofe. "You're absolutely fine. You're safe. You're absolutely safe." I say it over and over, until the words have lost their meaning. And I know, as O'Hare finally pulls free from the church, I don't believe a thing I'm saying.

I look back as we finally put some distance between us and the chaos. Russo is a black vulture, feeding on the crowd. And I wonder how many more times I can escape the mob's vicious hunger.

12

SAMANTHA

S onja calls before we're halfway home.

"I can't talk now," I tell her.

"Are you even *trying* to avoid reporters?"

The three weeks I've spent at the Rittenhouse have been the most quiet since this mess began. The hotel has no qualms about banishing paparazzi and protesters to the public park across the street. It's not my fault everything changed today.

I want to meet Sonja's attack with fire, but Aiofe is still curled against my side. I shift my phone to my right ear. "They ambushed me," I hiss.

"Do you understand how damaging it is even to *hear* those questions? Much less to realize you don't have a single good answer?"

"I'll call you when I get home."

"This is bad, Samantha. For our case, and for the criminal investigation too."

"I know it's bad. And it will be worse if I don't end this call now." I tap the red button and drop the phone into my lap.

Braiden is staring straight ahead, as if he can teleport us to the Rittenhouse solely by the fury of his gaze. I know the lion's share of his rage is for Russo, but I can't help but think some of it is for me. For my giving Antonio Russo a lever. For everything I did That Night. For everything I didn't do.

When we get to the hotel, Braiden takes Aiofe to her room. I lock myself in the bathroom of our Presidential Suite and return Sonja's call. When she answers, she sounds like a different woman. All the fight has drained out of her, as if someone pulled the plug in a bathtub. She doesn't even swear.

"You know how this works," she says. "Our job is to tell a story. We make the board understand why you were up on that mountain. How you made a mistake. How you've spent every day of your life since then regretting what happened. How you've fought to make amends."

"I know," I say, wishing I could paint the picture she wants to display. *I was there. I was wrong. I'm sorry.*

But in my heart of hearts, I know I never truly tried to make amends—not for the two cousins I killed. And not for the stranger who jumped in front of my car, the vagrant who ended up shattered and alone in a ditch.

If I had a time machine... If I could go back to that one night... If I could choose not to drink the watermelon vodka or the peach schnapps... If I could just pass the joint to the next person in the circle...

But that's all a fantasy. I can never escape my past.

Sonja drones on: "Every time these reporters get hold of you, they erase your story. They destroy the narrative. They change the focus."

"I know," I say again, even though I can't control where the paparazzi find me. I can't keep from being trapped.

"You have to seem innocent. Pure. People don't like women who end up with bad boys."

"Braiden's not—"

"Society doesn't approve of women who have sex."

"Every woman—"

"Board members don't want to know you faked your marriage."

"I didn't—"

"You can't—"

But I can't let that one go. I shout over her: "I didn't fake my marriage!"

"So we can sue the papers for defamation?"

The question hangs in the air, naked and vulnerable. I want to say yes. I want to say I didn't know. I want to say that I'm the victim here, that I didn't fake anything, that it was Braiden who lied.

But I know what Sonja will ask next. She'll want to know why I haven't left him, now that I know the truth. She'll ask why I'm living with him in the Rittenhouse. Why I was just photographed with two of the most notorious criminals in Philadelphia's long history.

And I won't have an answer.

Sonja finally says, "Braiden Kelly has a child, right?"

"Aiofe's not his child. She's his ward."

"Even better. She's an orphan?"

"What's *better*?" I don't like the freshly kindled excitement in her voice.

"Bring her down to Delaware tomorrow. We can hold a press conference. Explain that you're taking care of her. That the media are terrifying her. That you're being abused, and an innocent little girl is being hurt. Do you have matching outfits? No, that might be too much. Can you both wear jewelry, one of those necklaces? She has one half of a heart, you have the other. That's fucking perfect! I'll get one delivered overnight."

"Sonja!" I shout. "Stop!"

Her silence is hostile.

"I'm not bringing Aiofe to Delaware. I'm won't use her like that."

"If you don't write the story, it will be written about you."

"Aiofe has already been the subject of too many stories."

"You're boxing me into a corner."

"I won't do it."

Another long silence. Then, finally, Sonja says, "You have three weeks before the hearing."

"I know."

"We can prep twenty-four hours a day, but if the facts are against us and the law is against us, none of it will matter."

"I know," I say again.

"If you lose the ethics hearing, Teddy Newland will be hogtied in your criminal case."

"I understand."

She sighs. "Let me pull together a file. I'll draft key points. Everything your testimony needs to convey."

"Thank you," I say. I've done the same for my clients count-less times.

"You'll have to know it perfectly."

"I will."

"You can't sound rehearsed."

"I won't."

"This would be so much easier, if you'd just give me one hour to talk to the girl."

"No."

Sonja sighs. "I hope this doesn't come back to bite you in the ass."

"I hope it doesn't either."

This time, I'm not angry when I end the call. I'm exhausted. I already know what Sonja hasn't precisely put into words.

I'm going to lose my ethics case. I'm going to lose my license. I'm never going to practice law again.

But I won't destroy Aiofe as I circle the drain.

13

BRAIDEN

After Russo's little game at St. Columba's, my first instinct is to lock Samantha and Aiofe in the Rittenhouse and keep them from the light of day until Aiofe's old enough to drink.

But Samantha convinces me I'm wrong.

She doesn't try to use her collar. Instead, she uses years of legal training.

The Rittenhouse is a public business. It can bar access to anyone it chooses, but I—as a guest—can't force them to keep Russo outside. Even if I bribe the doorman and the front desk clerk and the concierge, they're under no binding obligation to me. They might take more money from Russo, giving him access to the lobby. To the public corridors. To Samantha.

So I settle on a new house without delay. It's in Ardmore, not far from Thornfield's remains. It's got five bedrooms, four baths, and it sits at the end of a cul de sac. Some architect I've never heard of built it on spec, layering in so-called biophilic designs, smart technology, and a hundred shades of beige. He's been using the place as a showcase, trying to impress future clients, so it's already filled with furniture, dishes, and enough stark, modern furnishings I almost wish my corneas were seared again.

All I need to do is overpay by a hundred thousand to get the closing done in forty-eight hours. I drag Sawyer Best's guy up from D.C. to overhaul the security. Some of what he recommends will take time, but getting bullet-proof glass in the windows is an easy, if expensive, fix. I hire extra security from Sawgrass to police the grounds until satisfactory fences can be built.

Wolf comes up the Saturday after the title transfers. He reworks the security system, taking out some backdoor access to the code. While he's at it, he looks at the firewall I'm running for all the computers on-site. In the end, it's easier to trash my whole system and go with what he uses at his own home.

Samantha is happy—she's out of the Rittenhouse for good.

Aiofe is happy—she's got a room overlooking the garden, complete with a pink canopy over her bed.

Fairfax is happy—he's got a bigger, newer kitchen than the one he had at Thornfield.

And I suppose I'm happy too. Almost ten million dollars poorer, but I've kept my promises to the woman I love. I'll figure out some way to make the books balance. I always do.

I'm still not putting Samantha back in her collar. I'm her Dom. I have more control than she does. But it's more and more difficult to ignore that emerald necklace—especially now that I have a bed with a cast iron headboard, perfect for securing cuffs. And a matching footboard, ideal for tying my sub spread-eagle. And a dresser drawer that I've already begun to fill with all the tools I need…

No.

Not yet.

But soon my own right hand won't be enough. And God save Samantha Kelly when I put her on her knees.

~

Of course the house isn't enough.

I've been played like an Irish fiddle—this time, by Fairfax. He's the one who found the Ardmore house. He walked me through the property, pointing out how it meets every one of our needs.

But he waited until after we moved in to show me the church, one block west of our new home: St. Agnes. By sheer coincidence—some might call it by brutal manipulation—St. Agnes runs a school, kindergarten through eighth grade. And for a generous donation to their building fund, they can find an opening in their summer school program for rising fifth graders.

I dig in, even though I know I can't win when Fairfax, Samantha, and Aiofe all join forces.

I tell Fairfax he can't walk Aiofe to classes. I need him at the house. Aiofe is too frail to carry her book bag. The public streets aren't safe.

Fairfax negotiates with Rory O'Hare, and O'Hare assigns his best enforcer to drive Aiofe to and from school.

I tell Fairfax Aiofe can't manage speaking to strangers. She's suffered more trauma in her short life than most adults. She's only been talking for a month. She may not be able to communicate effectively with the sisters if anything goes wrong.

Fairfax meets with Sister Immaculata, the headmistress of the school, who administers a placement test, focusing on Aiofe's language skills. Aiofe ranks in the ninety-fifth percentile for girls her age.

I tell Fairfax Aiofe faces too many threats. Paparazzi might follow her to the playground. Russo might get at one of the teachers, or a janitor, or even a parent of another student.

Sister Immaculata agrees to let O'Hare's man sit outside

Aiofe's classroom. He can go to the cafeteria, too. He can stand on the playground at recess. The nun's only restriction is that no student see any weapon he carries.

I tell Fairfax he's overstepped his bounds. He's in charge of the house only, nothing on the outside. He shrugs and bakes a batch of Aiofe's favorite biscuits.

I tell Fairfax I'll dock his pay. He whistles and shifts laundry from the washing machine to the dryer.

I tell Fairfax I'll send him packing. He laughs and makes a sack lunch for Aiofe to carry the next morning.

I won't tell Fairfax I can't handle the donation. I shift funds about, borrowing from Peter to pay Paul—or Agnes, as the case might be. I write a check with far too many zeroes.

And on Monday, June 3, eleven-year-old Aiofe Máiréad Mason heads to St. Agnes for her very first day of school, ever.

Aiofe's at her feckin' school.

Samantha's working in her office upstairs.

Fairfax is in the kitchen, clattering pots and pans like he's trying to raise the dead.

I can't take the noise. I can't take the waiting. So I grab the keys to the Jeep and head downtown to the new construction site for the Hare and Harp.

When we found the location, I gave half a thought to renovating the old bar that already sat there. But there was dry rot in the joists and mildew in the walls. I had to finish the basement, building out the special room my business requires. So, in the end, it was easier to take the whole thing down and start fresh.

There are perks to running one of the largest construction firms in town. I put my best foreman on the job, raised the budget by twenty-five percent, and told him to finish up six weeks early.

Money. It's only feckin' money.

The Hare is still a hard-hat site, and I'm not about to chance ruining a bespoke suit on a stray nail or two. It feels good to wear jeans and work boots. I like talking to Jack, the head carpenter, hearing his explanation for why they're bumping the ceilings up six inches on the second floor. The electrician is there as well, excited to show off his wiring diagram.

Supervising new construction isn't a complete distraction. I check my watch half a dozen times, noting when Aiofe's in first period class, when she's at recess, when she's at lunch. I know the tracker I put in her backpack can't confirm no one's dragged her off school grounds, but at least the bookbag is still at St. Agnes.

When the construction crew takes their late-morning break, I head down to the basement. The drain there is deep and wide, just the way I ordered. The floor has a gentle slope. Once it's tiled, with the grout sealed, it will be easy to clean. A network of pipes wait for heavy-duty shower curtains—more clean-up considerations—and the joists have been reinforced so a heavy man can be suspended two feet off the floor.

I'm just testing the pulley hanging directly over the drain when I hear footsteps on the stairs. "Jack!" I call. "You've done good work here."

"I'm glad to hear it. But I'm not Jack."

I knew it wasn't Jack from the first syllable out of her mouth.

Samantha's not as concerned about ruining her clothes as I was. She's wearing one of her skirts—the first one I ever gave her. It's pink and covered in flowers that match her soft short-sleeve sweater. She's wearing knee-high lug-sole boots I've never seen before, which is an oversight, because they make me want to push her up against the wall and fuck her till she screams.

I clear my throat. "You're supposed to have a hard hat."

She crosses the basement floor, and there's no reason her hips have to sway like that. "Whoops," she says. Her fingers are steady as she takes the hat off my head. She puts it on, settling it too far back on her own head for any real protection. "It's a good thing *you* always follow the rules."

"How did you know I'd be here?"

"I figured you needed a little distraction on Aiofe's first day in school."

"I have a dozen projects in the city."

"Not ones that make you feel like you're in control."

"You're not dressed for a construction site."

She looks down at her pink-on-pink clothes. "Whoops," she says again.

When she kisses me, she tastes like honey and sweet cream and the coffee I poured for her this morning, when I pretended Aiofe's school uniform wasn't breaking my heart.

Lips still pressed to mine, Samantha leans into me. She tangles her fingers in my hair and walks me back to the unfinished wall. "You should wear jeans more often," she says against my mouth.

"You should wear boots." I close my hands on her hips, pulling her against my hard-on.

She laughs and reaches for my belt buckle.

I shift my fingers to her wrists. "You're playing with fire, *piscín.*"

"Hush," she says. With my buckle undone, she twists the button loose on my jeans.

"I'm your Dom."

"And I'm your sub. I'll always be your sub. But let me do this for you now. Let me help you. Just this once."

She has my zipper down, and she's reached inside my boxers. Her fingers are soft and hard, cool and hot, and she knows exactly how to use them. I drop my head back against the wall and she squeezes my cock, easing it over the elastic band.

"Sweet Jesus," I breathe. "The men will be back any minute."

"Then I guess we'd better hurry," she says. Still holding my cock with one hand, she raises her skirt with the other. I get one quick glimpse of her bare hip—she isn't wearing panties—and then she's guiding me into her ready cunt.

My hands grip her arse, but that's not enough. I spin us around so her back is against the Drywall. The hard hat topples to the floor, clattering on the concrete. She splays her knees, giving me a deeper angle, and I plunge into her like I'm trying to knock her through the wall.

She grunts, and I think I've hurt her, but then she groans, "More."

I give her more. I give her six sharp thrusts, each one forcing air from her lungs. My bollocks rise, and the base of my spine burns, and I know I should slow down, should reach between us and find her clit, should give her a chance, a prayer to catch up, but she tilts her hips and flexes her thighs and I drive home one last time before I explode.

Her hand finds the back of my neck and her lips seal my mouth and she's hotter and wetter than my dreams. Each pulse of my cock devastates the heat inside her.

She waits until I'm empty before she pulls her lips from mine. I'm still breathing like an overworked compressor when she slips away from the wall. Twitching her skirt back into place, she kneels and retrieves the hard hat from the floor.

As she settles the hat onto my sweaty hair, I try to catch her wrist. "Wait," I say. "You didn't—"

Come, I'm going to say.

But she smiles like a saint and says, "The men will be back any minute."

"Fuck the men."

"You don't really want me doing that."

"Samantha..." Her name is part-warning, part-prayer, part-apology.

She tucks me back into my pants with an efficiency that should be embarrassing. Zipper up, button done, belt buckled, she brushes one more kiss across my lips. "I'll see you back at the house," she says. "Don't be too long. Aiofe should be home by now, and Fairfax promised to make all her favorites for dinner."

I check my phone after Samantha disappears up the stairs. The tracker in the backpack has safely returned to the new house in Ardmore.

14

SAMANTHA

When I get home from the construction site, I get past the paparazzi in record time. Maybe that means they're getting tired of my story. Life might return to normal sometime soon.

Yeah. Right.

I hear Aiofe in the kitchen, talking to Fairfax. Her voice is light and happy, like the chittering of sparrows. I want to hear about her first day at school, about her friends and classes.

But I have another obligation.

Standing in my closet, I stare at the racks of clothes. I long to be the woman who wears pink cashmere sweaters, who dresses in flowers and plays with knee-high boots. But I need to look professional. I need protection as I go into battle. I need armor.

Regretfully, I shed the clothes I wore to Braiden's worksite. I pull on a pair of white cotton panties. I add my most supportive bra. I step into black Givenchy trousers and a draping white top.

By the time I shrug on the pants' matching blazer and add my Dolce and Gabbana three-inch heels, I feel like a fucking warrior.

I stride down the hall to my new office, where Declan set up my computers over the weekend. He had a lot to say about the work Cole Wolf did, but I gather our information is more secure than ever, even if Declan's feelings ended up mangled. I'm able to reach out to Sonja with a single tap of a button.

"You're late," she says as she answers the video call.

By three fucking minutes.

"Sorry. I was caught up in a meeting I couldn't leave." For just a moment, I feel Braiden's weight, pushing me into the unfinished wall in the new Hare's basement. I hear his breathing, harsh and desperate. I smell the dust and sweat in his hair.

"Let's get started," Sonja says, and I'm more grateful than ever that I left my pretty pink flowers behind. "As you know, I won't be able to make any arguments for you tomorrow. I'll be present solely as an advisor. After I introduce myself, I can't make any statements to the panel. You can ask to speak with me in private, but I strongly recommend against doing that."

"I understand."

For the next four hours, Sonja Heller grills me. She takes me through the testimony we've prepared, asking questions in order. Then, she jumps around, pounding the most condemning facts. She pressures me for details, ridiculing me when I say I can't remember aspects of the tragedy that cost three innocent people their lives. She lures me with supposed understanding, then springs traps when I use phrases like "I think" and "I guess".

She's a brutal, efficient lawyer, perfect for my case.

And when we're done, I'm certain I don't have a prayer of succeeding.

"All right," Sonja finally says, sounding as exhausted as I feel. "Let's call it a day. I'll meet you outside the hearing room at noon tomorrow. By three o'clock, this will all be over."

One way or another. She doesn't say it, but we're both thinking it.

By the time I get to the dining room, Aiofe is polishing off an ice cream sundae. She's drowned it in gallon of multi-color sprinkles, and she's using her spoon to emphasize a statement: "Sister made us sit quiet for ten whole minutes! Not a word out of anyone!"

I slip into my chair and put my napkin on my lap. My plate is filled with food—roast chicken, potatoes, and carrots, a grilled quarter lemon, and a perfectly shaped Parker House roll. I'm fairly certain I'll puke if I try a bite of anything.

Braiden sits back in his chair at the head of the table. His own plate has been cleared. It looks like he skipped dessert, but he's eyeing me like I'm his next course.

"Don't start," I say. It's one of his favorite phrases, one of the ways he rules over all of us. I'm fully aware of how many rules I've broken tonight, coming late to dinner, wearing black and white, skipping a skirt, wearing underwear.

"Some people have the mistaken impression they can bank favors," he observes, his tone so mild I know I'm in trouble up to my neck. Deeper even. Far over my head.

But I say, "Some people have never lived with a tyrant."

Aiofe glances between us, a frown twisting her lips. "Sister Mary Elizabeth says it's not polite to tell secrets in front of other people."

Maybe Braiden was right. Maybe we never should have sent Aiofe to school.

But Braiden keeps his tone light as he says, "One more minute to finish that sundae, little one. And then it's time to get ready for bed."

"It's not even eight o'clock! Jeannie's bedtime is nine o'clock. And Nicky gets to stay up as late as she wants."

"Jeannie and Nicky don't live in this house." But he cuts off further rebellion by adding, "If you're in bed by quarter past, you can read till nine. You can tell Fairfax I said so."

Aiofe wolfs down the syrupy dregs of her dessert. Dropping her spoon on the table, she springs up from her chair and bounces over to Braiden. She throws her arms around his neck and kisses him on the cheek. "Thank you, Uncle Braiden," she says. "Thank you for letting me go to St. Agnes."

He hugs her with one arm. "I'm glad you had a good day. Tomorrow will be even better."

She crosses behind him and gives me a quick hug. "Good-night, Samantha. I love you."

The words seem to fall out of her mouth by accident, but she doesn't bother picking them up. "I love you too," I say, and she's gone with a smile and a twirl of her plaid uniform skirt.

"Why isn't Aiofe required to change clothes when she gets home from school?" I ask.

Braiden looks at me levelly. "Don't change the topic of conversation."

"I wasn't aware we were conversing."

"Eat your dinner."

"It's cold."

"I'll call Fairfax and ask him to heat it up."

"I'm not hungry."

"Enough." He says the one word quietly. As if he's answering a question.

He's still wearing his jeans, still wearing his plaid shirt, and I know when he gets close enough, he'll smell like dust and sweat and sin. I want to sit and stare at him. I want to remember how he moved inside me, losing control in the unfinished basement of his bar. I want to remember how it felt to do one thing right, to distract him when he needed distraction, to help him when he needed help.

But he says, "Still trying to control everything?"

"I'm not—"

"I've warned you too many times. Subs don't decide when and how they get punished. And make no mistake. You will be punished. Do we have to review the rules?"

"Jesus Christ," I mutter. "Work ran late tonight. I came down to dinner because I wanted to hear about Aiofe's first day at school. I didn't change my clothes because I knew it was almost time for her to go upstairs. Not everything is about you. Not everything is a grand challenge to your precious alpha dominance."

He waits a moment, as if he's actually curious to hear what else I have to say. But I know I've already pushed him too far.

"I should make you sleep in the guest room tonight," he finally says.

"Braiden—"

"But I won't. Because tonight you need this more than you need to learn a lesson." He pushes back from the table and takes three steps to the doorway. Looking over his shoulder, he says, "*Piscín?*"

And God help me, I follow him upstairs to our bedroom.

My collar is heavy around my neck. The platinum is cold, until it's hot. I feel the emerald every time I swallow.

This is the first time Braiden has tied me up in this room. The first time he's used the toys in this dresser. It's the first time he's brought me to the edge here, held me for an eternity here, left me wild and raw and desperate here—but he does it again and again and again.

This house doesn't have Thornfield's soundproof walls. It doesn't have long corridors, perfect for muffling noise. Our new home doesn't have a separate cottage for Fairfax—only a suite in the basement, two floors away and not far enough.

I do my best to swallow my moans. To muffle my groans. To scream inside the trembling darkness of my throat, smothering all my sounds. But when Braiden finally opens the clamps on my aching nipples, when he sets aside the pinwheel, when he slaps the riding crop against my clit one last time, I can't help myself.

I call out his name. I pant about God. I sigh and I cry and I stutter as he brings me to a quick second peak and then a long, drawn-out third. That last one pulses through my entire body, from the roots of my hair to the curl of my toes, an endless wash of release.

He brings me a glass of cold, clear water. He feeds me the darkest chocolate I've ever tasted. He holds me close and wipes tears from my cheeks, which doesn't make sense because I don't remember crying.

"I can't do it," I finally whisper in the shadows that have swarmed since sunset.

"You can do anything."

"The hearing. Tomorrow. It'll be a disaster."

He spreads his fingers across my hip. "It won't be. You'll be brilliant, *piscín*. And then it will all be behind you." He pulls me into the curve of his body, molding my spine to his chest. "You can do this, *mo chailín maith*."

I want to believe him. I want to know he's right. So I close my eyes. I relax in his arms. And I let him hold me until he falls asleep.

15

BRAIDEN

It's been six weeks since I've done the milk run. Six weeks since Madden cleared out my accounts, picking up all my cash-filled envelopes.

Rory and Seamus have been keeping me informed. Rory has done the run twice himself, making sure people understand he's my most senior enforcer in Philly these days. Seamus confirms everyone's following the rules, handing over what they should. He also, though, has told me we're entering the lean months— summer, when kids are home from school and families travel on vacation and men with wicked tastes have neither time nor cash to indulge.

So I plan a route and take the Jeep out after breakfast. Driving around the city is a better way to spend the day than waiting for Samantha to call, to tell me her hearing went fine and all her nerves were for nothing.

Mikey's waiting at the bar when I get to his underground gambling den. He looks like he's coming off a rough night; he's already sipping a glass of the black stuff. I wave off his offer of a Guinness of my own, even as he calls out, "If it isn't Himself!" Just like he's pleased to see me. He almost makes me feel like a friend.

The envelope he hands over is half what it once was.

"How's business?" I ask, because that's more polite than making threats.

"Going to hell in a handbasket." He sounds like someone poisoned his dog. "We put Cillian Ryan in the ground last Friday, may he rest in peace."

As he crosses himself piously, I tap his envelope against the counter. "Ryan's not responsible for all the shortfall."

Mikey scowls. "He's not. But his son is. And all his grand-sons too. Not one of them knows what to do with an honest bookie. If they can't place a bet on their phones, they won't bother. It's sportsbook this and betting kings that, with a dozen fancy lines you need NASA's computers to understand."

I've heard the complaint before. Now that sports betting is legal everywhere, casual gamblers stay away from joints like this.

But all us businessmen face pressure. "I've got a floor, Mikey. I need to see a minimum, or we'll find ourselves in trouble."

"I'm working on it, Boss. But I've gotta be honest. Regulars are pretty spooked by the Italians."

He pronounces it like my da always did—Eye-talians. "Spooked?" I ask. "Why?"

He looks like he wants to spit, but he'd only have to clean up the mess. "No one's told you what's going on? They're doing their best to scare folks off. Driving down the middle of the street after midnight, two men flashing machine guns in the back seat. Standing on the corner and greeting regulars by name. Last week, they wrote down license numbers, like they were the fucking cops."

"Goddamn Russo."

Mikey sits back in his chair. "I thought you two had a truce."

"We do." But that's not the truth. Not anymore—not after

he turned Madden. And not after the truckload of electronics went missing. Definitely not after he threatened Aiofe on the steps of St. Columba. "Why didn't you say something to O'Hare?"

Mikey shifts his weight and fiddles with his glass. "I hoped it could wait till Moran was back."

Patrick. He wanted to confess to someone he knew.

"Moran might not be back. Not for a while. You don't trust O'Hare?"

Mikey answers so quickly he swallows half his words. "O'Hare's fine. He's fair. He doesn't lean too hard, not like—"

He stops short. From the pure panic on his face I know what he hasn't said. *Madden.* O'Hare's not like Madden.

He's right. But I'm glad he didn't say the words out loud. Because we're still living the lie that my brother might walk through the door any minute, and I don't want to be forced to defend the dead dry shite's honor.

I slip Mikey's envelope inside the breast pocket of my jacket. "Let O'Hare know if Russo steps up his game."

By the time I get to the door, Mikey's drained half his glass. He freezes when I turn back, foam on his upper lip. "But I need a full share next Tuesday, Mikey. Business is business."

I wait for him to nod before I leave.

Mikey's story is repeated, stop after stop. Business is off. Marks are scarce. Russo's men are hanging around like a bad smell in the jacks.

The goombahs aren't entering my buildings. They aren't taking over my games, my bars, my girls. They aren't doing anything I can call them on, as a mob boss or as a legitimate businessman with lawful concerns on the streets of my adopted home of Philadelphia.

At the end of the day, though, the effect is clear. I'm short nearly half my feckin' take.

I call Seamus as I'm driving home. I go with a burner, because I'm pretty sure we'll say things that shouldn't be overheard. When I report my haul, he says, "That's worse than it has been."

"I need to get Patrick home from Boston."

"You can do that. But it won't change the take. This is about Russo. This is about planning a war."

"Are we ready to fight that?"

"Financially? You don't want to hear this, Boss. But the answer is no."

He's right. I don't want to hear it. But I grunt so he'll go on.

"It's not just the drop in income. We started the year short because of that container that went missing. And your outlay of cash in the past six months has been...extreme." As if I didn't know. But he's my quartermaster, so he doesn't stop there. "The property for the Hare, building out the new place, tipping staff..." That's the inspectors we've paid off, the commissioner we've bought. "Holing up at the Rittenhouse wasn't cheap, but compared to buying the new house... And underwriting that church's building fund..."

"I'm a billionaire," I remind him, same as I reminded Samantha. "I can buy a new house."

"You are. And you can. But it's my job to warn you. I'm already managing some cash flow challenges. And if you and Russo shift to open warfare, those challenges will turn into full-scale obstacles."

He doesn't know the half of it. Ever since the Diamond Ring went golfing at Augusta, I've been toying with the idea of making a run at the Union. I want to be own boss. I want to be the General.

But dreams like that cost money. And time. And energy. All things that Russo threatens, just by being alive.

So I focus on first steps, getting the Fishtown Boys out of debt. I ask Seamus, "What do you need to make things right?"

"Honestly? Twenty-five mill would fill all the holes and leave us with a little room to breathe."

Twenty-five million dollars. He says it like he expects me to empty my pockets and count up loose change. But Seamus Campbell knows better than most what he's asking. And he's got a Harvard Business School degree to back him up.

"Let me think about it," I say. I break the burner when I get to the next traffic light. Half goes in a storm drain. The other half flies out my window once I'm on the motorway, heading back to Ardmore.

My pockets won't yield any twenty-five million dollars. A lifetime of counting up envelopes like the ones I collected today wouldn't get me to that number. I could wait five years or longer for another shipment like the cocaine Russo boosted a few months ago. Gambling and cigarettes and producing porno movies—the profits dropped out of all those schemes years back.

But I've got one extraordinary asset sitting in my gallery at Diamond Freeport. It's an illustrated medieval manuscript that Patrick smuggled out of Ireland for me, a few months back. There's a limited market for art treasures without a proper provenance, a record of prior ownership. But that market isn't nonexistent.

The freeport gives a built-in advantage if the seller is already a client. Or willing to become a client, to keep their new-found treasure on the premises. The sale will be tax-free, just pure profit going to the seller. To me.

When I get to my home office, I check for a message from Samantha. It's only half past one, though. Her hearing's barely begun.

So I sit at my desk and pull up photographs of the book I looted from Ireland. Samantha's already briefed me on the legal consequences of bringing the Book of Skreen to auction. Alix Key, the freeport's auctioneer, has advised me to wait until November, when the most valuable rare objects are usually brought to market.

I can't wait until November.

Not anymore.

I place a call to Alix at the freeport. "Braiden!" she answers. She has a gift for making every client feel as if they're the tax haven's premier client. "To what do I owe the pleasure?"

"The illustrated manuscript that we talked about a few months ago…"

"The one we're taking to auction in November?"

"I've had a change of plans. I want to sell it now."

"By *now*, you mean?"

"No later than the end of this month."

She's so quiet, I wonder if the line has dropped.

"Alix?" I finally ask.

"Sorry. I'm just thinking through the variables. We can run the auction, that's not a problem. But with a turn-around like that, I don't know how many large institutions we can get to bid. Museums, libraries, that sort of thing."

"But you can get the word out to private collectors, right?"

"A good number of them."

"And private collectors are likely to pay more than museums?"

"Generally speaking. But with a treasure of this magnitude—"

"Do it." I cut her off.

Another silence, but a much shorter one this time.

"Of course," she says. "Let me check dates, and I'll get back to you."

I hang up the phone with the impatience of a child waiting to open presents from Father Christmas. Now that I've decided to sell the book, I want it out of my gallery immediately.

I want my twenty-five million dollars.

I need them.

Now.

16

SAMANTHA

I've spent enough time in courtrooms to know when judges hate the arguments they're hearing. I can tell the three board members on the ethics panel despise my case from the moment they walk into the room.

They're wearing business suits instead of black robes, and they sit behind a table instead of on a raised platform. But these three people will decide my entire future, based on whatever I say during the next two hours.

Sonja introduces herself and me. I'm invited to make an opening statement—the one Sonja and I rehearsed for so long yesterday.

"Good afternoon," I begin. "May it please—"

"Is it true, Ms. Kelly," starts one of the board members, but then she interrupts herself. "Or should I call you Ms. Canna? That is your name, isn't it? Before you changed it to misrepresent your connection to the dangerous Russo crime syndicate?"

"I changed my name because—"

"How much of your current legal practice involves repre-senting figures involved in organized crime?" asks the second member.

"The identity of my clients is confidential," I respond.

"So you agree that you are employed by Mafia dons, Irish mob bosses, and the like." That's the third member, peering at me over her cat's-eye glasses.

"No! I'm employed by Diamond Freeport."

"A tax haven organized under the laws of the state of Delaware—"

"Yes, the—"

"—specifically to thwart the enforcement of United States tax statutes and regulations." Board Member Number Two speaks over me, reading from some document. And then he says, "I'm surprised to hear you admit it." He sounds like I barbecue babies for breakfast.

"The freeport is organized—"

"Ms. Canna," the first one interrupts. "Are you directly or indirectly responsible for the deaths of anyone other than the three individuals listed in the ethics complaint we're deciding today?"

The hearing goes downhill from there.

When I was in law school, I was taught to appreciate inter-ruptions from judges. Their questions offer opportunities to explain my case, to clarify my clients' points of view. Questions prove judges are engaged, are actively considering every argu-ment made.

The ethics panel doesn't give a damn about how I answer their demands. It's clear all three of them made up their minds long before they entered the room. If they weren't inclined to yank my license when they first heard about my case, they were absolutely certain I needed to be disbarred after they read the recent newspaper coverage. I'm only grateful this proceeding is closed to the public.

After forty-five minutes of making no headway explaining

even one of my points, I ask for a recess to consult with Sonja—the one thing she said we shouldn't do. She waits until we're outside the conference room, standing in a corner of the all-too-public hallway before she mutters something.

"Excuse me?" I ask.

"You're fucked," she announces.

"So what do I do?"

"Go back in there, spread your legs, and think of England."

"This is what I'm paying you for?"

"And I can promise, you aren't paying enough. Because after we walk out of here today, I'm pretty sure I'll never be able to bring another client in front of that board. Lube up. This won't be pretty."

She's right.

It's brutal. And two hours later, when they've dragged me back and forth over the facts, when they've ground my answers into powder, when they've willfully misinterpreted every single word I've said and cut off every attempt I make to rephrase, Board Member Number Two leans back in his chair with a sigh so heavy I wonder if he has extra lungs where his heart should be.

"All right, Ms. Canna. We'll take some time to confer among ourselves. You can expect our written opinion within ninety calendar days."

Ninety days. I wonder why they don't just shoot me in the head right now.

Sonja and I shake hands outside the hearing room. I ask her to send her final invoice, and then I pretend to need the restroom so she can take the elevator downstairs on her own.

I realize I should reach out to Teddy Newland. Tell him about this disaster of a hearing. Warn him that my criminal case just became infinitely more difficult.

I don't have the heart.

When I finally get out to the street, I'm surprised to see Liam Murphy waiting at the curb with the new Bentley. I actually forgot that he drove me down from Philly four hours ago. A lifetime ago.

He's leaning against the sign that says, "No Stopping. No Standing." The instant he sees me at the top of the stairs, he opens the back door of the car. He must be able to read my face as he hands me in, because he says, "There's a cooler on the seat. Ice, Jameson, and soda. Himself said you might want a snort when you were done."

My laugh sounds slightly hysterical. I want to ask if Braiden thought I'd be celebrating or drowning my sorrows, but it's not fair to put Liam on the spot. "Thank you, but I'm fine," I lie. "I do need to stop by the office, though, before we head home."

I don't need anything at the freeport. But I can't bear the thought of sitting at dinner with a busy, happy Aiofe. The idea of yet another perfect meal from Fairfax turns my belly to stone. I can't imagine how I'll tell Braiden I've failed.

Liam doesn't care about any of that. He just makes his confident way through afternoon traffic, getting me to the freeport in record time.

My assistant, Mary, has taken the afternoon off for a dentist's appointment. Liam settles into his chair outside my office, beyond my range of view.

That means I can sit at my desk without interruption. I stare at the walls, not seeing the files around me. I count my breaths, starting over from one every time I lose track.

I'm finally up to twelve when there's a light knock on my open door. "Oh," Alix Key says. "I didn't expect you to be here."

"I am." My voice sounds strange. High. Thin. Like I'm trapped on top of Mount Everest.

"I was going to drop off these brochures with Mary, so she could send them up to Philadelphia. I want Braiden to see how we've promoted similar auctions in the past."

"Auctions?" I ask, because I think I'm supposed to say something.

"He called this morning to say he—" She cuts herself off. "Are you okay?"

I shake my head. "Sure," I say. I realize something's wrong there, that I was supposed to nod, but there isn't an easy way to make things right.

Alix shuts my office door and comes to sit in one of the chairs across from my desk. "Sam?" she says. "You're scaring me."

"I'm sorry," I answer automatically. "I won't do that anymore."

Alix puts a stack of brightly colored papers on my desk. "What's going on?" she asks.

"I had my hearing this afternoon. For my bar license. It didn't go well." There. I thought it would be hard to say those words: *It didn't go well.* But it's so much easier than I thought it would be. It's such a short sentence to say my life is changed forever.

"Did they issue their decision?"

"Not yet."

"How long until they do?"

"I'm not sure. Three months at the most."

"If it's bad, can you appeal?"

"It'll be bad."

"Can you appeal?" she repeats.

I blink. "No. All decisions are final."

Final.

Alix sits back in her chair. She's Chief Operating Officer at the freeport. If her General Counsel is about to be disbarred, she needs to hire a replacement. Immediately.

But after a moment, she says, "So what do you do now? When you know you can't fail?"

I shake my head. "I failed. I'm going to lose my license to practice law."

"You're *going to* do that. But you haven't yet. And no one can

stop you right now. Not until you get your official notice about
the hearing."

"Alix, you're not listening. They're going to disbar me. I
won't be a lawyer anymore."

"*You're* not listening to *me*. You've got a window of opportu-
nity here. A get-out-of-jail-free card. What's the last thing you
want to do as a lawyer? The most dangerous thing. The thing
that could get you disbarred."

Get Russo.

The answer's waiting for me, without a second of hesitation.
He's the one who told the world about That Night. He's why the
panel decided against me before I ever entered the hearing
room. He's the reason I fled to New York in the first place. He
murdered my parents. He killed my cousin. He's done everything in his power to take down the man I love, and I'm still not
sure Braiden will come out ahead in their ongoing battles.

"I want to destroy Antonio Russo," I say.

Alix nods slowly. She doesn't know everything that's
happened in my life, but she reads the newspapers. She's heard
the gossip. "So what do we do?" she asks. "To make sure that
happens?"

We don't do anything.

I do.

I walk into Russo's lair as if I have every right to be there. I
gain the bastard's trust. I learn his deepest secrets. I bring all of
it back to Braiden, so Russo is destroyed, once and for all.

Yeah. Right.

"Braiden would kill me," I tell Alix. I don't mean that liter-
ally. I think. But talk about taking control where I know I have
no right to run things...

"I don't believe that for a second," Alix says.

"What would Trap do if he found out *you* worked behind his
back to take down his worst enemy?"

She purses her lips. "Good point. So you'll have to tell him
beforehand?"

"What?" My question cracks with disbelief.

"Tell him what you're planning. Work with him to make it happen."

I shake my head. But even as I reject her suggestion, I wonder if I actually *can* convince Braiden. If the lure of taking Russo down, once and for all, is enough for him to let me do it.

It's impossible.

It's the only thing that makes sense.

I have to try.

Russo murdered Eliza, the last of my cousins. He ended the story I began That Night, eleven years ago. I need to destroy him. It's the only way I can give any meaning to those bodies I left on the mountainside.

It's the only way I can atone for my past.

17

BRAIDEN

L iam phones me from the freeport. He tells me things didn't go well at the hearing, that Samantha seems stressed. Stunned even. I tell him to get her home when she's ready. Not to force her. I can wait.

Last night I told her she could do anything. Tonight I'll tell her I love her, no matter what she does. No matter what happens.

Of course she misses dinner. She's still dressed in black and white when she comes to my office. She's ignored her skirt, broken every rule I've put in place, the ones I enforce for her own good.

Without me, she destroys herself from the inside out. She works too many hours. She misses too much sleep. She skips meals, forgets snacks, lives on caffeine and adrenaline alone.

And Jesus, she's wired tonight.

"I shouldn't be telling you like this," she says. "I should have taken some time. I could have drawn up a presentation, the way

I did for your Irish imports. Alix came by my office, by the way. She wanted me to bring you some brochures. She said you're moving up the auction, from November to the end of this month."

"I am," I say, cautious because I don't know where this flood of words is coming from.

"I left the examples at work by mistake. I got distracted because Alix and I started talking. I should have put together some examples, some suggestions for my new idea. I've already drawn up a list of pros and cons. There are a lot of pros—I can count them out for you now. There are just a few cons. Really. And they don't matter. Not in the long run."

I lean back in my chair. Her cheeks are flushed. Her breath is coming short and fast. She looks like a woman who's been well and truly fucked, which doesn't make sense, because Liam said she was a mess after the hearing.

"What's your new idea?" I ask.

Her fingers twist around themselves, over and over like she's washing her hands. Looking down, she realizes what she's doing. She catches the hems of her sleeve like she's a little girl caught outside in a snowstorm, suddenly cold in a gust of wind.

"Speak," I say, layering in my Captain's voice. I know she can't refuse.

She takes a deep breath. "We've known since that night in the safe room. Madden told us. Sure, *he* hired the waiter at the party. He delivered the fake documents to the freeport. Madden made sure I went to the tent, and he had his waiter ready, gun in hand."

I feel my face flush with every fact she recites. I want to cut her off, to make her stop. My brother suffered before he died, but I should have drawn out his last few hours. I should have made him pay more for what he did to Samantha. For what could have happened. Choking on his own cock was too good for Madden Kelly.

But he's dead now. Gone. Burned. So I ask, "What do you want with Madden?"

"Not Madden!" she says, and she sounds surprised. She walks over to the window. Stares out at the yard. Talks to her reflection in the glass as she says, "Russo."

"Samantha…" I warn her.

"Madden knew you'd kill him if he made a move against me. You'd already broken his jaw. Laid down the law. But he did it anyway. He risked his life. And that was because Russo played him. Madden probably didn't even realize it at first, didn't know he was being used. But Russo was behind that attack at the freeport, as clearly as if he hired the waiter himself."

My finger tightens around a remembered trigger, a pistol lodged in the mouth of the man who threatened Samantha. I'm the one who demanded the shitehawk waiter say who sent him. I'm the one who blew off the back of his head when he refused to answer.

Just like I let Madden go too soon.

"Think about it," Samantha says. "You and Russo had a truce. He couldn't act directly, not without starting a war. Not without getting his own boss to weigh in. That's what happened at the Rittenhouse. Those were the rules he was working under."

I pinch my lower lip. She's right. Russo's hands were tied.

"But when has Antonio Russo ever shown an ounce of patience?" she asks. "He used Madden. He tried to kill me. It was Russo all along."

She looks at me. She stops fiddling with her sleeves, stops pacing like a junkie, stops rolling over her own words like a child telling the plot of a movie.

"You can strike back," she says with perfect poise.

"Russo's wife is dead." As if I have to remind Samantha. Russo shoved a gun up his wife's cunt and pulled the fucking trigger. But I don't say that. Samantha doesn't need her mind filled with that image of her murdered cousin.

"You could go after one of his mistresses," she offers.

"That isn't the same."

"One of his capos, then."

"Not even the same playing pitch."

She nods, and I have the strangest feeling I'm making her arguments for her. She says, "What if I found you the perfect target? You strike hard, and you succeed where he failed. What happens next?"

I don't answer. I don't want to believe her. I don't want to hope.

When I don't play her game, she picks up the thread again. "Russo hits you again. That's what happens. And that's not all. He bankrolls someone to head up the GIU. He convinces the other captains you're not fit to run the Fishtown Boys. He uses everything Madden told him, every truth, ever lie."

My hands curl into fists so tight my knuckles stand out like commas. A tic twitches beneath my right eye, and my jaw aches. I force myself to count to ten.

"But it doesn't have to be that way," she says, her voice low and soothing.

"What do you want, Samantha?" I sound like a man staring at my own grave.

"Let me invite him into the freeport."

I make a strangled noise, but she goes on before I can interrupt.

"We'll set up a gallery for him. Give him a trading account. Get him into the Diamond Ring."

"Over my—"

"I'll meet with him," she says, not letting me build up a full head of steam. "The same way I meet with any client. Always at the freeport. Always surrounded by security."

"Freeport security is shite."

"It's better now. You know that. And I'll have Liam with me. Along with any other guard you say I need."

My jaw works, but I let her go on.

"I'll collect information about Russo. About his business. About his plans. I'll do presentations for him the same way I have for you."

"Not the same way," I growl. But God help me, I'm listening to her. I'm considering every word she says.

"I'll learn where he's vulnerable, domestically and internationally. That book you're going to auction by month-end exposes you to what? A hundred years in prison and a million-dollar fine, if you're caught breaking Ireland's antiquities laws? We'll get leverage like that on Russo."

"It's too risky."

"I'll get tax documents. Bank account information. You'll fund the Fishtown Boys for a decade."

I dangle my hands between my spread knees because I don't want to hope. I shake my head. "Even *if* you got out of there alive, you'd be breaking every ethical rule in the books."

"So?"

"So what will you do when they yank your law license?"

She stares at me like she's waking up from a very long nightmare. Her throat works, and it takes her three tries to speak. But when she finally gets the words out, her voice doesn't shake. "They're pulling my license anyway. I've got ninety days or less."

I refuse to listen. "We'll get you a better lawyer."

"I already had the best." She swallows hard, but she's brave enough to go on. "There's no coming back from this. Trap will have to fire me. He won't want to, and he'll put it off as long as possible. But clients won't invest billions in a company with a disbarred General Counsel."

"You can sue the freeport. Say it's discrimination. Harassment. You can keep a case going for years."

She shakes her head. "I wouldn't do that to Trap. He's been too good a boss." When she finally looks at me, her eyes are calm. Her gaze is steady. "I've worked this problem in my head for weeks. I've studied all the facts. I've applied all the laws. There isn't any other end."

I'm used to bowling over my opponents with raw power. My feckin' Irish charm when I can. Stacks of cash when I must.

But here, there's no one to intimidate. No one to charm. No one to buy off.

Samantha's fate has been sealed since she drove down that mountain eleven years ago.

"Let this be the last thing I do as a lawyer," she says. "Let it work for both of us."

And God help me, I agree. "Do it," I say. "Tell me what you need and we'll take him down together."

18

SAMANTHA

~

I'm going to reach out to Russo. Me. Alone.

I'm no longer the little girl who watched her parents die in a fireball of shattered glass. I'm not the terrified young woman who fled a drunken mistake. I'm not even the adult lawyer who heard her cousin die in the most horrific way imaginable.

I'm scared. Any reasonable woman would be. I'll be matching wits with a psychopath.

My spacious office in the new house feels positively claustrophobic. My stomach churns with too much coffee and not enough courage. I'm staring at my phone like it's a coiled rattlesnake, and for just a moment I consider flushing it down a toilet so I can't make the call.

I'd rather face the paparazzi jackals at the end of the driveway than follow through with this.

"You don't have to," Braiden reminds me.

"But I do."

I don't know how long I have. Ninety days is the outer limit. The ethics board can come back with its decision at any time. So I swallow hard and force myself to say, "And Russo has to believe I'm changing sides. He has to think I'm betraying you. I have to give him a reason."

For just a heartbeat, every muscle in Braiden's body goes stiff. But his voice is perfectly level as he says, "Tell him I'm marrying Fiona."

The suggestion's absurd, and I start to laugh. But Braiden isn't joking. "What do you mean?"

"I'd be consolidating power inside the Union. If I control Philadelphia and Boston, the other captains would have to make me General. I'd never have to bend a knee to anyone again. I'd never have to worry about someone taking over the Fishtown Boys."

"You can't—" I start, but I'm afraid to finish that sentence. He can marry Fiona if he wants to. He's got a signed annulment to his marriage with Birte, locked inside the safe in our bedroom closet. And we both know his marriage to me was never valid and binding.

"You wouldn't—" I try again, but that sentence isn't any better.

"You won't..." I trail off.

"Will you?" I finally ask.

"*Piscín*," Braiden says, and his palm is warm against my cheek. I'm surprised by how much I need his touch, how much I need to hear him say my pet name. "I'll never marry Fiona," he says. "But you can make Russo think I will."

I'm shakier than I should be, like I've just slammed on the brakes to avoid a deer in the middle of the road. *If Fiona marries another captain... If someone else becomes General... If someone comes for the Fishtown Boys...*

"I'll never marry Fiona," Braiden says again.

I nod, because voicing all my other fears will get us nowhere. I jam confidence into my words, pretending I believe them.

"Russo will buy that. That I'm turning on you because of her. But I still need to give him something specific. Something worth a lot. He has to think I stole it from you out of spite."

I'm right.

Braiden knows I'm right.

But this is hard enough that he forces himself to his feet. He paces my office with a grim determination. He looks out at the yard. At the neighbors' homes beyond our strip of green. He studies the sky, as if the clouds have written him a secret message.

"Roy Krakower," he finally says.

"Roy Law-and-order?" The press has been all over the new commissioner of prisons. In his first three months on the job, Krakower has seen two Black men die in city jails, he ordered a pregnant prisoner shackled to her hospital bed during delivery, and he made sure three gay men were sent to solitary confinement when they complained about being assaulted.

Braiden says, "Krakower has a brand-new penthouse two blocks from City Hall. He likes the view as a backdrop when he makes home movies."

"Movies?" A fresh surge of acid in my stomach warns me I won't like what comes next.

"Boys," Braiden says, then shrugs. "Men. Old enough to work construction, anyway. He likes them in hard hats. Lug boots. Two, three, four at a time."

"You have proof?"

"Kelly Construction built the penthouse. Most profitable job we had last year. It's amazing where you can hide cameras these days."

"Jesus," I say, because not a single class in law school prepared me for the casual blackmailing of a city official.

Braiden says, "If Russo plays his cards right, he can use the story to muscle in on Paragon. Take the whole project from Kelly Construction."

Paragon is Roy Law-and-order's program to upgrade one of

the city's jails. The fifty-million-dollar contract hasn't formally been awarded yet, but Braiden's company placed the leading bid. He's likely to see the payout over the next five years. "You can't give up that much."

Braiden's shoulders twitch. "What option do I have? If I give you one of my clubs or a contact at the port or a gambling book, it'll take months for Russo to see a profit."

That's true. But I have to say, "You can't pass up fifty million dollars. You need the money."

His lips twitch in a grim smile. "I'm selling the Book of Skreen. That'll make up some of the shortfall."

"But fifty—"

"Russo has to know you're a valuable asset from the moment you place that call."

So he doesn't kill you.

Braiden doesn't say it out loud. He doesn't have to. Antonio Russo has to get more satisfaction out of keeping me alive than he would by murdering me.

"All right," I finally say. "I'll give him Krakower."

And I need to do it now. Because once the ethics board issues its decision, my power to do anything involving the freeport is destroyed.

My palms are sweating. I wipe them on my jeans and reach for my phone. "You don't have to stay for this," I say.

"Not a feckin' chance I'll go."

I'll lose if I argue. So I tap the screen and find the private number Russo fed me months ago. I place the call on speaker.

Russo answers part-way through the first ring. "Giovanna. What a pleasant surprise." He doesn't sound surprised. He sounds like a man cleaning his gun.

"Don Antonio," I say.

Braiden's jaw clenches at Russo's title, but I need to make this pitch as appealing as possible. Antonio Russo is a lazy tomcat, and I'm one of those feather toys, tied to a fishing pole.

I need to flutter, to flail. I need to look so much like a wounded bird that Russo can't resist pouncing.

"I thought everything would blow over," I say, allowing my voice to quiver. "The information you released about my graduation night... But you heard Braiden, that night at the Rittenhouse."

I don't know who the fuck you are.

From the expression on Braiden's face, he remembers exactly what he said. His fingers flex, and I know he remembers clamping down on my biceps. He dragged me to our suite, where we both used words like knives, slicing fast, stabbing deep.

And now I'm carving us again. I hope—I pray—that I'm using a scalpel this time, sacrificing as little flesh as possible. But even a scalpel can be deadly. Braiden executed his brother with one.

"I would never let a *frocio* like that say such things to my woman," Russo says.

Braiden doesn't need to understand Italian to know his manhood is being questioned. Russo's tone is enough to drive Braiden back to the window. Every line of his body is a master class on rage.

I swallow hard and tell Russo the truth: "Braiden lied to me."

"What lies did he tell, Giovanna?" There's a hunger beneath the question, a bottomless pit I'll drown in if I'm not careful.

"Y— You already know about Birte. And now he says he'll take another wife. Fiona Ingram. He thinks that will make him General of the Grand Irish Union."

"That *morto di figa* should be put down like a mad dog," Russo says.

Braiden whirls from the window and tries to swipe my phone off my desk. I block his hand with my arm and point toward a chair with a commanding finger.

If Braiden truly were cunt-struck the way Russo says, he'd

obey me. Instead, he stomps back to the window. I raise my voice, praying Russo can't hear the angry footsteps.

"I can't live like this, Don Antonio. The shame... I want to hurt him. I want him to know what it's like to lose something that matters to him. Something he cares about."

"This is a lovely story, Giovanna. But why are you telling it to me?"

"You can help me, Don Antonio."

"I do favors for my family, Giovanna."

"I understand that now. I made a mistake. I want to come back. I want to be your family."

Silence, while Braiden glares out the window.

I worry that I've said too much, too quickly. That Russo smells the trap. I force myself to go on, testing the ground with every word, trying to find a path through a forest of hate.

"Don Antonio... I— I know people in your family bring you gifts. Things to show gratitude for all you do. I would like to give a gift to you."

"I have no use for another man's *puttana*."

Braiden growls, and I try to cover the sound by pleading, "Not my body, Don Antonio. I know I lost that chance when I walked away before. It's information I want to give you. Facts you can use to beat Braiden at his own game."

Silence again, but he's the one who breaks it this time. "I am listening."

"If I could just see you... If we could talk..."

"You know where I live, Giovanna. In the same house where you came to take my money the night you killed three people."

The house where he murdered Eliza. I'll never go there. Not even to get revenge.

But I'm so close to landing him. So close to getting what I need... I leak out a little more real fear, hoping it sounds like uncertainty. "Braiden's men watch me all day, every day. They'll kill me if I try to come to you." And then, like the idea has just come to me, I say, "Maybe... No..."

"What are you thinking, Giovanna?"

I make my voice soft, like a child asking Babbo Natale—Santa Claus—for a gift. "Could you come to the freeport? Meet me in my office there?"

"I am a very busy man, Giovanna. I do not have time to go to Delaware."

"Please," I say. "I'll make it worth your while. I'll set up an account for you. Give you a gallery in the warehouse. All the tax benefits of doing business through the freeport..."

His silence stretches out to nearly a minute, my first glimmer that this ploy might actually work.

"Don Antonio," I say, drawing out the title he loves so much. "I'll talk to my boss. He has a special group of investors... The richest men at the freeport. Braiden's there, and Connor Boyle too, the Irish boss from New York. I'll ask if you can join the Diamond Ring. For you, I'll beg."

Beg.

I use the word because I know Russo will love it.

But Braiden doesn't. He's reached the end of his tether. He calls from the window, as if he's walking down the hall, "Samantha?"

I glare at him, but I try to turn his interruption to my advantage. "Don Antonio," I whisper. "I have to go. Please say yes. Say you'll meet me at the freeport. Monday, Tuesday, any day next week."

"Samantha!" Braiden calls again.

I raise a silent middle finger to him as I plead, "Don Antonio..."

"Fine," Russo says, grudging. "Wednesday afternoon. I will come to your freeport then."

"Thank you, Don Antonio. Thank you. You won't regret it. I promise."

"Be certain I do not." He ends the call before I do.

I double-check that the connection is severed before I say to Braiden, "What the fuck was that?"

"I got you what you wanted, didn't I?

"You almost scared him off."

"That shitehawk doesn't scare. Don't forget that, *piscín*."

I stare at Braiden levelly. "I'll never forget *anything* about Antonio Russo."

He crosses the room faster than I think is possible, and his fingers close around my chin like he's disciplining a naughty dog. "But you'll beg for him?"

I toss my head, trying to break free, but Braiden only tightens his grip.

"Let me go!" My words slur because of the pressure of his fingers.

"Beg," he orders, using the Captain's voice that destroys me. "Beg *me*."

So I do. I beg with words. I beg with my fingers. I beg with my lips and then with my entire body. And whatever doubts Braiden has about the plan we've hatched, they don't keep him from taking his slow, sweet revenge for my seducing Antonio Russo.

19

BRAIDEN

Samantha's not accustomed to using evil criminals' greed against their own self-interest. She offered Russo too much, too fast.

She flattered him with his feckin' title. She fed him shite about me marrying Fiona. She said she'd bring him into the freeport, setting him up with all the tax dodges a criminal mastermind could desire.

She didn't have to give him the Diamond Ring. If she'd held her ground, he would have come around without it.

But she's had a lifetime of fearing Antonio Russo. I can't blame her too much for sweetening the pot.

Even if she offered something she has no right to give.

Trap Prince keeps the Diamond Ring close to his chest. The twelve of us men have secrets. We've seen things. Done things. He's not going to open the door to just anyone, even if Samantha does the asking. She overstepped her bounds.

But I've got a little leverage I can apply.

So I tell Liam to take the day off on Monday. I drive Samantha down to the freeport myself. I see her safely settled in her office, and then I go off to find Prince. Some conversations have to be held in person.

He's at the back of the property, watching a cement truck shite out the foundation for a new helicopter pad. I take up a position beside him at an orange mesh fence, watching the pour and waiting for a pause in the action.

Prince nods companionably. We supervise four men spreading the thick mixture across rebar. The wooden form for the pad is deep enough to bury a body.

The first truck leaves. Another one pulls into position. I wait for the back-up alarm to stop beeping before I remind Prince: "My boys helped you out of a jam last year."

He winces and rubs his arm, as if it's still bleeding. We lost the element of surprise that night, and Prince was shot up bad enough to need Doc Kelleher's needle and thread.

Now he says: "To the tune of twenty keys." That's his way of reminding me I ended up with twenty kilos of high-grade cocaine at the end of the night.

"The newspapers never managed to catch my good side." I can't let him forget the owners of that coke got revenge. My name was splashed across every paper from here to County Limerick, connected with a bloody crime I had nothing to do with. No one believes a Mob boss when he says he's an innocent bystander.

Prince looks over at me. "I assume this conversation ends with you asking for a favor?"

"Bring Antonio Russo into the Diamond Ring."

"That Mafia motherfucker?"

I manage one tight nod.

Prince looks back at the helipad. "Russo's not a client of Diamond Freeport."

"He will be."

Prince raises both eyebrows. "First I've heard of it."

"Samantha extended an invitation last Friday."

As Prince turns to study me, something happens on the pad. One man gestures with his concrete-covered brush, shouting at another in Spanish. There's an extensive debate over who is responsible for what at the site. I catch enough to understand sisters are involved in the division of labor, and possibly mothers.

The first man points toward Prince. The second cuts off his shout mid-word. They both go back to work.

Prince glances at me, side-eye, and says, "Bringing Russo here is a shit-for-brains idea. From everything I've heard, the man's a fucking psychopath."

"Everything you've heard is right."

"I don't want Best cleaning up any more messes on freeport property."

"That's not the sort of mess I plan on making."

Prince shakes his head. He watches the men diligently spreading concrete. He runs his fingers through his hair, and he narrows his eyes. But he finally says, "If Samantha brings him in, I'll ask him to join the Ring."

"I owe you one." I mean it.

"If that jizzstain hurts her—"

"I protect my own." I'm hurt that I need to say it, and my words come out hot.

But Prince doesn't give two shites about my feelings. He says, "I hope you know what the fuck you're doing."

I do too. But Samantha has a plan, and that's good enough for me. So even though I want to tell Prince where he can shove his skeptical concern, I manage to keep my mouth shut and turn back to watch the concrete flow.

Prince mutters under his breath, just low enough that I can pretend I don't hear. I clench my fists, though.

Prince apparently can't help himself—he says something else, and this time I catch the phrase *motherfucking Mafia prick*. I'm in complete agreement with his assessment, but the words sound like a challenge to me. I'm just deciding I can't ignore them when Prince shakes his head and stomps back to the main building. It's like he's got a billion-dollar empire to run or something.

I take a few deep breaths, then wait a bit before I head back to his office tower. I'm giving both of us a little time to forget how close he came to openly questioning my honor. When I get back to Samantha's office, she looks up from her computer screen.

"Everything okay?" she asks.

"Everything's fine," I answer tightly.

"Trap stopped by. He said he's asking Russo to join the Diamond Ring."

"Good."

"He dropped this off too. Said he wanted you to have it." She passes a bag across her desk, the plastic kind you get at a grocery store.

Inside is a fine-grain wooden box. The word *Jameson* is burned into the front, along with a familiar coat of arms. A label boasts that the whiskey inside has been aged for eighteen years.

I shake my head, wondering how many different peace offerings he keeps on hand. But I'm not about to toss it back.

"Do I have to be worried?" Samantha asks.

"Not about this," I tell her. And when she still looks concerned, I repeat myself. "Not about this." And I add a word, so I know she'll believe me. "*Piscín.*"

20

SAMANTHA

Outside the freeport conference room, Liam eyes Don Antonio, automatically registering all the places where the Mafia boss could hide a holster—shoulder, waist, and ankle. Russo tolerates the exam with cool disdain, unbuttoning his double-breasted jacket and twitching the hem of both pant legs high enough to show his smooth silk socks, both free of ankle holsters.

"Will you join us?" he asks my bodyguard, contempt dripping from each word.

"That won't be necessary," I say, my voice shaking. I'd give almost anything to have Liam stay beside me. But Russo has to think he's won.

So Liam takes his usual seat outside the conference room. And Trap waits inside, along with senior staff from every major department at the freeport.

Trap and I have led meetings like this dozens of times. We work well together, showing off the freeport's business. Trap presents the tax haven's history with his usual blunt efficiency. We pride ourselves on secrecy—our client list is confidential—but Trap can truthfully say we protect the wealth of senators and princes, of Fortune 100 self-made billionaires and trust-fund nepo babies.

I've memorized my lines for today like an Oscar-award-winning actress. I can cite statutes and regulations from state and federal governments, along with the legal codes of Palermo, Rome, and Milan. I love this part of my job, highlighting the challenges we help our clients navigate.

But it's hard for me to concentrate today. The entire time I speak, Russo eyes me without blinking. The corners of his mouth curl in the slightest hint of a carnivorous smile.

This is the man who had my parents murdered, planting a bomb in their car on a knife-sharp New Year's Eve nearly twenty years ago. A headache starts to gnaw at my right temple, and I can't resist the urge to try rubbing it away. My scars from that night feel like worms under my fingertips.

The freeport's head of accounting presents the usual charts and statistics like they're the key to solving climate change. Our director of import-export, our chief curator, our head of information technology—they all follow the script like Russo is an ordinary man. Like he isn't capable of ordering every one of them dead by morning, along with their families and friends.

I do my best to pull on the camouflage of a good freeport employee. I laugh at my colleagues' harmless jokes. I frown at their tales of government overreach. I nod when I should and shake my head when it's appropriate, all the while trying to forget that the monster across the table shoved his pistol between my cousin's legs and pulled the trigger.

Finally, finally, *finally*, Trap wraps up the dog and pony show, saying to Russo, "As I'm sure Samantha's told you, we have a special group of freeport customers, our wealthiest clients who have some unique needs. I'd like to personally welcome you into the Diamond Ring, Antonio."

It's the longest speech I've ever heard Trap make without swearing. He stands and extends his hand.

My boss abhors human contact. His left hand is shoved in his pants pocket, deep enough to hide five quick contractions of his fist. I've worked with Trap long enough that I barely register the tic.

But I see Russo catch it. The don's eyes narrow a tiny fraction as he stores away the gesture, filing it for future use. I didn't think it was possible to hate myself more for bringing this killer into our midst.

Not one of my colleagues—not even Trap—sees the red lasers skittering across their chests. They don't know Russo has marked them as prey. They hand the Mafia boss their business cards as they leave, telling him they're happy to help anytime, anywhere, with anything that will make his time at the freeport more pleasant.

I can't say the same. I can't follow them out of the room. I'm the only one who understands the true danger, and I'm the only one who has to stay.

When it's just the three of us—Trap, Russo, and me—my boss gestures toward the door, toward the lobby and freedom. "I'll just show you out—"

"Giovanna can do that," Russo says.

Trap gives no sign of being confused by the unfamiliar name. "If you'd like to visit your private gallery, I can have security—"

"That is not necessary," Russo says.

Trap looks directly at me. "Sam?"

That one syllable is my ticket out. I can escape this room. Or I can ask Trap to stay. Ask him to send in Liam. Ask, beg, plead not to be left alone with the demon who wants to possess me.

"I'm fine," I lie.

"Close the door as you leave," Russo says, as if he's dismissing some kid selling rip-off magazine subscriptions.

Trap bristles. "Sam?" he asks again.

I force myself to nod. "You can close the door."

He doesn't want to. But he trusts me. He leaves.

Russo barely waits for the door to latch before he stalks around the table. I don't move quickly enough, and he backs me into my chair.

Heat radiates off his body, singeing the space between us. I catch my breath too sharply, and my lungs are filled with the stink of lemon-soaked lumber, his Acqua di Parma cologne.

"You got me to your freeport, *cara*. To your fancy Diamond Ring. Now you must convince me to stay."

This is where I tell him Braiden's secret. This is where I share the truth about Krakower, about all the ways Russo can extort his way to millions. I must convince Russo that I've truly abandoned Braiden, that I've returned to the fold of my childhood. If I don't, the past three hours mean nothing.

But Russo expects me to satisfy him another way. He shifts his weight forward, rocking onto the balls of his feet. The motion brings his belt buckle level with my throat. Even as I swallow, I can make out the bulge of his erection behind his zipper. I try to look away, but his fingers close around my jaw.

"I can't," I tell him. "Not here. Not where I work."

"My sweet Giovanna," he says tightening his grip. "You can. And you will."

He has to think he's beaten me, but I won't let him see me cry. I push some of my desperation into a single word: "Please…"

An ugly light kindles deep inside his flat, dark eyes. "Please, what?" he asks.

I know how to beg. Braiden taught me. But with Braiden, I always have a safeword. I can always escape.

Russo has no limits.

"Please don't make me do this." And then, as if a brilliant idea has come to me for the very first time: "I can give you something else. Something better."

He moves faster than my eyes can follow, shifting his grip to the back of my neck. Bending me over the table like I'm a plastic doll, he plants a paralyzing elbow in the small of my back. "Your tight little *figa*? That would be better."

For the past six months, I've wondered how I can kneel, how I can beg, how I can submit to Braiden's commands. I've been shamed by the longing he ignites in me. I've been embarrassed by the needy heat he kindles between my legs, by the slick dampness of my panties every time I think about giving him control. I've questioned how I've turned into a creature who lives to be dominated.

But Russo's taking the upper hand turns me to ice.

I don't crave being mastered.

I crave *Braiden*.

"Please," I beg. "If you let me go, I'll tell you one of Braiden's secrets."

Russo freezes, his belt buckle half undone. "What kind of secret?" His breath stinks of stale coffee.

"The kind worth money. Lots and lots of money."

The swell of his cock presses into me. "Enough money for me not to fuck your *culo*?"

I'm shaking now, every inch of my body reacting in primitive, instinctive fear. I want him off my back, across the room, far enough away that he'll never touch me again.

But Russo must believe he's broken me completely. So I leak a little of my nerves into my voice, letting my words tremble as much as my body. "Oh, God. Braiden will kill me if he ever finds out. Forget it. No. I can't betray him like this."

"You will deceive him either way, Giovanna. With your body or with your words. What do you hold most dear, sweet girl? What will hurt the most?"

His fingers are tight around my neck. I know he's leaving bruises. That's the only way he'll believe he's running this, that he will think he's won.

So I gasp.

I cry.

And when he finally thinks I'm broken, that I'm utterly destroyed, I whisper in my softest voice, "Roy Krakower."

"What about him?" Russo snarls.

I tell him all the words Braiden gave me. I hand over the dynamite and unwind the fuse.

Russo pulls me to my feet and makes me repeat my story. He tests me on the details, going over the facts a third time, a fourth, a fifth. He pinches the small bones in my wrist, daring me to recant, but I grit my teeth against the agony and hold fast.

And finally Russo buys it, every word. He counts the millions he'll get from blackmailing Krakower. He accepts that I've betrayed the man I love.

He thinks he's safe. He thinks he's strong. He thinks he's the one I've chosen.

And now I'll be able to dig for all the facts, for all the gritty details I'll use to destroy Antonio Russo forever.

"That *testa di*—" Russo gloats, but I never learn if he's cursing Krakower or Braiden.

The door flies open before he can finish. The heavy metal bounces off the wall behind it, and Braiden Kelly storms into the room like an avenging angel.

21

BRAIDEN

S amantha's face is streaked with tears. Her neck is marked with scarlet fingerprints, and her jaw too. Her top is pulled out of her trousers.

I was a fool to let her leave home this morning. I should have locked her in our bedroom. Tied her to our bed. Poured sugar into the Bentley's petrol tank.

It's my job to protect her. I'll give my life to keep her safe. And if that means driving all the way from Philly to knock Antonio Russo's too-white teeth down his feckin' throat, I'm ready, willing, and able.

"Braiden!" Samantha says, her voice high and tight. She looks as guilty as a nun caught with her lips around a priest's prick. Refusing to meet my furious gaze, she staggers back a few feet.

Good girl. She's given me room to shoulder between her and the goombah shite who's shrugging his jacket back into place. As Russo shoots his cuffs with careful precision, I see

Samantha wipe the back of one hand across her lips. If that shitehawk forced his tongue down her throat, I'll rip out his diamond cufflinks and jam the metal posts through his eyes.

Better yet, I'll slice his throat open, and spit down his windpipe while he bleeds out on the freeport floor. Executing the shitehawk now just seems like efficient time management. I know I'll have to finish the job one day or another.

Samantha tweaks the waistband of her trousers, straightening the seams that animal twisted, and I actually see scarlet.

"Braiden," she says again, and this time I catch a hint of warning in her tone. I twitch her tentative fingers off my arm, using the motion to better block Russo from so much as glancing at her.

The gobshite is smart enough to notice my balled-up fists. But he's fool enough to say, "Giovanna was just welcoming me to the freeport."

"I'm sure *Samantha* was doing her job."

"It is fascinating, the things a girl can be paid to do these days."

He's calling my wife a whore, and I barely keep from smashing the shite-eating grin from his face. But Samantha has a plan. Samantha has a goal. If I can manage not to murder the fecker, she'll see Russo in jail for a very long time, stripped of his money and his power.

I won't be satisfied until he's feeding catfish at the bottom of the Schuylkill River. Preferably after every joint in his body is broken and he's been carved into bite-size pieces.

But I promised Samantha I'd try her way first. Forcing myself to relax my hands, I cast a quick glance over my shoulder. "Ready to go home, *piscín?*"

Samantha is wary, like a cat in a room full of strangers. She says, "I need some files from my office."

"I'll wait for you here." I won't let Russo follow her out of this room.

She leaves the door open, probably thinking that will keep

me from murdering the goombah prick. She should know better than that by now.

I try to sound like I'm talking about the weather when I say, "Touch my wife again, and I'll have your hands for paperweights."

"Which wife is that?" Russo asks, his voice like the slick of oil on top of bad pizza. "You already killed the madwoman in your attic. I hear you mean to wed the Boston girl, the one who broke your *coglioni* at the Rittenhouse. Or are you talking about my Giovanna?"

"Her name's Samantha Kelly. And she's mine."

"Are you sure she knows that?"

His smug smile makes my knuckles itch. But I answer with words instead of the haymaker I'd love to plant on his cleft chin. "*She* chose *me*. A concept you might understand if you ever had a woman you didn't need to buy or shame or terrify to get into your bed."

Russo clicks his tongue like he's talking to a naughty child. "Always about the sex with you. A woman can be good for more than tickling that *pisellino* between your legs."

"Don't pretend you know anything about what a woman's good for."

"Some women are very good at telling stories," he says. "My Giovanna, for example. Once upon a time, the worst story Giovanna knew was about the laws she broke. But now she tells me more. Much more. She tells me about laws *you* have broken."

Samantha told him about Krakower—that was our plan.

But Russo wants me to believe she's told him more than that. She's babbled about the Fishtown Boys, about deals we've made, jobs we've pulled. But I know Samantha better than that. She won't betray me. This gobshite can't break that bond between us.

"She was not willing to speak at first," Russo says, as if he's read my mind. "But after she found out about your first wife, the one in the attic... And then that Boston bitch... Let us just say my sweet Giovanna has found a whole new use for her pretty little mouth. Asking for help from a real man."

The sound that rips my throat isn't human. I forget why I'm not allowed to destroy this piece of shite, why I can't shove my fist through his fucking sternum and squeeze his heart until he screams for mercy.

Russo's not an eejit. He put a chair between us before he yanked my chain, but I'm mad enough to think I can hurdle over the leather to reach him.

"What the fuck is going on here!" The cry comes from the doorway, deeper and louder than anything I'm expecting.

I wheel by reflex, arm already pulling back to land a blow. As soon as I get rid of the intruder, I can get back to my true enemy. But I recognize the voice even as I'm shifting my weight. I can't fight Trap Prince in his own conference room, inside the freeport he owns.

"Back it up, motherfucker," he roars at me, shouldering past. "That's right." He growls, pointing to the foot of the table, behind me. "Over there."

I stalk across the room like it's my own idea.

Prince rounds on Russo before I can change my mind. "You too, cocksucker," he says to Russo, pointing to the other end of the table. And when Russo doesn't move fast enough: "Now, asshole!"

All three of us are breathing like rutting bulls, but Russo follows orders. Prince plants his hands on the polished mahogany, making a wall out of his body. "I'm only saying this once," he snarls at both of us. "Your investments in Diamond Freeport can make us all a lot of money. And your membership in the Diamond Ring can be a benefit to you, to me, and the ten other men in the group. But I've had bodies carried out of this place before. And I'm not afraid to do it again."

I've been present for two of those corpse removals. I don't know if there've been more, and I don't actually want to find out.

Prince goes on. "Sam Mott is one of the smartest women I know. She says she can work with both of you, and she says the two of you can work together. Don't make her a liar."

I want to correct him—her name's Samantha Kelly. And from the look on Russo's face, he's getting ready to test Prince himself, to call her Giovanna.

But neither of us gets a chance to make his point. Instead, Prince says, "I don't trust either one of you to do what's fucking right. So let me give you both a little motivation even you dickheads can't ignore. Whoever lands the first blow is out of the freeport forever. I'll lose out on some income, but you'll be paying tax consequences a hell of a lot longer."

He glares at Russo first, then at me. "Questions?"

When neither of us responds, he says in a louder voice, "Do either of you have any fucking questions?"

"No," I say, feeling like I've been whacked on the palms with a ruler.

"Not one," Russo says, his eyes narrowed and his lips tight.

"Good," Prince says. "Now get the fuck out of here, Kelly. And Russo, I was just coming down to see if you'd like a tour of the garage and the racetrack."

I stride out of the room before Russo can accept his feckin' engraved invitation.

I could find my way to Samantha's office wearing a blindfold. Liam stands as I approach, stepping forward like he's about to give a report. As I slam my hand down on the knob to the office door, Samantha's assistant calls out: "Excuse me! She's on the phone!"

I compromise, closing the door behind me softly, instead of slamming it. I *can* be reasonable.

Samantha takes one look at my face and says, "Alix, I'll call you back." She cradles the phone as I close the distance between us.

I don't want to talk. I don't want to strategize. I don't want to think about the ugly purple marks on her neck.

"Did he hurt you?" The question burns my lips like paint thinner.

"No," she lies, and I hate myself because I *know* she's lying, and I know why she's lying, and I have to admit that I'd lie too, if it was me answering the question.

"Did you tell him about Krakower?"

She nods like she's afraid of me, like I might make her pay for what I once gave freely.

"And what else?" I demand. "What else did you give him?"

"Nothing," she says.

This is my one true wife, paperwork and priests aside. This is the woman I love. I need to protect her. I'll shelter her with my body, with my bones, even if it costs me every penny I've ever invested in the freeport.

So I have to test. "Russo says—"

"Russo lies."

"He—"

She cuts me off with her lips on mine.

I pull away, because my body still thrums with all the adrenaline I need to kill a man. "He says," I get out, but this time her tongue tangles with mine.

My cock is ready to be done talking. My bollocks ache. But Samantha doesn't make the rules between us. She doesn't get to decide when we're through talking.

I hold her fast, my arms tight around her biceps. "Russo says you gave him dirt on the Fishtown Boys."

"I didn't. I promise. I swear."

I believe her, but I still want to kill someone. I settle for swiping my hand across her desk, sending documents flying. Pens and paper clips hit the floor, and a computer keyboard clatters after. Samantha's spluttering for words when I force her to lean over the edge of the desk.

"Braiden, no, you can't—"

But she's wrong. I can. I can shove my hand beneath her

and tear open the button at her waist. I can force her zipper down and slide her trousers over her rounded arse.

And even as she protests, my *piscín* raises her hips for me. She braces her arms for me. She waits for me to take her, so hot and ready I can smell the honey between her thighs.

I lower my own zip and free my raging cock. "I can," I tell her, sinking deep enough and hard enough and fast enough that she groans. "You're my wife," I say, setting a punishing pace. "Say it."

"I'm your wife," she whispers.

"Louder," I demand, picking up speed, because I might be a grown man, but she strips away every last shred of my restraint.

"I'm your wife," she says again.

"I can't hear you."

"I'm your wife," she repeats, but she's not any louder because her voice is shaking too much. She's as close to breaking as I am.

I reach around and catch the hot button of her clit between my forefinger and my thumb. I squeeze, hard enough to make her cry out, and then without my ordering her again she chants as she shatters: "I'm your wife I'm your wife I'm your wife I'm your wife I'm your wife."

I crash into her one last time, before I start to spasm in time to her promise, her prayer. I clutch her hips until I'm empty, and then I collapse on top of her, wanting to pin her, to splay her, to melt into her forever.

"I'm your wife," she whispers one more time.

I kiss her neck, softly now, gentle where Russo left his marks. I smooth her hair to one side. I help her up, and then I guide us both behind her desk, to her mesh-and-metal executive chair. I pull her onto my lap, folding my arms around her and holding her close enough to feel her heartbeat.

I whisper that I need her. I whisper that I love her. I whisper that she's mine. And I close my eyes to offer up a prayer that we both stay safe from the predator we've unleashed inside the freeport.

22

SAMANTHA

Two weeks after the freeport conference room was used to welcome Antonio Russo, the space has been converted into an auction house. The Book of Skreen, Braiden's Irish treasure, is displayed at the front of the room inside a custom-made bulletproof case. Velvet wedges support the ancient wooden boards that cover the hand-lettered pages. One example of the book's ornate Celtic knotwork is projected on a huge screen. The gold-lined image is twelve hundred years old, but it looks like it could have been painted yesterday.

A buzz of excitement builds as Alix Key enters the room. She's been conducting auctions at the freeport for a couple of years now, bringing in stunning results for our clients.

I smile as she comes to stand beside me, next to the display case. My role today is primarily moral support. I've already drafted the contract and the lengthy disclosure statements that will make the sale official. "Ready for showtime?" I ask her.

She glances at the clock on the wall. "We'll keep them

waiting an extra ten minutes. Build that last-minute excitement."

"Just in case the Morgan Library changes its mind?"

She offers a rueful grin. "Not likely."

In a perfect world, the Book of Skreen would cause a bidding frenzy between the world's most prestigious collectors of illuminated manuscripts. New York's Morgan Library is famous for a collection build in the nineteenth century. The Metropolitan Museum of Art, the Getty Center… Museums have built entire rooms around treasures like the Skreen.

But every one of Alix's advances to public institutions was politely declined. Aside from the shockingly short timetable, museums and libraries are frightened off by the book's sketchy background. Braiden can't prove his property wasn't removed legally from Ireland. There are no prior sales documents to show it wasn't stolen.

But the room of speculators around us proves private collectors aren't as concerned by legal uncertainty. Plenty of millionaires—and billionaires too—are willing to take a risk, just so they can claim ownership of one of the most beautiful books in the world.

Alix says, "Wish me luck."

"You don't need luck," I tell her. "You're the best in the business."

As she takes her place at the lectern, I head to the back of the room. Braiden sits in the last row, a look of impatience marring the effect of his perfectly tailored suit. "Ready?" I whisper, as I slide into the empty seat beside him.

"I just wish…" He trails off, making a fist of his right hand.

He just wishes he could bid on the book. Or that I could. Or Trap, or Alix, anyone he knows and trusts. But he's known the rules all along. Once he consigned the Skreen for auction, he gave up all control.

And Braiden Kelly hates to lose control.

The crowd is getting anxious. I glance around the room, trying to figure out how many of them will actually bid.

Cole Wolf sits near us in the back. He collects Impressionist art; he bought the Monet that was on the block at Alix's first auction. He won't bid today; he's not interested in manuscripts. Instead, he's here for the pure sport of today's contest.

Same with Connor Boyle. I've never seen him at a freeport auction. But maybe he came to Dover on other business, and the book is Irish, and the caterers are waiting with vintage champagne, so why not waste an hour or so watching other people spend their money?

Braiden shifts his weight, broadcasting frustration like a radio signal. I close my fingers over his fist and squeeze gently. We both sit a little straighter as Alix greets the crowd. She opens the bidding at an easy ten million dollars.

A woman in the third row raises her paddle. Marti Kingston is a relatively new freeport client; she joined us about two years ago after making a fortune leading a New York hedge fund. Now, in retirement, she spends her time decorating her seven homes. She must see the Skreen as a beautiful curiosity.

"Thank you for getting us started," Alix says with an easy grace. "We've got ten million, do I hear ten one?"

A man wearing a long white robe and matching headdress gets in on the bidding. Mohammed Bakir has bought a dozen top-quality paintings at freeport auctions in the last year. He's rumored to be building a museum in Saudi Arabia.

Alix acknowledges him with a nod. Bidding is brisk for nearly ten minutes, with eight potential buyers. Alix jumps the price steadily, easily clearing fifteen million. Eighteen. Twenty.

Four of the bidders drop out. Alix raises the price to twenty-three million dollars. Another bidder passes. Twenty-four. Twenty-four five.

As sometimes happens at these events, the final bidding is between the two who started. With the entire room watching,

Kingston and Bakir alternate bids. Alix guides them up the ladder to twenty-six million dollars, to twenty-seven.

"Thirty million dollars," comes a bid from the side of the room.

My heart seizes in my chest, even as Braiden half-rises out of his seat. Both of us recognize the voice. Antonio Russo is bidding on the Book of Skreen.

The crowd murmurs in thrilled surprise. No new bidder has raised a paddle for minutes. Kingston turns in her seat, an expression of annoyance on her Fifth Avenue features. Bakir merely sets his paddle in his lap, retiring the fight.

For the first time since taking the stand, Alix hesitates. But then she clears her throat and says, "The current bid is thirty million dollars. Do I hear thirty million, five hundred thousand?"

Kingston says, "Thirty million, five hundred."

Russo counters. "Thirty-two million."

Alix raises her eyebrows at the jump. Russo's bid doesn't make sense. Kingston might be at her limit. He might be able to get the book for less.

The bid doesn't make sense for other reasons as well. To my knowledge, Antonio Russo has never expressed the slightest interest in art of any kind. I was in his home when I was a child, and I don't remember paintings, much less astronomically expensive rare books.

Even if Russo has discovered a love of illuminated manuscripts, he surely doesn't value Irish work. The man has built his entire illegal career on his Italian heritage.

There's more at stake here, though. Because Russo might have become an art collector. And he might have a soft spot for Irish manuscripts, But there's no way in hell that Antonio Russo would ever put a penny in Braiden Kelly's pocket.

From the tight line of Braiden's jaw, he's come to the same conclusion. He climbs to his feet, as if he's trying to get a better view of the proceedings. Of course, with his height and his broad shoulders, he looks intimidating as hell.

Marti Kingston goes to thirty-three.

Russo hesitates for just a moment. He reaches into his breast pocket, as if he's checking to make sure he brought his wallet. But instead of taking out a billfold, he takes out something smaller. Something shiny. Something silver.

For one horrified second, I think it's a weapon. But Russo has cleared extra security to get into today's auction. He had to pass through a metal detector in the lobby.

His hand works the rectangle of metal like a fidget toy, passing it over his fingers and under, over again and into his palm. He seems unaware of what he's doing, but that's a lie, because Antonio Russo has never been unaware of his own behavior, not once in his life.

Alix stands at the front of the room. "The current bid is thirty-three million dollars. Thirty-three million dollars for the Book of Skreen. Do I hear—"

"Forty million dollars," Russo says.

As the crowd gasps in amazement, Russo leans back in his chair. He fiddles with the box in his hand. He glances over his shoulder, looking directly at Braiden. And he rolls his thumb over the edge of the box, sending a long finger of flame from the cigarette lighter he holds.

23

BRAIDEN

The shitehawk is going to burn the Book of Skreen.

He doesn't care about the hand-lettered pages. He doesn't care about the decorated margins—people and animals and buildings showing how villagers lived twelve centuries ago. He doesn't care about the eighteen full-page drawings—knot-work so intricate it can scarcely be followed with the naked eye.

Irish monks gave years of their lives to make the Skreen. Some of them likely went blind painting its pages.

But Antonio Russo will pay an obscene amount—half again the most generous estimate of the manuscript's value—just so he can burn it in front of me.

And there's not a thing I can do to stop him.

I glance at Samantha. Her head is bowed. Her eyes are closed. She might be reviewing every statute and regulation she's ever read, but I'm willing to bet nothing will save the Skreen.

Caught at the front of the room, Alix Key looks like she's

trapped in a nightmare. She can't do anything to stop Russo either, not if he's willing to pay.

"Marti?" she asks.

But the woman in the front row shakes her head. She slips her paddle under her seat, as if she's afraid she might make a bid by accident.

Alix looks at me, stricken. But she knows the rules as well as I do. I'm the consignor. I can't bid.

"F— Forty million dollars," she says. "Going once. Going twice—"

"One hundred million dollars."

The bid lands like a ton of rain-soaked wool, sodden and dark and far too heavy to shift. Connor Boyle stands as the crowd swivels. His shoulders fill the space of two ordinary men. He's nearly a head taller than anyone else in the room.

He nods to Alix, eyeing the ceremonial gavel in her hand.

She startles and gets back to work. "One hundred," she says quickly. And before Russo can decide it's worth an extra sixty large to ram his prick up my arse, Alix ends the auction: "Going once. Going twice. Sold to Connor Boyle."

"*Puttaniere!*" Russo shouts. Even furious, though, he's not stupid enough to go after Boyle. Instead, he shoulders his way out of the room, sending a waiter flailing to save a tray of champagne flutes.

The freeport explodes in reaction. People ask each other if they actually saw flame coming from that lighter. Small groups gather around Marti Kingston and Mohammed Bakir, consoling them about their respective losses.

Other people converge on the lectern, congratulating Alix on the auction. A couple of freeport clients shake her hand, and I suspect that her composure has gained her at least one more sale on her increasingly busy calendar.

Samantha still sits in her chair. Her head is still bowed. Her eyes are still closed.

I settle a hand on her shoulder. "It's over, *piscín*." I pitch my voice just loud enough for her to hear.

When she looks up, her eyes are haunted by a lifetime of fear. "He would have done it, just to spite us."

"It doesn't matter. He lost this round."

I can see she wants to argue. But people are gathering, reaching out to shake my hand, congratulating me on the sale.

Samantha takes a deep breath. I watch her transform like a flower going from bud to blossom. She physically sets aside the ghost of Giovanna Canna and puts on Samantha Kelly like a feckin' crown. She makes her way to the front of the room, where she has paperwork to manage.

Waiters approach with champagne. I take a glass, and then I carry one over to Connor Boyle, who's surrounded by his own sudden fan club.

"To Connor Boyle!" I announce, raising my glass. "Proud new owner of the Book of Skreen!"

"To Connor Boyle!" the crowd salutes. Boyle looks me in the eye before he drains off half his glass.

It's half an hour before I'm able to speak with him alone. "I never knew you were interested in manuscripts," I say.

"I wasn't, before today."

"You chose a deadly one to start with." Deadly—I mean it in the Irish way. A good one. A great one.

He hears something different. "I'm not afraid of Russo. Any guinea gobshite who thinks he can burn Irish treasure needs a lesson."

"You delivered him one today."

He eyes me for a long moment. "Don't be thinking this changes my thoughts on the Union," he warns. Before I can assure him the Union has been far from my mind, he says, "I'm still thinking Reardon's the man for the job."

"You've got your right to vote."

He nods toward Samantha and the table she's commandeered at the front of the room. She's got a dozen different documents, all of them in triplicate—for the freeport, for Boyle, and for me. "Your woman has some things for us to sign," he says.

"Worse than buying a house," I say. I glance at the book, locked in its bulletproof box. "What will you do with it?"

"For now?" he asks. "Put it in my gallery, here at the freeport. That's the way we turn a profit, right?"

After what he's paying today, it'll be a long time before he profits on the Skreen. But I say, "That's the way."

I let him lead the way to the front of the room.

24

SAMANTHA

~

Last Friday, Russo lost the Book of Skreen.

This week, he gets his revenge, running me ragged.

On Monday, he requires my presence as he takes delivery of the first shipment destined for his gallery. Other tax haven clients manage loading in without the direct oversight of Diamond Freeport's General Counsel, but I give in because I think I might see something, evidence in the case I'm building against him.

In the end, though, I only witness several hundred cases of laundry detergent, stacked to the ceiling by hard-working young men. I'm sure the jugs fell off a truck somewhere along the Eastern seaboard, but it's hardly the type of theft that would put Russo behind bars for a lifetime.

On Wednesday, Russo demands my company again. This time, the shipment is barrels of olive oil. I'm certain the liquid in those drums is nothing but cheap vegetable oil with a bit of green food coloring. But, again, no agricultural fraud will put Russo away for life.

On Friday, Russo keeps me waiting all day, but no shipments make it through the freeport gates.

Russo blames the fuck-up on Independence Day, which falls on Saturday, but I'm certain he's testing me. Figuring out how much time I'm willing to give him. How long my leash is from Braiden's controlling hand.

Throughout the week, I remind myself I'm not just doing this for Braiden. I'm doing it for me. I'm destroying Russo because he killed my parents. I'm getting revenge for what he did to Eliza.

The fact that my husband wants his head in a sack and his body at the bottom of the Schuylkill just makes the job a little sweeter.

So far, though, I have nothing to report to Braiden. That makes breakfast a rather tense meal, the Monday after Independence Day.

I enter the dining room, briefcase in hand. Liam waits in the Bentley outside, but I'm willing to uphold house rules, at least to grab a bite of breakfast before we hit the road.

"No," Braiden says, barely looking up from the first of his newspapers.

"Good morning to you, too," I say. I pour myself a cup of coffee and grab a piece of toast from the silver rack on the table.

Braiden sets his teacup onto his saucer with the precision of a watchmaker. "You won't be going to the freeport this morning."

I glance at Aiofe, who is watching us with the rapt attention most children reserve for video games. If she's nursing a sugar hang-over from polishing off Fairfax's July 4 cherry pie, she's hiding it well.

"I'm already late for a meeting," I say evenly. I retrieve a peach from the bowl on the sideboard, as if that will appease my over-protective husband.

Braiden takes his phone out of his pocket and taps an already-stored number. After a gap that must cover four or five rings, he says, "Mary, this is Braiden Kelly, calling for Samantha. An emergency has come up at home, and she won't be able to make it in this morning. Please cancel all of her meetings, and she'll reschedule at a future date."

"You controlling bas—!" I only cut off my shriek because Aiofe's eyes have gone as wide as her plate of eggs. Furious, I collect my briefcase and head for the door. I can set my assistant straight once I'm in the car.

Which is a great plan. I just don't take into account how quickly Braiden can move when he's motivated. His hand falls heavily on the front door, slamming it shut before I can slip outside. When I whirl to face him, he uses his body as a cage, capturing me between his arms.

"Let me go!" I shout, not caring anymore if Aiofe overhears. Fairfax either, for that matter.

"No."

The same one-word dismissal as when I walked into the dining room—no explanation. No justification. No argument.

But this time, he shifts his weight. He moves his hands from the door to my wrists, pinning my arms in place. He rolls his hips, trapping mine against the door. I turn my face to the side.

For just a moment, my concentration is shredded by a gut-punching memory of what we did Saturday night, after our happy-family evening watching fireworks from the back porch, as Ardmore celebrated our country's independence.

Braiden trails his cat o' nine tails across my belly... I strain against the leather cuffs keeping me spread-eagled on the bed... A pleading growl rises in my throat...

My cheeks flush as I force away the image. Pressing my thighs together, I concentrate on what I need now. Of course Braiden feels my motion, and he forces more of his weight onto me. My hips turn traitor and rock toward him, needy and desperate, even through my tailored suit.

Braiden's lips find the exposed line of my jaw. The tip of his tongue ignites my jugular.

I take a deep breath. "I don't know how long I have before they take my license. I have to go to work today. I need to be at the freeport."

"For Russo," Braiden says, like he's biting into a bar of soap.

"For *us.*"

"I don't trust him," Braiden says.

I cut off a dismayed laugh. "I don't trust him either. But you agreed… This is what we have to do."

He shakes his head. "That was before I spent every day last week imagining everything that can go wrong."

"Nothing will go wrong. Between Liam and freeport security… I'm safe."

Braiden stares at me for so long I think I've lost. He cares more about controlling me than he does about getting vengeance against Russo.

But then he crushes his mouth against mine. His tongue demands entrance as his fingers tangle in my hair. He's taking, drinking, consuming me like he's a starving man and I'm a feast.

When we have to breathe, when we're both gasping like frantic animals, his teeth close on my lip, sharp enough to make me moan. He tightens the bite for just a heartbeat, and then he backs off, touching his forehead to mine.

"Wear your collar when you meet with him," he says.

Shock stiffens my body. This time it's my turn to say, "No."

"Just today," he says, his thumb tracing my swollen lips.

"I can't."

"You won't."

"You've always said it was only in our bedroom."

"*You* said that. *I* said you'd get no argument from me if you want to wear it elsewhere. So wear it today. When you're with Russo."

It's the symbol of my submission. The outward expression that Braiden controls me. That I belong to him, and him alone.

Swallowing hard, I imagine the weight of the emerald against my throat. I want to please Braiden. I love him. I want him to be happy.

But he's asking the impossible.

I speak slowly. "The freeport is business. Not—" I shrug, gesturing helplessly between us. "This."

He backs away, and the air in the foyer is suddenly so cold I have to clench my jaw to keep my teeth from chattering. "Go," he says.

I clutch his arm, trying to make things right. We both stare at my fingers. At the gold band he gave me when we married. "I'll wear the collar tonight," I say.

He shakes his head.

"I promise," I say.

He moves toward the center of the foyer.

"I love you." I've said the words before. We both have. But they've never sounded so desperate, so heartsore, so raw.

Braiden stops, so I know he heard me. But all he says is, "Get out of here."

He goes back to the dining room.

I do as he says. I leave. But every step I take out the door, down the steps, to the car, I pray he'll change his mind and follow me. He doesn't, though. Not even when the braying paparazzi slow my departure for nearly half an hour.

I tell myself it doesn't matter.

I tell myself everything will be fine when I get home tonight.

I tell myself...

It doesn't matter what I say. I don't believe my own lies.

25

SAMANTHA

~

With Liam driving, I take out my phone before we hit the freeway and leave a message for Mary: "Hey there! Braiden was fooling around when he called this morning. Of course I'm coming in—no need for you to cancel anything. See you soon!"

My voice is so chipper, I nauseate myself.

For the rest of the ride, I study the documents Russo provided the freeport when he completed his membership application. I need to dig deeper into all the accounts he gave us, all the papers he filed, all the shipments he's started running through Dover.

I should concentrate on following those leads. But I keep replaying my conversation with Braiden, trying to figure out what I should have said, what I could have done—short of wearing the symbol of my submission—to make it right.

I love you.

Get out of here.

By the time we get to the freeport, I'm questioning every choice I've ever made. But I'm so close to gaining Russo's trust... Last week, he showed me his small scams—detergent, olive oil. Any day now, he'll give me the weapon I need to destroy him forever.

I've come too far to back down now.

After I check in with a bemused Mary, Liam escorts me to the warehouse building, where freeport clients maintain their personal galleries. If he notices my fingers shaking as I press the button for the third floor underground, he doesn't say a word. But he insists on taking point as we approach a waiting Russo.

"I'm sorry I'm late, Don Antonio." The title scratches my throat like a toilet brush, but it does its job. Russo puffs with pride and stops looking at his watch.

"We have a lot to do today," he says before he jams his finger onto the biometric pad. He's leaning forward for the retina scan when Liam moves into position between us.

Russo steps back, a frown pursing his thin lips. "Your services are not required today," he says to my bodyguard.

Liam ignores him, staying planted firmly in front of me.

"Giovanna," Russo says. "Send your dog to his kennel."

Liam's neck tenses, but he knows better than to say anything out loud. "That won't be possible," I say to Russo.

His only reply is to state his name for me again, his tone full of warning, like a teacher disciplining a disobedient student: "Giovanna."

I want to cross my arms over my chest, folding away from his disapproval. But I force myself to stand firm, settling my hands on my hips. "I'll leave you to your work, then, Don Antonio. If you need me, I'll be in my office."

His laugh ripples like the scales of a snake. "My sweet Giovanna," he says. Before I can remind him that I'm not his sweet anything, he reaches into his breast pocket. Liam shifts his weight, clearly ready to deal with a weapon, but Russo only produces a sheaf of paper, folded lengthwise.

"I hope we can discuss these documents, Giovanna," he says, handing me the top page. "Surely you understand my need for privacy."

I'm staring at a federal tax form. It looks completely legitimate—last year's date in the upper left corner, with Russo's name and address typed into the appropriate spaces. A nine-digit Social Security Number is listed on the proper line.

"Let us not waste any more time," Russo says.

He turns back to the gallery door, clearly assuming I'll obey him. Returning his finger to the electronic pad, he lowers his face to the retina scanner. But when the door glides open, I say, "Let Liam clear the gallery. Once he's confirmed there are no weapons in there, he'll wait outside."

It's a dangerous compromise. Even if Liam confirms there are no weapons in *sight*, the gallery holds hundreds of cases of stolen goods. Any one of them could hide a firearm—and I have no doubt Russo can kill with his bare hands.

But that tax document… The chance to verify I'm on the right path as I work toward Russo's downfall…

He pauses with his hand on the doorknob. "I am afraid that will not—"

Liam bulls past him.

It's clearly against freeport policy, invading the private gallery of a client. But Russo's reaction shoots a warning arrow down my spine. He bellows in outrage at Liam's interference: "You have no right!"

A bitter taste numbs the back of my throat, and my fingertips tingle. Every cell in my body orders me to flee.

But if I flee, I'll never know what happens to Liam.

I won't know if Russo will actually fire the pistol he's raked from the small of his back.

And I'll have no idea who the man is standing inside the gallery. The one beside the hospital table, wearing a white coat. The one holding a gun of his very own.

26

SAMANTHA

L iam produces the pistol I've always known he keeps in a
shoulder holster under his jacket. He's aiming it now, arms
rigid with his two-handed grip. His attention shifts from Russo
to the stranger inside the gallery and back again, but then he
settles all his concentration on the Mafia boss.

"Get out of here, Samantha," he says, not bothering to look
at me.

"That would be a mistake, Giovanna," Russo says, like we're
doing nothing more important than swapping recipes. He's still
pointing his weapon at Liam.

Without shifting his own aim, Liam juts his chin toward the
unknown man. "Put it down and back away from the table."

The man does nothing.

Continuing to aim at Russo, Liam orders the stranger: "Put
it down, shitehawk!"

The man remains frozen until Russo says, "Put down the
gun, Paolo."

The stranger—Paolo—places his weapon on the table before he backs away. He takes three large steps with his hands over his head.

"You do not understand," Russo says to Liam.

"I understand you wanted Herself in here. Without me. Alone with you and that dry shite."

Russo glances at me. "Pat your dog on the head, Giovanna. Give him a bone and send him away."

"Why the hell would I do that?" My voice is steadier than I expect after a lifetime of dreading Russo.

"Because I will not explain a thing while a gun is pointed at me. Because you want to know what I have to say."

"Who is that man?" I ask, nodding toward Paolo. "What were you going to do to me?"

"Nothing you do not allow," Russo says.

"Bollocks," Liam says, which makes Russo frown, as if he smells sewer gas.

My cousin Eliza didn't consent to Russo shoving a gun between her legs. "What *permission* can you possibly think I'll give?"

"Permission to bear the *segno*. Like your father did before you."

Holy shit.

That's not a pistol Paolo set on the table. It's a tattoo gun.

No wonder Liam has kept his own weapon focused on Russo.

I shake my head, dimly aware that I'm not thinking clearly. Maybe my brain is flooded with adrenaline. Maybe I have a life-time of conditioning regarding Antonio Russo and the East Falls Crew. Maybe I remember the mark of the Crew on my father's back.

I only saw it a few times—at family gatherings in the summer, swimming at Zio Matteo's cabin in the Poconos. The tattoo was as long as my hand. It sat at the base of my father's spine, just above the elastic band of his Speedo bathing suit. It was a line drawing, black against his swarthy skin: the head of a Medusa, snakes and all, framed by three bent legs.

The trinacria. Ancient symbol of Sicily. Emblem of Russo's Mafia family.

"Why give me the *segno*?" I ask him now. "I'm not part of your Crew."

"You are not," Russo agrees. "But I will not show those papers to anyone who has not sworn an oath of blood."

I have a crazy image of Eliza and me, huddled beneath the quilt on her childhood bed. She stole her brother's Swiss Army Knife, and we held the small blade over a match, sterilizing it before we pricked our thumbs. We said we'd be true to each other forever.

Eliza. The woman Russo murdered.

"Enough with guns," Russo says. He holds his finger from the trigger of his own weapon as he lowers it to the floor. "Giovanna?" he asks, after he stands.

"Liam," I say. From the set of his shoulders, my protector loathes giving in. But he does it because I ask him to. Because he's loyal to me. He puts his gun on the floor by his foot.

"Excellent," Russo says. "Now, Giovanna, you will accept the *segno*, and then we will discuss these documents. Or I will leave and tell the world your freeport is a sham. That you offer services you fail to provide. That your auctions are frauds, with winning buyers chosen in advance."

So that's what has brought us to this. He's getting revenge for Connor Boyle outbidding him for the Book of Skreen. Russo was embarrassed in public, and now he needs to rebuild his ego.

I have no doubt he can do everything he threatens. He's built an empire through blackmail and extortion. He can devastate Diamond Freeport and Trap Prince before the end of this fiscal year.

"You ask too much," I say.

"Your father took the oath. Your cousin, too, before she

betrayed me. Once you are part of my family, I will share the documents with you. All you must do is take the oath."

Take the oath. Let a stranger tattoo me with the symbol of Sicily, of the Mafia's ancient home.

"Liam stays here," I say.

Russo's flat gaze gives away nothing. "If you wish."

Liam says to me, "The boss won't——"

I cut him off. "The boss isn't here."

"I'll call him," Liam says.

"You'll do nothing of the sort."

Russo says, "Giovanna? We have wasted enough time this morning."

Liam stares at me, pleading. It isn't fair, putting him between Braiden and me like this. But Russo is losing interest. He's turning toward Paolo. He's glancing at the gallery door.

I say to Liam, "I take full responsibility."

"You know the boss——"

"Then leave!" I cut him off. "Go on! Get back to Ardmore."

He shifts his weight. He looks from Russo to Paolo to the tattoo gun. "Jesus, Mary, and Joseph," he swears, half under his breath. But then he moves toward the table. "Go on, then," he says to Paolo. "What does she do to get ready?"

I strip to my underwear. It hurts to take my clothes off, a physical pain, like I'm peeling away flesh instead of fabric. But I have to do this. I have to meet Russo's demands. This is the only way he'll trust me, the only way I'll get the evidence I need to lock him away forever.

Fighting panic, I lie on the table, flat, on my stomach. I pull my hair to one side. I try to relax the iron muscles of my back.

Looking over my right shoulder, I see Russo. He's staring at me like I'm a side of beef and he's the butcher. His eyes measure my bra straps. He studies the elastic band of my panties with clinical expertise.

I turn my head to the left and start to shiver like I'm stranded on an ice floe.

"Get her a blanket," Liam orders.

"You think you are at the Ritz?" Russo asks.

Liam swears, in Irish this time, and he strips off his jacket. I can feel the warmth of his body as he settles it, cross-wise, over my shoulder blades.

Paolo sets one palm in the middle of my back and lowers the tattoo gun to my spine, a hands-breadth above my hips. "This will hurt," he says, just before he switches on the device.

He lies.

Hurt is too small a word for the agony I feel. The first punch of the needle echoes all the way to my brain. I scream, but Paolo only shifts the palm he's using to brace himself, and then he settles down to serious business.

It's agony.

Torture.

Fire fans out from my spine to my flanks, an impossible flame that freezes everything it touches. My stomach lurches, and I'm grateful my breakfast was nothing more than coffee and toast. I regret I had that much.

I want to sob. I want to beg. I want to plead with him to stop, to set me free, to let me get off the table.

But if I do that, if I give in, I'll never capture Russo. So I set my jaw. I hold my breath as long as I can. I close my eyes. And I endure.

After a century or two, Liam says, "She needs a break."

"No break," Paolo says.

Part of me wants to argue. But I know that if he stops, I'll never find the courage to let him start again, and then all of this will be for nothing. I'll never get Russo.

I close my eyes. I count to one hundred. Again. Again. Again.

And finally, when I've lost track of who I am, of where I am, of why I ever agreed to do this, the needle stops. The room falls silent, except for a harsh, tearing sound, which I finally figure out is my own breathing.

Paolo moves toward my head, and I realize he's holding a mirror. Clenching my teeth, I angle my chin for a better view.

The black ink stands out against the smooth flesh of my lower back. It's faintly rimmed with red, where my skin protests the abuse. But however brutal Paolo was, he had a steady hand.

The line drawing looks like it belongs in a history book about Sicily, or maybe a textbook on witches. The snakes of Medusa's hair twist around the three bent legs. The bizarre design is perfectly legible.

I nod, because I don't trust myself to speak. Paolo looks across to Russo and grunts something in Italian, in a dialect I no longer understand. Steeling myself, I turn to face the Mafia don.

"*Sì*," he says to Paolo. And then to me, "My sign looks good on you, Giovanna." He waves a dismissive hand to Paolo. "Cover it up," he says.

Paolo rips open a paper packet and settles a clear dressing over the tattoo. "You keep for twenty-four hours," he says. "Then wash. Careful." He thinks for a moment, then chooses another word. "Gentle."

"Tw— Twenty-four hours." My voice is sandy with exhaustion.

Liam is the one who helps me sit up. He retrieves my clothes like a trained nurse, and he helps me to dress. By mutual agreement, we don't tuck in my smooth silk top. I hand him back his jacket once I'm fully clothed.

And then I turn to Russo. "All right," I say. "I got your tattoo. Now I can advise you on those tax documents."

I hold out my hand, but he shakes his head. "I do not think so, Giovanna. You are tired, and—"

"I'm fine."

He goes on as if I haven't interrupted him. "These papers are not urgent. They can wait until you are recovered."

"I don't need any recovery," I say.

He clicks his tongue, like a parent correcting an overtired

child. "It would be cruel of me to expect you to work, after such an experience. Next week," he says. "When you have rested."

I want to protest. I want to tell him he's mistaken, that I'm fine, I'm fresh, I'm ready to provide legal advice on any document in his possession.

But I can't afford to make him suspicious. So I incline my head and feed his ego. "You are too kind, Don Antonio."

His crocodile smile says he knows I think otherwise.

I have no other option—I let Liam help me from the room. He takes me directly to the Bentley but when he opens the back door, I say, "Please. I'll sit up front."

He clearly considers protesting, but in the end he opens the front door. He turns on the heater before we reach the highway, even though it's July. That's the only thing that makes me realize I'm shivering. The sun sets as he drives me home, and neither of us says a single word for the entire ride.

The paparazzi are gone when we arrive at the Ardmore house. The porch lights are on, but every window is dark. "Want me to come in with you?" Liam asks.

I shake my head. "I'm fine," I say, the same lie I used with Russo.

"It's no problem."

"I'm fine," I repeat, my exhaustion sounding like annoyance.

I open my own car door. I take the steps carefully, as if they're slippery with ice. My key catches in the front door, and for just a moment, I think Braiden changed the lock, but then I find the right angle. I take a deep breath and head inside.

Braiden sits in the foyer. He's dragged an armchair out of the dining room, placing it at the foot of the stairs. His legs are spread, like he's anchoring the world. His hair is mussed, and I wonder how many times he's run his fingers through it. My collar is draped over the fingers of his left hand, the emerald shining like a beacon in the light from the porch. Braiden holds a tumbler in his right hand, and the smell of whiskey slaps me like a wake-up call.

I close the door, shutting out the bright lights on the porch. Now we're illuminated only by the soft glow that sneaks inside the windows.

"Wh—" I hate that my voice shakes. "Where is everyone?"

"I sent Aiofe and Fairfax to the Rittenhouse. So we could have some privacy."

"And the paps?"

"I had Best send out a dozen of his best men. Told them to patrol with machine guns for a couple of hours. I guess there are easier stories to land."

I want to laugh, but I'm too exhausted. "What are you doing here?"

"Waiting for you."

"Why—"

"*Piscín.*" The word is rough on his lips. He holds out my collar, and the gem glints in the dim lights. It's an invitation.

I take it. I cross the foyer and sit on his lap.

His arms fold around me, pulling me close to his chest. My spine unzips, releasing a weight I didn't know I carried. All the tension, all the fear, all the pain of today boils up inside me, breaking free in a trembling sigh.

"*Mo chailín maith,*" he whispers against my hair. He brings the glass of whiskey to my lips. As he tilts it gently, I take a sip and the warmth thaws the still-frozen places inside me.

"I was wrong this morning," he says. "I was worried." I hear his heartbeat beneath his crisp white shirt. "Angry," he says. "Jealous."

I can count on one hand the number of times I've heard Braiden admit he was wrong. His fingers shift on my hip, as if he thinks I'll try to break away, but I don't ever want to leave this place. I never want to lose this feeling of shelter, of absolute safety. My collar hums between his palm and my flesh.

I tilt my head and raise my chin, finding his mouth.

It's a sweet kiss at first. Chaste. A solemn pledge never to repeat the morning's fight.

But the energy between us has never been innocent. From the moment we looked at each other in that elevator door at the Delaware Division of Revenue, I've been falling, tumbling, spinning out of control. Now I open my lips first, and he's there, waiting to swipe his tongue deep. I moan because this is what I've always wanted—this power, this heat, this searing, overwhelming need.

The glass of whiskey clatters to the floor. Braiden tangles one hand in my hair, pulling my head back, arching my neck as if he's a vampire ready to drink. His other hand presses my collar against my thigh.

His erection feels like a tree trunk beneath my leg. I shift my weight so I can stroke him through his pants. Before I can slip, he grabs me, clamping my collar against the small of my back.

I cry out as fire ignites my spine.

"What—" he asks, but his fingers are already moving beneath my silk top.

"I can ex—" I start.

"What the hell?" He's found the bandage, the slick plastic Paolo used to cover my tattoo.

I tug my top down, but I'm not strong enough to defeat his grasp. He yanks up my shirt and twists my body like I'm a ratty scarecrow.

"Samantha?" he asks, the three syllables an entire treatise on disbelief. My collar clatters to the floor, freed from his loose fingers.

"Russo—" I start to answer, but he cuts me off by standing so quickly I have to scramble to keep from sprawling beside the tangle of platinum and emerald.

He grips my arm like he's going to tear it off my body. "What did you let him do?"

27

BRAIDEN

~

My *piscín*.
My beautiful girl.
Ruined.

I rip the dressing off, ignoring Samantha's hiss of pain, and her tattoo sours the whiskey in my belly. That woman's face in a nest of snakes... Those three legs, bent like they've been cut off crazy circus girls...

Of course I've seen the mark before. All Russo's men wear the monster.

But my Samantha...

I drop her arm and stagger back, putting the chair between us. "What the hell were you thinking?"

"I was *thinking* I need Russo to trust me if we're going to put him away." She tugs her top back into place, yanking hard to emphasize her words. The fabric must be rough against her sensitive skin, because she winces.

I say with deadly calm, "If you want that shitehawk to trust you, then flatter him. Use your words. Not your fucking body."

"Sometimes words only go so far. Sometimes people need symbols." She bends at the knees, graceful as a swooping hawk, and she retrieves her collar from the ground. Holding it out to me, she adds a single syllable, pointed and heavy: "Sir."

I swipe at the necklace, sending it back to the floor. It lands in the pool of whiskey that spilled from my glass. "Fuck symbols."

"Braiden," she says, her voice low and dangerous, warning me I've gone too far.

But she didn't warn Russo. She didn't tell that dry shite to stop before he marked her permanently. So, I point to the necklace. "Pick up your fucking collar."

Her chin tilts up, and her shoulders stiffen. My cock presses against my zipper, even harder than when I held her on my lap. "Or what?"

"Or I'm shoving you out that door so fast you'll be halfway back to your dago boss before you catch your fucking balance."

"Jesus Christ!" she explodes. "Madden said the same thing for months, and you *know* he was a fucking liar. For the last time, in short words you'll be sure to understand: Russo is not my boss. Russo has never been my boss. I want to lock up Russo as much as you do. That's why I did this. That's why I got the tattoo. So I can see his papers."

"Fine," I say. "Let's see them."

"What?"

"Let's see the papers. Show me what the gobshite's been hiding."

She wipes her hands down the front of her trousers. "I don't have them yet."

"*What?*" The question rips out of me, so loud and sharp she jumps like I slapped her.

"He says he'll give them to me next week."

"And you *believe* him?" My Samantha's always been stubborn, but she's never before been stupid.

"Of course I don't believe him!" she shouts, almost loud enough to match my rage. "But what was I supposed to do? How was I supposed to convince him, without giving away the entire game?"

"This is all a game to you?"

"Don't be a fucking idiot," she says.

"Watch your mouth," I warn her.

"Or what? You'll spank me? Tie me up? Beat me with a cane?"

"I'm your fucking Dom."

"Watch your mouth," she says sweetly, mimicking a bratty sub.

I snap my fingers, giving her one last chance. "On your goddamn knees, *piscín.*"

She laughs, a hollow sound that echoes to the center of the earth. "That ship just sailed, motherfucker. You're a bully, Braiden Kelly. I swear to God I can't tell where you stop and where Antonio Russo begins."

"Here's a hint: I've never shoved a pistol up your gowl."

"No. You're more the mind-fuck type. Call me a whore, because Russo makes you feel like a weak little man. That's *your* game, isn't it? You led Fiona on because you were afraid of Kieran Ingram. You kept Birte locked up, because her brother shamed you. You can't manage the men in your life, so you take it out on women. And the whole time you're fucking us over, you tell yourself you're such a big man, such a kind man, such a brave man. But you're really just a scared little boy who can't get his peepee up unless your woman's tied like a Sunday roast."

"Jesus Christ," I say. "You're a vicious cunt."

She still hates the word.

That's why I use it.

She settles her hands on her hips but thinks better of the gesture when it pulls her top against her damaged skin. Shifting her weight instead, she balances on the balls of her feet and looks me in the eye. And then she says, very low and perfectly even: "Fuck you."

"No," I say, and I don't care that I'm standing in spilled whiskey, that I'm grinding the platinum chain of her collar beneath my heel. I pinch her arm between my fingers, hard. "Fuck. You."

She kicks at my shoe, at the necklace trapped under my sole. But when I don't release her arm, she wipes all hint of emotion from her face. She ratchets her voice into a robot's creaky tone. "Whatever you require," she says. "Sir."

Blindly, mechanically, she reaches for my trousers. She purses her lips like a blow-up doll and says, "Let me make you feel good, Sir. Fuck me real hard, Sir. Want me on my knees now? Take me up the ass? Want to hit me hard? Sir?"

I drop her arm like it's riddled with disease. "Get the fuck out of my house."

She twists her fingers together, one hand over the other, and it takes me a moment to realize she's wrestling with her rings. There's the Fishtown knot I gave her when we faked our engagement in front of Russo. And there's the gold band I put on her finger at St. Columba's.

Is liomsa tú, the second one says. *You are mine.*

But that doesn't keep her from throwing both rings at my face.

I don't give her the satisfaction of watching me duck. After hitting my cheek, the gold clatters on the floor, like a boxer's teeth knocked out in the final round.

Samantha doesn't look down. Instead, she moves toward the door with her head high and her back straight. She doesn't deign to straighten her clothes, so I can still see that fucking tattoo where her top hitches over her trousers.

Her fingers settle on the doorknob.

This is it. This is the moment I can say I was wrong, that I spoke in anger. I can change everything by dropping to my knees, by begging.

But I'm her Dom.

I don't beg.

Instead, I say, "Walk out that door, and you're never setting foot in this house again."

She flexes her wrist, and the knob turns.

"You're on your own with Russo."

She opens the door.

"You'll never see another penny from me."

That makes her stop. She shakes her head like I'm a drooling eejit. Or like she pities me.

"Don't even start telling yourself that lie. It was *never* about the money, Braiden," she says. "Not ever."

And she's gone.

28

SAMANTHA

Of course, Liam's waiting outside. He's leaning against the hood of the Bentley, arms crossed over his chest.

"How much did you hear?" I ask.

"Nothing." But he's lying. Rovers on Mars heard some of what we shouted.

I'm shaking—a low, steady tremble that makes my ankles totter in my shoes. Every breath feels like it's going to trip a circuit breaker in my lungs. My spine vibrates, each little spasm shaking loose more of my self-control.

"Get in," Liam says. "I'll drive you wherever you want to go."

He would, too. But I can't let him do that. He's one of Braiden's men. The Fishtown Boys are the only job he's ever had, the only thing he ever wanted to be when he was growing up on the streets of Philadelphia.

I hold out my hand for the keys. I don't want to take Braiden's car. I don't want to owe him for anything. But he hasn't left me with any alternative. My Mercedes is still stranded at the burned-out husk of Thornfield.

I don't have a car. I don't have a home. I don't have clothes or a computer.

This is the third time Braiden and I have fought. The third time he's reduced me to a helpless, homeless girl. The third time he's transformed me from Sam Mott, independent attorney, into Samantha Kelly, humiliated mob wife.

I can't take this anymore. I won't do this again. I'm done, forever.

"Come on," I say to Liam, because I need to hit the road.

He wants to argue. But he knows I'm right. He gives me the keys.

Somehow, I drive all the way from Ardmore back to Dover without causing a crash. My body functions like a machine, using my mirrors, looking left, looking right to check blindspots. I don't process. I don't think. I just act.

It's back to the Hilton Garden Inn for me. I don't know if the night clerk recognizes me. It's been two months. I collect my electronic key card and one of those packets they give unfortu-nate travelers who've lost their luggage at the airport—tooth-brush, toothpaste, and a comb.

My second-floor room is safe and clean. I kick off my shoes and strip down to my underwear, just like I did in Russo's gallery. Shaking my head in fruitless hopes of driving away the image, I collapse backward on the bed.

That's a mistake. My tattoo ignites under the weight of my body. For the first time, I wonder about the consequences of losing Paolo's protective dressing. Pain, I can manage. Infection is something else entirely.

I roll over to my side and pull a pillow to my chest like I'm hugging a teddy bear. I need to sleep. I need my body to recover. I need my mind to stop replaying images from my fight with Braiden.

Pick up your fucking collar.

This is all a game to you?

You're a vicious cunt.

I can't recall when I last ate a real meal, but I remember every hateful word Braiden said to me tonight. Every bitter response I threw back.

I stare at the clock until my eyes feel like they've been battered and fried. I roll to my other side and study the wall for what feels like hours, but when I check, barely twenty minutes have passed. I lie on my stomach, trying to relax every muscle in my body, one by one, but I can't get past the iron bar of my diaphragm.

At 4:30, I give up and take a shower, pitifully grateful for the hotel's shampoo and conditioner. When I dry myself, I dab at my tattoo carefully. The towel comes away clean—one minor mercy.

I'm at my freeport desk by 5:30. If Mary's surprised when she gets in at eight, she covers it well.

I do my best to turn myself into a machine. Answer email. Draft a contract. Review a brief. Think about the law, think about the freeport, think about our clients, but don't ever allow myself to feel.

I'm not perfect. I close my eyes over my fourth cup of coffee, and I can see my collar trapped beneath Braiden's shoe. I reach for a trademark file and my back twists; I wonder if that cursed symbol on my spine is bleeding through my top. I read a proposed tax regulation for the seventh time, and I taste the whiskey on Braiden's breath when I first arrived home, when he kissed me, when he still loved me.

It's dark outside when Mary comes in, securing a stack of corporate filings with her chin. "These have to be finalized by next Tuesday," she says. "Do you want to take them with you or should I overnight them up to Ardmore?"

"I won't be working at Ardmore anymore."

Her eyebrows leap, but she's too well-trained to say anything out loud. It only takes her a few seconds to regroup. "I'll just need your local address then."

I think I'm fine. I think I have this all under control. I think I'm managing the absolute destruction of my life perfectly.

But Mary's matter-of-fact request sparks tears in my eyes. I try not to blink, try not to give in, and I could probably succeed if I'd had even an hour of sleep last night. If I'd had anything to eat today. If my tattoo wasn't burning like Russo branded me, instead of forcing ink under my skin.

"Sam..." Mary says as I start to cry.

"I'm fine," I lie.

She puts down the filings and studies my desk. When she doesn't find what she's looking for, she hurries out to her own station. She comes back with a jumbo box of Kleenex.

"I don't need that," I lie again.

"What happened?" she asks, perching on one of my visitor's chairs and folding her feet beneath her—crisscross, applesauce.

"I..." I don't know where to start. I can't imagine how to explain. So I just skip to the end. "It's over."

"Again," Mary says, because she's heard this twice before.

"For real, this time. He said..."

I can't even put together the words he said. But Mary puffs up with indignation, like a robin fending off a bitter wind. "That bastard!"

I shrug. Maybe Braiden *is* a bastard. Maybe I'm a bitch. Maybe we were doomed from the start, from the moment he held back my hair as I vomited into the snow in front of the Delaware tax office.

"You gave up your condo, didn't you?" Mary asks, like I'm doing my part now, holding up my end of our conversation.

I nod, because that's easier than words. I didn't want to let it go. I didn't want to be alone. I only got rid of it because Braiden wanted...

Braiden wanted... Braiden said... Braiden did...

All those sentences are dead ends now. I need to surgically remove them from my life.

"Well, get your purse," Mary says.

I finally find the will to say something. "Why?" I ask.

"You don't want to leave it overnight."

"I'm going to work a while longer."

"Not tonight."

I gesture at the stack she just delivered. "There's so much to do…"

"There's always so much to do. And it will be there tomorrow, and the next day, and the next."

"I'll just get started—"

"No," Mary says, her voice incredibly gentle.

That makes me cry again, because the last person who told me no was Braiden, just before he said, "Fuck you."

"Let's go," Mary says.

"Go where?"

"To my house."

"I can't stay with you!"

"The place has four bedrooms. I've got two roommates. We just put up ads for a fourth."

I can't think of a kinder offer. "I can't… I shouldn't… I won't…"

"You can and you should and you will. Stay for a few days. Just until you get your feet under you."

I shake my head, because I've forgotten how to argue.

"Come on," she says. "Where's your suitcase?"

I look around, as if one might materialize if I stare in the corners long enough. "I don't have one," I finally say.

Once again, Mary mutters, "That bastard." But this time, she steps back, placing her hand on the light switch by the door. Then she speaks in the bright voice of a kindergarten teacher convincing a child her scraped knee won't require amputation. "All right. Let's go. You're really lucky. Tonight is spaghetti night, and I make a mean marinara."

I grab a handful of Kleenex for the ride to my refuge.

29

BRAIDEN

~

I 'm going after Russo.

I call Seamus Campbell, my Quartermaster. I need all the funds he can spare.

I call Rory O'Hare, my Warlord now that Patrick's gone with Fiona. I need all our soldiers ready to fight.

I call Declan Fitzgerald, the man who makes the computers run as they should. These days, half our battles are won with online attacks, not bullets.

And then my finger hovers over Samantha's name.

Despite everything we said last night, I want her here.

I want her brains.

I want her courage.

And yes, I want her body. I want the sheer release of ordering her to please me. I want the victory of making her come, over and over and over again, until she's soaked and spent and *mine.*

Fuck. She isn't mine anymore.

I don't know if she ever truly was. She topped from the bottom every time I took her. She was never made to be a true sub.

Now she has Russo's brand on her back. And she always will.

My cock has never failed me when I've been with a woman. But the thought of looking down at those snakes... The idea of grabbing Samantha's hips and making those three tattooed legs stretch and move... That ink unmans me—and not because of the hateful words she spat before she walked out the front door of the house I bought for her.

Samantha's gone. And the sooner I accept that, the better, for all the men I captain. For me.

I jam my phone in my pocket and wait for Seamus and Rory and Declan to arrive.

The Fishtown Boys are going to war.

30

SAMANTHA

~

L ife is calm in Mary's house.
  Miraculously, the paparazzi don't follow me here.
Maybe it's because the final episode of the Mousetrap podcast
aired over a month ago. Maybe they don't think Mary's home
photographs as well as one of Braiden's mansions. Maybe
they're all distracted by new stories—the high school senior
claiming Mayor Thompson fathered her twins, the man found
with three scalped heads in his freezer, the movie star who
claimed aliens possessed her as she drove her car into the
Schuylkill.

I don't know who claimed their attention. I'm just grateful to
have some peace and quiet.

All three of Mary's roommates trade off making dinner—
simple, nourishing meals designed to stretch a dollar. A chart on
the refrigerator lists rotating household chores—wash the dishes,
clean the bathrooms, mow the lawns. A folder on the counter

holds receipts for groceries, utility bills, the occasional pizza ordered as a special treat.

My room is the smallest, at the back of the house. The double bed makes everything a tight fit. The dresser only has three drawers, and a milk crate stands in for a nightstand. The house is too old for closets, but four wooden hooks jut from the wall.

We all share the one bathroom at the top of the stairs. I buy a plastic bucket to hold my shampoo and conditioner, my toothbrush and toothpaste and hairbrush.

I rescue my suits from the closet in my office. I pick up a packet of white cotton underwear and two plain, matching bras. I sleep in an over-size gray T-shirt that was on sale at Wal-Mart.

Mary is gentle. Her roommates are kind. No one fights; no one even raises their voice. I feel like I'm wrapped in tissue paper, covered by bubble wrap, surrounded by packing peanuts.

There are no sharp edges to life with Mary Rivers. No passion, certainly. But no danger either.

Back at work, I write an article about a proposed new federal tax on luxury goods. It's a long shot the bill will get through Congress, but I send my summary to every freeport client. I add a personal note to Russo: *Depending on your personal inventory, this might be a concern.* I don't dare say more. I don't want to spook him, don't want him to think I'm prying.

I don't add a note to Braiden's copy.

While I wait to see if Russo will bite, I live my life. After a week, Mary and her housemates fold me into the household schedule. I cook dinner on Mondays. I take out the trash on Wednesdays. I unload the dishwasher on Fridays.

It's all so simple. So easy. So safe.

At the freeport, I complete my final review of Trap's plans for the monthly gathering of his richest clients. Diamond Ring activities always require sign-off from Legal. I decide if we need to contact our insurance providers or if we need local lawyers on call with bail money. The July get-together is costly but simple: A finish-line suite at the Miami Formula 1 Grand Prix.

The Friday before the race, I renew my argument that I should be there. Our clients might have questions about their gambling winnings, about how large windfalls are handled by the tax code.

Trap finally agrees. I tell my housemates that I'll be away for the weekend. On the Friday before the race, Trap takes a photo of us standing beside his private plane and texts it to the entire Diamond Ring.

TRAP

> Your freeport team ready to serve.

When we touch down in Florida, Trap passes me his phone. There's a text from Braiden:

BRAIDEN

> Sorry. Emergency at work. Can't make it.

There are a million emergencies that could be real—shipments gone astray, soldiers out of line, city inspectors getting too interested in the Thornfield ruins.

But I'm pretty sure *I'm* the emergency. Braiden won't come to Miami because I'm here.

At least we won't have to keep a medical team on standby, with Braiden and Russo in the same suite.

On Sunday, race day, I get to the track early. I'm working, so I wear my gray suit and a white top. My hair is pulled back in a neat French twist. I carry my briefcase.

Russo is the last of the Ring to arrive, except for Braiden. Trap is busy chatting up other clients, so I greet our final guest alone. "Don Antonio," I say. Even though it's early afternoon, I hand him his favorite cocktail, a negroni.

188 | ALIX KEY

"Ah," he says, after sipping the blood-red drink. "You remember, Giovanna."

I make a point of looking down, of clutching my hands together. It's not difficult to seem nervous; just standing next to the man who murdered my cousin sends my pulse into overdrive.

"But please," Russo says. "I do not wish to keep you from the race."

He gestures toward the window that looks over the track, where twenty spider-like race cars are taking up positions for the formation lap. I have no choice but to walk in front of him. His palm settles over the small of my back, over my hidden tattoo. A wave of nausea rolls through me, so strong I stumble.

Russo's flat fingers clasp my elbow. "Careful, Giovanna."

I don't know if he's telling me to watch my step, or if his warning means something more. He doesn't release his grip until we join the others, and it takes all my willpower not to glance down at my sleeve, to see if the fabric is actually charred or if the stink of sulfur is only in my mind.

An hour and a half later, Red Bull has won the race. Ferrari takes second, and McLaren an unexpected third. I'm back at the bar, pouring a bracing tonic and lime, because I don't trust myself with the Jameson I crave.

I feel Russo behind me, as if my tattoo is equipped with a silent alarm. He reaches for the Campari to build himself a fresh drink. I'm effectively trapped against the bar.

"Where is your so-called husband, Giovanna?"

We both look at my left hand at the same time, at the faint band of white where I used to wear two rings.

"Ah, sweet Giovanna," he says, as if he truly cares. "The *stronzo* leaves his mate."

"*I* left *him*," I say, faster and angrier than I mean to. I try to temper my words by adding, "Don Antonio."

He leans in close. My *segno* kindles from his body heat, sending a dull ache up my spine to the back of my eyes. "If I had known, *cara*, I would have sent my jet to Dover. We could have traveled here together, you and I."

I have to swallow three times before I can speak, and then my words are only a whisper. "I wish you had, Don Antonio."

He laughs and traces my cheek with a finger. My stomach cramps, hard and sharp. I clutch my glass of bitter tonic and will myself not to vomit.

"Antonio!" Trap calls from the front of the room. "They're awarding the trophies."

My knees buckle when Russo leaves, and sweat pools in my armpits. I force myself to take slow, deep breaths until my body registers that the threat has passed—for now.

It takes an effort, but I finally rally my thoughts. This is necessary. This is what I have to do, if I'm ever going to convince Russo to trust me with his most damning documents.

The Mafia don collects his winnings from other members of the Diamond Ring. They ask how he knew to put it all on Red Bull, and he laughs. "They're gold and red. The colors of Sicily." The ache in my tattoo flares to a sharp pang, as if the lines are etched with acid.

Russo leaves after that, claiming he has other business at the racetrack. Looking back from the door to the suite, he skewers me with one last gaze. He points his finger at me like an imaginary gun, and then he's gone.

Back in Dover that night, Mary can tell I'm upset. She's become a friend, yes, but she's still my assistant at work. It would be unprofessional to tell her about the Diamond Ring, about the day at the races, about Russo.

So we pop a giant bowl of popcorn, and she sprinkles parmesan cheese on top, the stuff that comes in the round green can. We sit in front of the television, sharing a blanket across our laps, and we watch episodes from past seasons of *The Great British Baking Show*. There's plenty of room on the couch when our housemates get home, and by the end we're all casting votes for our favorite baker.

It's not until I'm curled up under my plain black comforter in my blank-walled room that I replay everything that happened in Florida. I want to stop. Stop waiting for the ethics decision. Stop putting myself in danger. Stop trying to make Russo trust me.

I started down this path so I could give Braiden something he couldn't get on his own, something he couldn't steal, couldn't buy. Now that Braiden is gone, it's stupid to risk my life for him.

But no.

I didn't go after Russo just to satisfy Braiden. I acted for revenge against the animal who murdered my cousin. Who killed my parents. Who disclosed my deepest secret and destroyed my life, my practicing law in the only job I've ever loved.

I want to—I need to—destroy Antonio Russo for *me*.

Even if it takes weeks, months, years, I won't give up until I see him brought to justice.

31

BRAIDEN

When Trap announced he was taking us to the Miami Grand Prix, I prepped for the outing. I added Formula 1 analyses to my breakfast reading. I studied the drivers, the pit crews, the team leaders. I planned my bets.

Sure, Russo would be there, but I could handle that.

We've been jockeying for position the past few weeks. It's mostly penny-ante shite, boosts that are more annoyance than anything else. I muscle in on his contracts for summer landscaping around the city, scaring off his men and replacing them with my own. He returns the favor, carjacking half a dozen vehicles in Fishtown, terrifying the ordinary men and women in my territory.

So, I knew Russo and I wouldn't be shaking hands in Miami. But with eleven other blokes in the room, I figured we could keep from murdering each other. Probably.

But then Trap said Samantha was coming along.

I won't be in the same room with her and Russo. Not when

that goombah gobshite will do everything in his power to yank my chain.

Not when Samantha wears his brand.

So I cancel at the last minute. And I place an idiot bet on my own, putting a hundred grand on one of the Mercedes drivers, because that's the car Samantha left at Thornfield.

I choose wrong. The Mercedes eejit leaves the track in a tight hairpin and loses a costly seven seconds, only to return with dirt on his wheels. He boxes late and picks up a ten-second penalty for leaving the pit too close to another car. His entire race strategy ends up banjaxed. His soft tires can't hold up, and he needs a second pit stop seven laps before the end.

He comes in dead last. So much for my hundred grand.

On Monday, I send Liam Murphy over to Thornfield with instructions to sell the Mercedes. He protests, exactly the way I know he will. He offers to drive the car down to Dover. He has the feckin' nerve to say Samantha's name out loud.

I give him a choice. Sell the car or hand in his Fishtown ring.

He sells the car. But he tells me *I* need to forge Samantha's name on the registration. He flat out refuses to do it on his own.

I sign, and I put the money into an account for Aiofe.

When Liam's still sulking a week later, I wake him at midnight and tell him to bring me Madden's McLaren. I don't need it. But Liam has to remember I'm his fucking Captain.

He calls me Boss as he hands over the key fob. But he leaves the car parked under the oak tree at the edge of the drive. When I come down to breakfast, a flock of crows has had at it. The roof is coated in shite.

I wash it down myself, because no one's supposed to think about Madden. When I'm done, I move it to the side of the house and cover it with a tarp. And I try to come up with the next degrading task to put Liam Murphy back in his proper place.

32

SAMANTHA

I go to work every weekday, and half the time on weekends. I come home to peace and quiet and gentle shared jokes with my housemates. I attempt to reach out to Russo as often as seems wise, once a week, never more, and I don't get angry when he ignores me.

A hollow space aches somewhere under my heart whenever I think of Braiden. He remains a client at the freeport, but he never sets foot on the premises. Instead, he contacts Trap directly for anything he needs.

Aiofe is already in her second month of summer school. I hope St. Agnes has continued to be a welcoming place for her, that she's making new friends and growing more comfortable in the wide world outside of Thornfield. I hope Braiden continues to send her to therapy.

I wonder if Fairfax has settled into the Ardmore kitchen. On the one hand, he has all new appliances and counter tops large enough to butcher a lamb. On the other hand, he's only cooking for three now. No matter how much I disliked Grace Poole, I know she was a companion for him. I hope he's not too lonely.

My life at Thornfield seems like a distant dream. I barely had a chance to move into the Ardmore house. I can't believe I ever wore skirts patterned with flowers. I don't remember what it was like having my evenings free from work. And my nights...

Of course I can't forget the things Braiden made me do. The things I wanted when I was with him. The punishment I craved, and the sweet, sweet release he always delivered.

But that's gone now. Impossible. Not after all the things he said to me. All the things I said to him. Not after the tattoo that stains my spine.

That part of my life is gone. All I have left is the desperate hope that I can cage Russo before I'm forced to leave Diamond Freeport forever.

33

BRAIDEN

F inally, a glimmer of good news amid all the shite.

Rory O'Hare gets news of a warehouse outside of Philadelphia—run-down, sagging roof, cracked foundation—the type of place I'd just as soon demolish as try to repair. But rumor has it, Russo's been using it for something.

Russo *should* be putting his valuables in the freeport now, storing them in his personal gallery and taking advantage of the tax breaks Samantha has worked out for all of us. So I tell O'Hare to take a drive by the warehouse after midnight, to bring a few men along, just to see what's what.

He's busy enough with other work that he asks if I can send someone else. He wants to know if I've been in touch with Madden, if my brother can make the run instead. I tell him Madden can't make it, but I'll call Patrick back from Boston if I have to.

O'Hare says everything is under control. He makes the run that night, to prove I can trust him.

The place is packed to the rafters with fireworks.

They aren't in the freeport because Prince won't allow explosives past the gate. In the most recent round of security updates, he added bomb-sniffing dogs; every vehicle is checked before it's allowed on the property.

Russo must have cleaned up after the Fourth of July, bought out everyone he could. Fireworks are legal in Pennsylvania, but not in Maryland or New Jersey. Come next Independence Day, he can drive his stash over state lines and sell them for a tidy profit, same as he would any contraband.

It takes Seamus twenty-four hours to line up our own warehouse—a newer one, a dryer one, and one we can easily keep a guard on. After that, it's easy enough to use Kelly Construction trucks and O'Hare's runners. The fireworks are cleaned out before Russo even suspects they've been discovered.

I authorize a few sales up in New Jersey. Independence Day is over, but people always want to make loud noises and see pretty lights. When a short shipment to Trenton sells out overnight, I tell Seamus to unload the rest of it—no need to wait until next July.

Seamus needs someone to coordinate driving, and I tell him to use Liam Murphy. I need to forgive the blighter. After all, the only crime Murphy truly committed was letting Samantha get that tattoo. I haven't forgotten how persuasive she can be. The fella didn't stand a chance.

A week after O'Hare found the warehouse, I'm a million dollars richer.

Better yet, I have other captains sitting up and taking notice. Reardon calls from Chicago to find out how I unloaded that many fireworks *after* the Fourth. Our counterpart in New Orleans chimes in too; he imagines he can build a new market shipping into Texas.

I'm not interested in setting up a consulting business, advising either one of those captains. But it's nice to know people are paying attention.

It's even nicer that I landed my million bucks when the Grand Irish Union is still in disarray. Without a general to claim his ten percent, I keep every penny.

So I'm feeling rather flush as I sit down to dinner with Aiofe. She, though, doesn't share my good mood. She spends the better part of half an hour pushing buttered egg noodles around on her plate. Every time she sighs, something twinges beneath my ribs. I'd rather be out on the front lines in my brooding war with Russo, than sitting at a dining room table with a moody pre-teen girl.

O'Hare reported Aiofe didn't say a word when he drove her back from her therapist this afternoon. She didn't push for a walk around the block to see the puppies at the home of one of her classmates. Instead, she went straight to her room and closed the door.

Gritting my teeth, I ask, "How was your meeting with Miss Sharon today?"

More poking at her plate. I wonder if Aiofe's decided she's through with talking. At least when she was silent before, she responded to direct questions with a range of expressions on her face. Hand signals, even.

"Aiofe?" I prompt, wondering how I should proceed.

She talks to her fork. "Miss Sharon said I should ask you a question if I want to know answers. Even if it's private. Personal."

I put down my own fork. Fairfax has given Aiofe an entire book on how her body works. I'd expect her to turn to him if she's confused. But I do my level best to sound open to whatever she has to say. "What question do you have?"

She takes her napkin from her lap. Folds it into quarters. Opens it again.

"Aiofe?" I ask again.

And in a tiny voice, so soft I have to catch my breath to hear, she asks, "Did Samantha leave because of me?"

The instant the words are out of her mouth, I'm bowled

over by a tidal wave of relief. I don't need to elaborate on Fairfax's book. I don't have to find words that work for a child.

But the relief is immediately swamped by shame. There's no reason on earth Aiofe should believe Samantha left because of her. I'm an eejit for not addressing the matter sooner. "No," I say, too fast. Too loud. "Samantha's leaving has nothing to do with you."

"She wasn't angry with me?"

"Why would Samantha possibly be angry with you?"

"Fairfax took me to the Rittenhouse. I went swimming in the pool, and I got to spend the night at the hotel. But Samantha had to work. She couldn't play with us. And when I got home, sh— she was gone."

She was gone because she and I fought in the foyer. She was gone because I couldn't hold my tongue. She was gone because I said things I'll never repeat to this child.

How long has Aiofe been believing she was at fault? It never dawned on me she might think Samantha would be jealous of yet another stay at the Rittenhouse.

"Samantha didn't leave because you went to the hotel," I say. "I promise."

Aiofe nods solemnly. But she whispers to her plate, "I miss her. A lot."

I want to say that's ridiculous. Aiofe lived with me for seven years before she ever met Samantha. Fairfax is still taking care of her, morning, noon, and night.

But Aiofe's lost a lot in the last few months—Samantha, sure, but Birte and Grace too. Aiofe's clothes burned at Thornfield, and all her sketchbooks too. She only kept her manky stuffed rabbit because she had it with her in Fairfax's cottage, the night of the fire.

She's suffered. And she's a child, who brought none of this on herself. So I answer with an honesty that catches me by surprise. "Yeah, little one. I miss her too."

"Where did she go?"

"She's in Dover. In Delaware. The place where she works, where Liam used to drive her."

"Where's that, on a map?"

I take out my phone. And before I can pull up a general map, I think of something that might comfort the girl. I open the tracking app, the one I set when we were in the Rittenhouse, when my eyes were burned and threats seemed to lurk in every unseen corner.

A dial spins on the phone screen, the app working its magic to locate the distant tracker. For a moment, I think Samantha's erased the connection on her end. There's no reason for her to keep it. She's not mine to follow any longer. She never truly was.

But the dial stops moving. A tiny red drawing pin hovers over a field of green labeled Diamond Freeport.

"There she is," I say to Aiofe.

The child levels a finger over the pin. When she finally looks up from the screen, she's smiling. "Thank you, Uncle Braiden."

"You're welcome," I say.

"May I be excused from the table?"

I should make her finish her dinner. I should tell her to carry her plate into the kitchen. I should warn her it's time to get ready for bed, and she has forty-five minutes for reading before turning out the lights.

But instead, I say, "You may."

And I stare at the screen long after Aiofe's left, wondering why Samantha's still working at a quarter past eight on a Monday night in the middle of the feckin' summer.

34

SAMANTHA

I worked until 9:30 tonight. It's getting harder and harder to draft updates for all the freeport clients. I'm running out of fishing hooks I can bait to lure in Russo.

Now, I'm lying on my bed, staring at the ceiling. When someone knocks on my door, I'm so tired I don't bother sitting up. Instead, I just call out, "Come in."

Mary pokes her head around the door, as if she's afraid of what she'll find. I try to picture the space from her perspective. There's nothing to complain about. I haven't put anything on the walls. My clothes are hidden in the dresser. If I weren't lying on this bed, no one would ever know I live here.

She frowns as I force myself to swing my legs over the side of the bed.

"What?" I ask.

"Nothing."

"It's something, or you wouldn't have knocked."

She sighs and steps into the room, closing the door behind

her. "We're friends, right? I'm talking to Sam, my housemate. Not Samantha Mott, Esquire, General Counsel of Diamond Freeport?"

"Of course," I say. But her words make me sit up straighter. I'm certain I don't want to hear what she has to say, but I've never run from a fight before. "What's wrong?"

She twists her hands like she's wringing out a dishrag. "I... You..."

"Mary? Keep this up, and I *will* dock your pay."

She laughs, a nervous little hiccup, which is what I intended her to do. But she also stares at the dresser, throwing out words like she's afraid they'll set the house on fire. "I know that when you came here, I called Mr. Kelly a bastard, and said you were better off without him. But it's been a month now, and nothing is getting any better. You aren't happy at home. You aren't happy at work. You're like some sort of ghost, or maybe a robot. There isn't any *Sam* there anymore. And I see when you're thinking about him, when your face gets all soft and dreamy and I wouldn't say this to just anyone, I definitely wouldn't say it to someone who wasn't strong and determined and just plain kick-ass the way you are, but I really think you should try getting back together with him. You should try going home."

She inhales a huge breath and then she stares at me, biting her lip, and I can't tell if she's trying to keep from saying more or regretting everything she's already said.

I sigh. "You've been thinking about that for a while."

She nods. "You deserve to be happy."

"Braiden Kelly won't make me happy."

"You say that, but..."

I *mean* that. "I can move out by Monday," I say.

"I'm not asking you to move!" It's the first time she's ever raised her voice to me, and I don't know which of us is more surprised. She goes back to twisting her hands. "You're welcome to stay as long as you'd like. As long as you need. But you aren't getting better."

"I'm not sick."

She ignores me. "What have you got here? You go to work. You come home. That's it. That's not a life."

"I'll help out more around the house."

"I'm not asking for more help!" I suppose it's easier to shout at me again, now that she's already done it once. And this time, she's frustrated enough that she paces my small room with tight, measured steps. "When you lived in Philadelphia, you smiled. You relaxed. It was like you went from those opening scenes in *The Wizard of Oz*, from life in black and white, to the part where everything's in color. You deserve that, Sam. Not for me. Not for Braiden Kelly. But for *you*. Because you're worth it."

I'm mugged by a memory, hit so hard I actually gasp. I *feel* a flowered skirt beneath my fingers, the silk sliding over my thighs, light and airy and alive.

"I'm sorry," Mary says. "I shouldn't have said anything."

"No. I appreciate your looking out for me."

"I'm sure you know what you're doing."

I wish *I* was sure. I wish I could read the Wikipedia entry for my life, so I could understand everything that's happened. I'd settle for being able to hear a musical score in the background of a film called *The Samantha Mott Story*, something, anything to let me know if this is a thriller or a horror movie, an Oscar-worthy epic or a love story where the hero and the heroine finally work out their differences and laugh like fools over all the time they wasted, not being together.

Braiden Kelly won't take back what he said, just because some script says he should.

Pick up your fucking collar.
This is all a game to you?
You're a vicious cunt.

And even if he did, that wouldn't solve my true problem. The clock is ticking toward the ethics panel issuing its decision. At most, I have six weeks before my license is pulled.

Six weeks to gain Russo's trust.

Six weeks to take him down.

I want Mary to be right. I wish I knew what I was doing. I'm close to tears that I don't. But I tell her, "Thank you. I know it wasn't easy for you to say all that."

She wrinkles her nose. "Yeah. Okay. Whatever." She stands up and crosses to the door. "There are leftovers in the fridge. Mac and cheese."

"Perfect," I say.

That's a lie. Nothing's perfect. But if I play this role long enough, maybe I'll finally start to believe it.

35

BRAIDEN

Fairfax enters the front door of the house, juggling four bowls and matching spoons. He's laughing to himself as he carries everything to the kitchen.

I call out from the recliner in the living room, where I'm finishing the newspapers I didn't get to this morning. "Those men get paid to guard the house, you know. You don't have to feed them too."

"Just some peach cobbler, to tide them over for the night."

I wonder if I can deduct the cost from the massive sum I'm handing over to Sawyer Best every month.

Fairfax pauses on his way into the kitchen. "You know, I made this with real Irish butter."

"Or so you think," I say, because he's been nagging about this for at least two weeks. Fairfax has looked the other way when I've extorted city officials. When I've traded cigarettes without their legal stamps. When I've boosted cars and run guns and sold kilos of cocaine.

But he draws the line at feckin' butter.

At my command, Seamus has finally followed through on his Irish butter scam. He's sourced counterfeit labels and bought up American butter, selling the so-called Irish stuff to a network of small grocery stores in the state.

The operation has been brilliant. Not the sixteen-billion-dollars-a-year brilliance the Mafia is seeing with its olive oil scam, but a cool three mill cleared after all our costs, which isn't bad for a trial run.

I've told Seamus to expand—more stores in Pennsylvania, then New Jersey and Delaware. Other captains are paying attention—Lynch in Baltimore is already making noises about my staying out of Maryland. Even Bowen, all the way out in San Francisco, has asked Seamus about printers for labels.

Fairfax is having none of it. He told me that he can taste the difference between Irish butter and the sorry American stuff, and he wouldn't use the latter to bake dog biscuits.

I've told him not to worry. If *I'm* running the scam, he'll always know who has the true Irish goods.

He said he'll pray for my soul.

Now, Fairfax moves into the kitchen, and I hear him filling the dishwasher. He runs water in the sink for a moment, and then he materializes in the living room doorway with another bowl.

"Here," he says, apparently deciding to declare a truce for the night. "You weren't forgotten."

"I don't need more." Aiofe and I already had cobbler with dinner.

"Maybe it'll sweeten your disposition."

I fold *The Irish Times* over the arm of my chair. "I'm sure you won't leave until you've told me the rest of what's on your mind."

"It's been a month."

I won't give him the satisfaction of asking a month since

what. Instead, I keep my voice mild. "If you think I'll spot you a raise because you manage to keep a calendar..."

"Aiofe misses her."

"So she's told me. Multiple times now."

"I miss her."

"I'm not sure why. She must have been a holy pain in the arse, with her leaving early and coming home late, upsetting all your carefully scheduled meals. And now you've only half the clothes to take to the dry cleaners."

"You miss her too."

I want to tell him he's wrong. The light summer duvet doesn't migrate from my half of the bed, now that I'm sleeping alone. The dining room doesn't stink of coffee first thing in the morning. My right hand is stronger than it's been since I was a teen-age boy.

Instead, I say, "There's no coming back from some things."

"Said every man who ever spoke too much in anger."

"She said things too."

"When Aiofe comes to me with cross words like that, she's sent to her room for an hour."

"Does that teach her a lesson?" I ask, honestly curious.

"No. But she usually gets bored and takes a nap, which puts her in a better mood when she comes back to the kitchen." He waits a moment. When I don't resume the conversation he says, "Call her."

I don't bother pretending we're still talking about Aiofe. "Not this time."

"You've worked things out before."

"Which is why both of us knew the best way to blow things up this time. For good."

He sets the bowl of cobbler on the table by my chair. "Not for good," he says. "For ill. And if you knew how to blow things up, then you know how to put them back together. Spend your time doing something productive, instead of plotting your next attack on the East Falls Crew."

He heads back into the kitchen while I'm still putting together my response to his utterly banjaxed theory—starting with the fact that it's pure productive, my going after Russo.

I eat the cobbler. And I finish *The Times*. And I take out my phone and watch the bright red drawing pin, anchoring a corner of Delaware that might as well be a million miles away.

36

SAMANTHA

〜

M ary is right.
     Not about Braiden. She doesn't understand a thing about my twisted marriage, about the relationship I thought would be my life.

But she knew I needed food, even if it was three hours after normal people eat their dinners. And after I eat, she knows I need a reason to stay out of my lonely bedroom, so she organizes a Scrabble tournament among all four of us housemates. She says it's a Friday night in the middle of summer. We can all sleep in tomorrow. So we click wooden tiles onto the board until midnight, toasting Mary with Diet Coke when she finally wins.

I'm actually smiling as I get into bed after taking my turn in the shared bathroom. I turn on a small fan, fighting the leftover heat of the July day. As usual, I toss and I turn, trying to punch my pillow into a more comfortable shape.

I could swear I never close my eyes, but when my phone rings, I don't remember where I am. Shaken from the absolute black of dreamless sleep, it takes me a moment to sit up in bed. I'm clumsy with confusion, and I almost drop my phone.

But I see the name on the screen: EC.

Elisabetta Canna.

A woman who will never use a phone again.

Abruptly, brutally awake, I tap the screen. "What?" I ask, because I know who's on the other end, and he knows me.

"Giovanna," Russo says. "My *uccellino* says the FBI meet Monday morning."

His little bird. He must keep a spy in the heart of the United States Department of Justice. "Meet about what?"

"Me. My business. My taxes."

"You need a criminal lawyer," I say, remembering to keep my voice steady, even as my pulse launches into triple time. Every synapse in my body says I've won. He's finally reaching out to me. I'm about to get the proof I long for.

"I *need* to shelter assets. And that means my tax documents must reflect certain…versions of reality. Before I meet with the FBI."

"Fine," I say, pushing back my sheets. "I can be at the freeport in twenty minutes."

"No," he says. "I will not go to Dover. You will come here, to Philadelphia."

Immediately, I try to think of someone I can call, someone who can keep me safe in Russo's lair. Trap. Liam. Braiden.

Before I can even begin to wrestle with the emotions of reaching out to any of them, with needing a man to keep me safe, Russo says, "Come alone, *cara*. Within two hours. Or I will leave the freeport forever."

37

BRAIDEN

I t's late by the time I finally head upstairs for bed. I checked the news after Fairfax's talking to. There was an article on *The Enquirer's* site, a story that won't be in print until tomorrow.

The Department of Corrections is moving forward with its Paragon plan, the project to renovate one of the state's oldest prisons. Ray Krakower held a press conference, expressing his enthusiasm for one of the city's newest business partners: East Falls Contracting Company.

Russo has finally leveraged the information Samantha gave him. Krakower has ducked public disclosure of his career in film. Kelly Construction has lost a fifty-million-dollar project that was virtually guaranteed.

I could hire lawyers. I could sue the DOC, demanding they re-compete the job. I could drag things out for years, maybe even a decade, and in the end, I might tear Paragon back from Russo.

But I won't.

No matter how heated things get with Russo's crew, I'll let him keep Krakower. I made a promise to Samantha, and I won't go back on that.

Once I get into bed, I can't fall asleep. Even with the air conditioner pumping out its frozen air, the bedroom is too warm. I turn on the ceiling fan. Tap the remote to make it spin faster. Tap again for the maximum speed. Turn the whole thing off, because it feels like I'm trapped in a wind tunnel.

I throw back the covers and stalk to the window, automatically taking shelter behind the curtains, so no one can see me from outside. Best's men are at their stations, two men each in two cars, one on either side of the street.

Still restless, I pull on the trousers I set aside when I got ready for bed. I slip into my dress shirt as well, but I don't bother doing up the buttons. I consider putting on my shoes and socks, but I'll be quieter in bare feet.

Something is off. Something is wrong. I prowl to the closet, stopping in front of the gun safe built into the wall. Setting my fingertips on the reader, I listen for the muffled click of the lock releasing.

Walther in hand, I make my way down the hallway. Aiofe's asleep in her bed, clutching her stuffed rabbit like it's a shield against bad dreams. My office is empty. Samantha's too.

The staircase at Thornfield creaked like a cheap mattress, but my feet are silent on the new steps here. The living room is just as I left it, my newspapers stacked beside my recliner. The dining room is empty, the kitchen too.

I ease the door open to the basement. I can hear Fairfax's snores from the top of the stairs. That doesn't mean an intruder's not lurking down there.

I'm quiet enough not to wake Fairfax, which is a good thing, because he'd somehow manage to make this about Samantha, if I gave him half a chance.

Back on ground level, I open the front door and step onto the front porch. I can hear wind in the trees. Cars on the cross street, four houses down. A dog barks somewhere in the next block, maybe farther away.

A shadow glides up the driveway. "Everything okay, Mr. Kelly?"

It's one of Best's men. His hair is cut military short, and he's poured into his tight black T-shirt with matching denim jeans. He's got one hand on his sidearm as he waits for my response.

"It's fine," I tell him. "I just couldn't sleep."

"I can move one of my men to the porch here. If you'd like, sir."

I nod. "Do that. And put someone in the back."

"Yes, sir."

He speaks into his radio—fast, efficient, trustworthy.

"Anything else, sir?"

"No." I shake my head. "Have a good night."

Back in my bedroom, I put the Walther on my nightstand. I tell myself to stop being an eejit, to trust the men I've hired, to get some sleep, because the Krakower news is sure to keep me busy tomorrow.

I pick up my phone before I shrug out of my clothes. My fingers move in the new habit I've set over the past four days.

I look for messages—none.

I check email—none.

I open the tracker app, confirming that Samantha's pin is centered in Dover.

It isn't.

Samantha's pin is winding through a tangle of Philadelphia streets. For just a moment, my shoulders rise. She's driving to Ardmore. She's finally coming home.

But I see my mistake almost instantly.

Samantha isn't driving to Ardmore. She's driving to East Falls. At this time of night, in that part of town, I have absolutely no doubt about her destination.

She's heading to Russo's compound.

I grab the Walther and shove it into the waistband of my

trousers. I pull on the shoes and socks I skipped before, when I wanted to be quiet. I throw on a jacket and snag my keys from the dresser and I'm halfway down the stairs before I realize my mistake.

Back in the bedroom, I ransack the nightstand, reaching all the way to the back. The key fob that waits there is heavy but slim. Clutching it like a lifeline, I whirl back to the stairs.

Best's man jumps to attention as I throw open the door. I shout something at him, tell him to keep an eye on the house, on Aiofe, on Fairfax. And then I rip the tarp from Madden's McLaren and race toward the city.

38

SAMANTHA

I look around Antonio Russo's study, wondering if I'm standing in the same spot my father did when he reported to his don. The room is smaller than I imagined. Darker. Warmer too, hot enough that sweat breaks out along my hairline.

Once, I vowed I would never come to Russo's home. I would never set foot over the threshold of the building where my cousin was murdered. But now, with vengeance so close…

I'll do anything to destroy the man before me.

Russo leans back in his chair like a lizard sunning on a rock. I don't know if he dressed specifically for me or if he attended a party earlier this evening, but he's wearing a tuxedo. He lost his tie somewhere along the way, though, and his shirt is open at the throat, revealing a mat of tight curls on his chest.

"I thought perhaps you had chosen not to come, Giovanna."

"I was stopped for speeding," I admit.

Russo seems to think this is the funniest thing he's ever

heard. He laughs until tears stream from his eyes. Eyeing me over his whiskey glass, he finally says, "You were so eager to see me, *cara*."

"I'm always eager to help Diamond Freeport clients." I try to make the words sound true. In reality, I lost track of how fast I was driving when I thought about getting my hands on Russo's tax forms, on finally getting the evidence I need. I pictured him in a courtroom, standing before a judge, bowing his head as he was sentenced to decades for federal tax evasion. Before I knew it, the Bentley's odometer passed eighty.

I'll gladly pay the ticket, even though it comes with the promise of my own visit to court—for reckless driving. The cop didn't arrest me on site, probably because I admitted exactly how fast I was driving.

"Your tax filings," I say. "Are those the documents?" There's a stack of official-looking papers on the corner of his desk.

"It is always business with you, my sweet Giovanna. If I had known how seriously you take your legal studies, I would have followed your career much more closely."

I bristle at the lie. Russo tracked me in law school. He knew exactly where I lived and worked. The entire time I thought my new identity was secret, Russo was monitoring my every step. I only learned the truth after he murdered Eliza.

"Those are the documents?" I ask again.

He nods with all the confidence of the pope. I sit in the chair across from his desk and reach for the papers.

"Not so fast," he says.

Caution slams into my brain like a meteor smacking the earth. This has all been too easy—Russo's midnight summons, being waved through by the guard at the front gate, the summary patting down by the two East Falls men in the kitchen...

"I need to review them now," I say. "We don't have much time to fix things before Monday morn—"

"*Basta!*" Russo barks.

I'm a trained lawyer. I'm devoted to my mission. I'm deter-mined to get those documents before I leave this house. But a lifetime of terror crashes down on me at the command. My throat feels like it's closing, and I freeze with my hand half-way to his desk.

"I told you before, Giovanna. My trust does not come lightly. I will see my *segno* before you take those papers."

My breath stutters in my lungs. The roof of my mouth goes numb. But very slowly, very carefully, I stand.

I don't want to turn my back on Russo. I don't trust him. But I recognize absolute command on the flat features of his face. His pupils are wide in the dim light. His dull eyes look like a snake's. Once I get that picture in my head, I can't budge it—especially when I realize I haven't seen him blink since I came into the room.

I don't have a choice.

I stand beside the chair. I face the door. I bite my lip and pull up the hem of my black knit top.

Russo laughs.

"That is not the view I paid for, Giovanna. Strip and show me your *segno*."

"Go to hell," I say, spinning back to look at him, because Antonio Russo hasn't bought me. I'm not his whore. I'm not his wife. And I'll never take my clothes off for him.

He moves faster than I thought possible, swooping toward a drawer in his desk. When he comes up, he's holding a pistol. Its tight little mouth points directly at my chest.

"Strip and show me your *segno*," he repeats. "*Puttana.*" There's no emotion in his voice. He might as well be placing an order in a restaurant. Instructing his barber. Commenting on a television show he wants to watch.

And standing in Russo's study, I finally understand what Eliza learned so many years ago when she married the don. I know the truth my father mastered as Russo's made man.

I have no options. I have no choice. If I want to get out of this room alive, I must do whatever Antonio Russo commands.

So I strip.

I step out of my shoes. I take off my black top. My matching jeans. My plain white bra and simple cotton briefs.

I face Russo, because I have to rebel that much. I fold each garment neatly, setting it on his desk next to the tax papers. My clothes look like an offering on an altar.

When I'm naked, I glare at him defiantly. His only response is to twirl his gun in the air, telling me to turn around.

I hate him. I hate his cruelty. I hate his certainty that I'll comply.

But I do it. I turn around. I feel his eyes on my *segno*. My back burns as if the tattoo ink has turned to acid beneath the surface of my skin. I feel each line of the design like a separate battery cable to my heart.

I complete my turn and gaze straight into his reptilian eyes. "I need to review the documents now," I say, as if I always intended to stand here nude.

That makes him smile. "Not yet, Giovanna," he says. His lips look oiled in the dim light, slick with his spit. "I want you on your knees." He uses the gun to point to the floor beside his desk.

"No," I say, because that won't be his last command. He wants me to suck his cock. He wants to rape me. He wants to destroy me, the way he ruined Eliza.

He barely twitches his wrist. The gun flicks toward the cold fireplace on the far wall, and my ears are filled with a single sharp report. I flinch as if I've been shot, and I hear pieces of brick crumble onto the andirons.

"Boss!" The door to the study flies open hard enough to hit the wall behind. The two goons from the kitchen tumble into the room, their own guns drawn, their eyes wild.

"I am fine," Russo says. "Leave us."

The men are already relaxing, confident once they see their

master with his weapon. I wonder how many naked women Russo has tormented here that neither soldier looks surprised to find me like this.

The men do as they are told. They leave, shutting the door firmly behind them.

And Russo says, "Do not keep me waiting, Giovanna. I have told you once. I want you on your knees." He sights casually down the barrel of his gun. "I will not ask a third time."

I believe him. I believe every word he says. He murdered my cousin for challenging him, for sleeping with another man. And in my heart of hearts, I know he intends to murder me.

But if I try to leave, he'll shoot. If I try to argue, he'll shoot. If I try to plead, he'll shoot.

I don't see a way out. I'll never reach the Bentley. I won't hit the interstate and make it back to Dover. But I have to do something. I have to keep moving. I have to give my brain a chance to unlock, to come up with a way out.

So I cross the room. I kneel in front of Russo. I'm light-headed, and I sway, and I put my hands on his knees to steady myself.

My fingers are dangerously close to the engorged rod I can see beneath his pants. I swallow hard and start to look away. But when I turn my head, I'm stopped by the pressure of his gun against my jaw.

I expect it to be hot from the bullet he fired into the fireplace. Or maybe I expect it to be hot because he's the devil. Or maybe because...

"Oh yes," Russo says, as if he read my mind. "This is the gun I used to kill Elisabetta. Can you smell her stinking *figa*? Can you taste her?"

He slides the barrel from my jaw to my lips. I try to pull away, but he grabs my hair with his free hand. Pulling hard, he forces my head into his lap, grinding my cheek against his pulsing hard-on.

I open my mouth to scream, and he shoves the gun past my

teeth. My lips are crushed by steel. I buck against his hand, but I can't get free. I try to thrash my head, but he only presses me harder into his thigh.

"Tell me, Giovanna," Russo says, as if we're chatting about the weather. "Are you afraid to die?"

39

BRAIDEN

Speeding along Highway 30, I discover how easy it is to break ninety with the McLaren's massive engine. I also learn that Madden kept a sawed-off shotgun under the passenger seat.

I glance at my phone as I cross into East Falls. The red drawing pin that marks Samantha is still now. She's arrived at Russo's place.

Four months of my brother's nagging chews at my brain. His ghost haunts this feckin' car.

Madden pulls at the cuffs that tied him to the table in Thornfield's infirmary. He whispers: Samantha started life as Giovanna Canna. She's been Russo's tool all along. That's why she refused to wear my collar to the freeport. That's why she took Russo's brand. That's why she's driven to the shitehawk's lair.

Madden fights the forceps I used to destroy the shattered bones of his face. He argues: No sane woman would face Russo in the middle of the night. She wouldn't enter his home. Wouldn't lock herself behind his gate, behind his security. Not unless she knew Russo wouldn't hurt her.

Madden writhes beneath the scalpel I used to dissect him. He howls: That's why she got the fucking tattoo. That's why she wouldn't drop her mad plan to get Russo's tax papers. She's been a Mafia plant all along, playing her Dom for a fool.

I don't want to believe him. I don't want him to be right. I want to find another reason Samantha's come to Russo's home in the middle of the night.

Madden screams: She's blowing him! She's fucking him! She's bending over and letting him take her up the ass!

I drive the scalpel into him again, severing his limp prick. He bleeds out in my brain when I'm a block from Russo's compound.

Pausing at a stop sign, I take a deep breath, using my exhale to saw off the spikes of adrenaline in my blood. I'm through with thinking. Through with feeling. It's time for cold, hard instinct to take control.

I offer up a prayer to whatever saint is responsible for wreaking bloody vengeance. If whoever's on guard tonight is new… If he doesn't recognize Madden's McLaren… If my brother didn't come here often enough for the guards to wave him through…

Maybe I do have a patron saint. Or maybe Samantha does, and everything Madden said is a lie, and she needs me more than she's ever needed anyone before. But the gate cranks open as I approach at a steady pace. My hands are at ten and two on the steering wheel. The Walther points to midnight.

The guardhouse door opens quickly, without any caution. "You've been a stranger, Kel—"

The rest of the guard's greeting is blown away with his face. That's why I like the Walther; it does a hell of a lot of damage at close quarters.

The guard slumps to the ground as the McLaren drills

through the gate. I hope Russo's neighbors have been bulldozed into accepting the sound of gunshots in the night.

Russo's house is in the city. He doesn't have a winding drive, the way I did at Thornfield. He doesn't have gardens and a greenhouse and cottages for staff.

Instead, a circular driveway curves in front of his pile of brick. My Bentley sits in the middle, blocking an easy path to the door.

A straight leg of asphalt runs up the side of the house. Declan has flown drones over here plenty of times. He's reported there's a garage in back, big enough for four or five cars. And there's a door into the back of the house—maybe an old servant's entrance, maybe straight into the kitchen.

I'm happy to play the role of hired help.

Parking the McLaren close to the back door, I use the car's body as a shield while I snug the Walther into my waistband. I'm racking the shotgun when the back door opens, framing a hefty shadow in a brick of yellow light.

"What the fuck, Kelly?"

The blast of the shotgun is even louder than I expect, echoing off the brick wall of the house. The recoil knocks me back a step, even though I'm braced for it.

A second guy appears in the doorway, gripping a pistol in both hands. He straddles the mangled meat that used to be his buddy, slipping in the mess. He can't see much out here with the light at his back. His eyes dart left to right as he tries to pick me up. I raise the shotgun like it's an extension of my own arm, ready for the recoil this time, and the second guy collapses in a rain of blood and bone.

I step over both corpses. The gears in my brain tick quietly, like an engine cooling in the night. Two hands of cards spread over the kitchen table. Two espresso cups sit in matching saucers. The dead men behind me were the only guards in the kitchen.

I rack the shotgun again and head into the house.

It's an old home in the heart of the city. It's built like all those colonials, with a central hall, rooms off either side. I clear each doorway like the trained killer I am, making sure no bogger will jump me from behind.

I know from the start where I'm headed. It's the closed door at the front of the house. A study or a parlor or a den. Dim light glows beneath the door, an open invitation to anyone paying close enough attention.

I raise the shotgun to my shoulder. I test the brass of the doorknob with two fingers and a thumb. I take a deep breath, shoving back all my thoughts about Madden, about Samantha, about my craving for revenge. I'm a machine again, a carefully balanced pile of gears and wires.

When I throw the door open, I duck a little, putting my head where a sure shot will least expect it. I come up with the shotgun ready, sweeping the room for my first target. I take in the leather couch, the matching chairs, the desk as big as a destroyer.

But none of that matters. None of that means a thing.

Because Russo is standing against the far wall. And Samantha is standing in front of him. Naked. He's got his arm around her throat and a pistol pointed at her head.

And she's staring at me, her eyes full of terror.

40

SAMANTHA

Nothing makes sense.

One moment, Russo has me on my knees. His gun is in my mouth, stinking like acid rain on a field of nuclear waste. I can't sob, can't pray, can't breathe, because I know what he did to Eliza. One twitch of his finger, and my brains will spray onto the wall. I picture him fucking my corpse with his pistol.

There's a sound outside—the short sharp pop of a fire-cracker. But that's not right; Independence Day was almost a month ago. It must be a car back-firing. That's why I hear an engine racing.

Russo hears it too. His hand jerks at the sound, banging the pistol against my teeth. Terror squeezes bile onto the back of my throat, and I start to gag.

I don't want Russo to be the last thing I see before I die—his cobra stare, his greasy lips, the knife-sharp edge of his jaw. I close my eyes and try to picture something else, anything else.

Braiden. If I have to die, he's the one I want to see.

Braiden's cobalt eyes, challenging me to stand tall. The quirk of his lips, like he's holding back a smile. The stubble on his cheeks after a long day's work, when his lips finds the tender spot beneath my ear, along my jaw, at the hollow of my throat.

There's another blast, much closer than the first, and another. Russo yanks me by the hair, dragging me to my feet. His arm is tight, pulling my body close to his, and that gun—that stinking, freezing gun—is pressed against my temple. He jams the barrel into the spiderweb of scars he gave me when I was ten.

His body feels like stone behind me, like I'm tied to a cement block, sinking to the bottom of the sea. Bitter cold spreads through my *segno*, icing my entire body. Russo's clamp on my throat cuts off my breath, and a hive of bees explodes in my brain, frantic, desperate to be free.

The door of the study flies open.

Braiden spins into the room as if I conjured him with my dying wish. His shirt is askew. His jacket flares behind him like a cape. His hair stands on end like coal-black straw, and he's the most beautiful man I've ever seen.

"Drop it!" Russo barks, and I realize Braiden holds a weapon. It's a shotgun, or it was, before someone sawed off a foot of the barrel. "Drop it," Russo says again. "Or I'll kill her."

He shoves his pistol against my head, hard enough to bring tears to my eyes, but I can't gasp, can't sob, because his grip on my throat is too tight.

Braiden shifts his fingers on the shotgun's stock. He holds the weapon out to the side, hand clear of the trigger. He kneels slowly, setting the gun on the floor. "Let her go," he says, once he's standing.

"*Vaffanculo*," Russo says. "Kick that over here."

Braiden keeps his hands high, proving he's no longer a threat. He kicks the gun hard enough that it comes to rest against my feet. Russo's grip on my throat eases just enough that I can swallow.

"Let the bitch go," Braiden says. "This isn't about her. It's never been about some slag."

"Easy for a man to say, when he cannot keep his wife in his bed." But the pistol eases away from my head. Russo no longer needs me as a shield, not with Braiden disarmed.

"You and me," Braiden says. "We don't need New York or Boston to tell us how to divide Philly. We'll work out our territory, once and for all. Just send the cunt away so we can talk like men."

"You hear that, *cara*?" Russo says. "This is what he thinks of you, the man you chose to marry."

Of course Braiden calls me that word. I came here in the middle of the night. I'm standing here naked, in the home of his enemy. I know what it looks like. I know what he believes.

There's no heat in Braiden's gaze. No anger. Nothing. He's a soulless computer, ticking through the options, adding up what he can get for his Fishtown Boys. He's buying and selling. Nothing more. Nothing less.

"Put the gun down," Braiden says.

"Easy for you to say." Russo shifts his weight behind me. "When I have a weapon, and you have none. In fact, I have a family, and you have none. I have a kingdom, and you—"

"Samantha," Braiden says, and his voice is different now. It's loud and it's sharp, and it rings with absolute authority. "Beg!"

I drop to my knees by reflex. That's the lesson Braiden taught me, the first night he spent in my home, when he ordered me to eat even though I couldn't stand the thought of food. It's the lesson I learned in the office he gave me, on the second floor of his home. It's the lesson I mastered in the greenhouse, in our bedroom, in the pool house I thought was my refuge.

He orders.

I obey.

And this time, I hit the floor so suddenly that Russo is taken by surprise. He's lost his shield, squandered his bargaining chip, the one thing he was so confident he owned that he dropped his guard.

And now that I'm on my knees, I can grab the shotgun. I've never fired a long gun before, much less an illegal sawed-off weapon that looks like it'll knock me flat with recoil. But my fingers know how to work a trigger, and I barely need to aim.

I clutch a single steadying breath and sweep up the shortened barrel. I jam it hard into Russo's crotch, digging deep into the soft pit of his balls. I slip my finger past the trigger guard and pull—slow and steady and absolutely certain.

The report is the loudest sound I've ever heard. It fills my head and stops my heart and folds my brain in cotton.

But I can smell—blood and shit and the gunpowder tang of sweet, burned plastic. And when I force my eyes open, I can see —shredded black pants and minced red muscles, streaks of bone and the pink-red-gray sheen of mutilated organs.

Somehow, Russo's still alive. His hands open and close over his chest like the claws of a blind crab, and I wonder if he dropped his gun before or after I shot him. Dark red bubbles spill over his lips, staining his chin.

I push myself to my feet and dig my bare toes into his side. I don't know if he squirms by reflex, or if he still has enough control over his body to try to get away. His movements, though, drown his lips in a sticky crimson river.

"That was for Eliza, you motherfucker," I say.

It was more than that. It was for my father, too, and my mother. And it was for me. But he's dead before I have time to say all that.

I stare at his mangled body like this is a horror movie. Like he might come back to life. Like he might torture the people I love, all over again.

"Samantha."

I hear my name from a distance, too far away for me to respond.

"*Mo chailín maith.*"

That's different. That's better than my name. That's a promise and a bond.

I look up to find Braiden on the far side of the desk. He has a gun in his hand, a pistol, and it takes me a lifetime to realize that he meant to use it. He ordered me to kneel so he could take out Russo. So he could save me.

A long, rolling shudder starts at the base of my spine, at the heart of my *segno*. It climbs my body like a time-lapse of ivy, weaving in and out of my ribs, my lungs, my heart. It ripples up my neck and across my head, and then it travels down my arms. My knees break, and I start to drop to the floor.

But Braiden's there. Braiden has me. His arms are around me and his body braces me and his lips touch the tangled scar above my temple. His hand is firm against the back of my head, and I'm safe and I'm warm and I'm his.

"Let's go," he says, when my legs are firm enough for me to stand.

I turn to the desk, to my neatly folded clothes. The thought of working buttons and zippers overwhelms me. I can't imagine finding my shoes and socks.

Braiden shrugs out of his rumpled jacket and settles it around my shoulders. The heat of his body melts into mine, and I fill my lungs with cedar and spice. He reaches past me and grabs my clothes.

I point to the papers. They're important. They're why I came here. They're what I have to do.

I see the flash of annoyance on his face. He wants to argue, because no documents are worth what we almost paid tonight. But they're here, and they're ours now, and he gathers them up with the rest of my things.

"Can you walk?" he asks.

I nod, not certain if I can. But he takes my hand, and he leads me to the study door, and I discover I'm not lying.

"Keys?" he asks. "For the Bentley?"

I had them. They're in the pocket of my jeans. I point, until he digs for them.

He leads me down the hall then, and through the kitchen, past two blasted bodies. Madden's car sits just outside the door, glinting in the light from the kitchen like it's been dipped in toxic waste.

Braiden takes a moment, propping me against the passenger door. He opens the driver's side, and he reaches into his pocket for a handkerchief.

I remember that night in a snowstorm, the night Russo murdered Eliza. Braiden had a handkerchief then, too. He gave it to me after I was sick in the snow.

Now, he uses the white square to wipe down the car—the steering wheel, the dashboard, the gearshift, the door. He wipes the shotgun as well and tosses it onto the driver's seat. He pulls a key fob from his pocket, cleans it, and leaves it next to the gun.

Then Braiden helps me around to the front of the house. He opens the Bentley's passenger door, and he guides me to the seat. He folds his jacket around me and buckles the belt across my lap.

I watch him cross to the driver's side, quick and confident, a panther returning from his kill. With a push of a button the car hums to life.

"Ardmore?" he asks before he starts down the short driveway to the gate.

I nod once. My voice sounds strange in my blasted ears, small and hollow and very far away. But I don't hesitate. I don't question. I only confirm my choice: "Home."

41

BRAIDEN

S amantha's steadier on her feet by the time we get to the new house. She's aware enough to pull my jacket around her before we get to Best's lads on the street. She unbuckles her own belt when I stop at our front door.

She follows me up the stairs like we've been doing this every night for the past six months. She glances at Aiofe's room, a faint smile ghosting her lips.

I lock the bedroom door as soon as we're inside. Samantha's clothes go on the dresser, along with the stack of papers she insisted we take. Nothing there is important, not with Russo dead.

First things first—my *piscín* needs a shower. She hasn't looked in a mirror; she doesn't know her face is spattered with Russo's blood, and her hair too. That means I'm a mess myself, because I couldn't keep my hands off her. I couldn't let her stand alone as the shock of what she did grabbed hold.

I make the water hot enough to fill the bathroom with

billows of steam. I slip my hands to her shoulders to help her out of my jacket, and she surprises the hell out of me by reaching for my belt. I let her work the buckle, and the button too, but I step back when she goes for the zipper, because the last thing she needs right now is a cock that won't mind its manners.

She feels it anyway, after I strip and take her into the shower. I'm at full mast when I stand behind her to wash her hair. And she can't ignore me when I soap her body. She'd have to be pure senseless not to know what's what as I take the spray in hand, as I rinse away all the suds.

"Braiden," she says, as I towel her dry, and I hear the question she's asking. But I try to be a gentleman as I take another towel to her hair. I find black silk boxers in the dresser and a plain white T-shirt, which should make her feel right at home. But when I hand them both to her, she shakes her head and says my name again.

"Not tonight, *piscín*. You've had enough."

"No," she says. "I haven't."

She walks to the dresser like she hasn't been gone for the past month. She opens the top drawer and reaches in like she owns the place. I watch confusion bloom on her face, unfolding like a flower in the sun. "It isn't..." But she's brave enough to meet my gaze. "Where's my collar?"

I could keep it from her. She's exhausted, physically and emotionally. It's not fair to lock that emerald around her neck, not right to make her do all the things I long for.

My job is to protect her. To set limits. To stop her when she's too headstrong, too determined, too stubborn to take care of herself.

That's why I make her eat breakfast.

That's why I make her wear skirts.

That's why I make her bend over a desk and take the spanking she needs, to understand that she's bold and fierce and wholly, unshakably strong.

But she executed her enemy tonight. She destroyed the man who killed her family. So my *piscín* is perfectly capable of making the decision to wear her collar.

I cross to my nightstand, where I've kept the box since the night she left. I place the black velvet on the bed. And then, before I can gather up the necklace, I reach for the second box I've kept hidden. The one I meant to give her the night we fought.

It looks small on my palm, like a soft, furry creature that could easily be stomped to death. I think about tossing it back it into the drawer forever.

But I want Samantha to have this. Even if she doesn't agree, even if this isn't the life she chooses, I want her to know I asked.

She's still standing by the dresser, exhaustion and confusion fighting over her face. Confusion wins as I cross to her and kneel.

Me. Captain of the Fishtown Boys. On my knees.

But I open the box, and then she understands.

The emerald isn't as large as the one in her collar, but it's been cut by an expert and set in platinum to match the necklace I gave her months ago. Light catches on the stone, kindling a fire deep inside its green heart.

"Samantha Mott," I say, because that's her name, until she says yes. "I made a mess of this once. And I don't deserve for you to give me the chance to make it right. But I'm asking you... I'm begging you... Will you do me the honor of being my wife? In the eyes of the law and standing before God, will you marry me?"

She didn't cry when a madman used her body as a shield or when she put down that blighter like a rabid dog. But now tears sparkle in her eyes.

"Yes," she whispers. "Yes, I will."

That's enough for me. I'm happy to call us married from this point forward. I don't need a priest or a clerk, any eejit with a collar or badge to make this official. But Samantha will, and I can live with that. I can wait till morning, when I'll drag her to a justice of the peace. I'll wait even longer, if she wants us back in church, if she needs to stand in front of everyone she knows.

Standing, I take the ring out of its box and slip it on her finger. I say the words I had engraved on the gold band I never had a right to give her: "*Is liomsa tú.*" *You are mine.*

And then I wait.

She's the one who was stripped naked. She's the one who was used like a Kevlar jacket. She's the one who shoved a shotgun into a man's bollocks and had the nerve to pull the trigger.

I won't risk pushing her too far. I won't take the chance of losing her again.

But she pulls me close for a kiss. It starts sweet, like we truly do stand in front of an altar, with priest and congregation looking on. But when she opens her lips, I accept the invitation. And when she presses her body close to mine, I figure she has her own plan for recovery, her own recipe for healing mind and body and soul.

My hands slip beneath the plain white cotton of the T-shirt she wears. Even though it's been weeks, my fingers remember the curve of her breasts perfectly, the weight of them, the jut of her nipples. I pinch hard, and I drink down her moan like a man dying of thirst.

My palm counts her ribs, then skims over the taut plane of her belly. She sucks in a breath like I've hurt her and I freeze, but only long enough for her to whisper, "No. Don't stop."

I know what I want to do to her, how I want to use her, but I still can't believe she's home. I need to know she wants it too, that she needs it as much as I do. I turn her around, her back to my front, and she lets me mold her to my body. I slip a hand inside the fly of the boxers she wears.

Her hips tilt like she's a jointed doll, pulling her higher on my body, letting her ride the massive hard-on she's raised on me.

I cup her, pulling her closer, pressing hard. My fingers find her hot, soft seam and then the slick honey that tells me she's mine.

"Braiden," she breathes as she takes my first finger. "Oh, God," she says when I give her the second. "Sweet Jesus," she breathes as I slip in a third.

She doesn't have words for the fourth, just stretches her mouth in a tight little O and I fuck her with my hand, driving hard, pressing her clit with the pulse point in my wrist.

I only slow my pace when she nears the cliff. I stretch out each stroke, lingering inside her, tapping my fingers against her deepest patch of nerves. She bites her lip. She holds her breath. She tightens her thighs and she waits, waits, waits.

But just before I give her what she longs for, just before I set her free, her fingers clamp around my wrist. She holds me fast, stilling my soaked fingers inside her. She whispers, her voice rough, like every syllable costs her a fortune: "Not yet. Not like this. I want to wear my collar."

42

SAMANTHA

∿

I'm greedy.

I don't want to come now and be done. I want everything Braiden can do to me, every way he can use me. I want to
know I have the strength—I have the power—to be the woman
he needs me to be.

The heel of his hand rocks against my clit as he slips his
fingers out of my drenched pussy, and the pressure is almost too
much. I nearly tip over, nearly lose control.

But I hold my breath. I bite my lip. I stiffen my legs and I
curl my toes and I shove back the wild flood of freedom.

He takes off my T-shirt like he's worshipping at an altar. He
slips his hands inside the waistband of my boxers, guiding them
over my hips, past my knees, down to the floor. I step free, and
I'm naked again, bare to the world.

Before I can think about it, before I can stumble over the
memory of Russo—what he made me do, what I did to him—
Braiden takes my collar out of its velvet case. He kisses the nape

of my neck and then he fastens the platinum clasp. He presses the emerald into the hollow of my throat with this thumb.

He stares at me fiercely, as if he can read everything that's written on the inside of my brain. *"Mo chailín maith,"* he breathes, and it doesn't matter that I stripped for Russo. It will never matter again, because now I'm naked for Braiden, and Braiden is my heart, and Braiden is the only man I've ever loved.

I nod once, and then he snaps his fingers in absolute command. "On the bed," he says. "On your back. Legs out. Arms out." And when I don't move quickly enough: "Now!"

I'm not surprised when he goes to the dresser or when he comes back to the bed with coils of cotton rope. He loops my left foot with an efficient knot, tying it off on the bedpost like he's a sailor. My right foot too, and I'm spread in front of him, bare, displayed, without even my hands to cover myself, because he ties my right wrist, and my left wrist too.

It's intoxicating to lie here. He has access to every inch of me. He can do whatever he wants with my body, and I'm powerless to stop him.

Except he says, "Red. Red if you want me to stop."

I shake my head, because I know I'll never say it.

But he grips my chin, tight enough to hurt. "This is important, *piscín*. This is how I keep you safe. Tell me you understand."

"I understand," I say, because that's what he needs. I only want to please him, only want to make him whole. I'll accept my safeword so he knows he can do everything he needs to do.

I expect him to go back to the dresser. To pick up a paddle or a cane. The riding crop. The cat o'nine tails, with its metal-studded leather straps. I know he's going to hurt me, and I want it, I *need* it, so much more than I'll ever be able to explain.

But he doesn't leave the bed. Instead, he shifts his weight and straddles me, framing my hips with his knee. He looms over me, his heavy cock jutting toward my face.

As I watch, he strokes himself. Long and steady and hard, his fingers work his cock. I whine because I want to touch him. I want to be the one pulling on that velvet. I want to take him between my lips, to feel him hit the back of my throat. I want him pumping hard between my legs, pinning me, filling me, making me his.

I beg. I plead. I stretch my arms, fighting to free my hands. But I don't control what happens. Not when I'm wearing my collar.

"Please," I say, when a drop of precum spatters on my belly.

"Please," I moan, when the tip of his cock flushes scarlet.

"Please," I beg, when he hisses as if his own hand scalds him on one last pull.

He explodes over me, pulse after pulse of hot, wet cum. He paints my belly. He soaks my breasts. He stripes my chin, my cheeks, my lips.

He's using me like I'm a centerfold he can rip out of a magazine, like I'm a video he can pause. I'm filthy. I'm raw. I'm gloriously, utterly alive.

And when he's done, when he's breathing like a stallion, when he's collapsed on top of me and seared those thick pearly ropes into my body, he whispers against the emerald on my throat, "You're mine."

"I am."

"No one else can do this to you."

"No one."

"I'm the only one who can have you."

"Only you."

He raises himself on his elbow, high enough to take my right nipple into his mouth. He sucks hard, lancing an arrow to my aching, needy clit. He works me with his tongue, and when I groan, he bites me.

I yelp, and he pushes off the bed. He slaps my flank with his open hand, igniting a whole new constellation of stars inside my head. I close my eyes to hold in the light, but I'm already trying to figure out how to get him to slap me again, how to set my world on fire.

If my eyes were open, he couldn't take me by surprise. If I were looking, I would know what he was planning. But I'm caught inside my head, lost in a forest of sensations, so I have no warning of what he plans.

My pussy fills with an impossible weight. Before I can protest, before I can scream, my entire body starts to shake, from the savaged place between my thighs to the hollow between my ears where my brain is supposed to be.

It's a vibrator. I understand that. But I've never taken anything that large before. I've never felt that constant roar of power. I'm splitting in two, ravaged into separate halves, speared and pinned and suspended.

He fucks me with the toy. He eases it out until it barely flirts with my slick lips. He waits for me to arch my back, to raise my hips from the bed, to plead with every muscle in my body. And then he slips that colossal thing back inside, deep, deep, deeper than I think I can stand. He changes the speed. He changes the angle. He plays me until I'm screaming, until I'm begging, until I'm sobbing and desperate for release.

He's taken all my words. He's taken all my power. He's in absolute control, and all I can do is offer myself up to the wild ride.

I don't come. He doesn't let me do that.

Over and over, he brings me to the edge. It's like he has a secret instruction manual for my body, like there's a hidden code inside me that only he can read. He knows when one more second will be too much. When one more breath will destroy me.

The fifth time he pulls away, I turn into an animal. I scream. I snarl. I bite the air, because he doesn't let me reach his cruel, cruel hands.

And there, in the heart of madness, in the grip of need, an evil creature telegraphs the most secret folds of my soul: *Of course he won't release me. I'm marked. I'm branded. I'm damaged beyond repair.*

Once the thought infects my brain, I'm trapped. My legs go limp. My arms sag in their bonds. My body is locked away from me, cut off completely. The only thing I can feel is Russo's tattoo at the base of my spine, gritty and greasy, like a scorched cinderblock dragging me to the bottom of the sea.

"*Piscín?*" Braiden asks, but I don't have words to reply.

"Samantha?" he says, but there's no point in responding to my name.

"Say it, *piscín*. Just say red." That's what he orders, but I don't care about colors, red or black or white, everything's the same.

I hear him at the nightstand. I feel him cut the rope. My hands are free. My feet are free. I can draw my knees together. I can hide. But there's no reason to bother. Not when I'm destroyed.

That's why he tied you up, the wicked thing says. *He needed you on your back. He needed to hide the mark.*

I want it to be wrong. I want Braiden to look at my back, to see my tattoo, to touch it and tell me he loves me. I almost find the strength to say that out loud. I almost tell him: "Turn me over. Fuck me from behind. Fuck me hard."

But I can't do it. Not when I'm wearing my collar.

I cannot, will not, *must not* top from below. I owe Braiden that. I owe myself that.

Even if that means I'm lost. I'm finished. We're done.

But Braiden is my Dom. He understands my mind. He understands my body. He knows me better than I know myself.

So without my saying a word, he folds his arm around my belly. He drags me to the edge of the bed. He swings me around, so my feet are on the floor and my chest is pressed into the mattress.

Once, I thought the most terrible thing about this position

was having my ass exposed. Now, I know there's something worse.

I look over my shoulder at Braiden looking down at me. At my back. At my tattoo.

I expect to see disgust. Revulsion. Hatred for the weakness I let destroy us.

But none of that is on his face. Instead, I see compassion. Understanding. Love.

He slips one foot between mine, tapping my ankles wide. He closes the distance between us, and his cock is hard again, hot, demanding. He grips my hips with both hands, tight, tight, tighter, until I feel the bruises bloom.

I catch my breath against the tendril of hope that uncurls in my belly. He fits his cock to my straining pussy lips and drives in just the way I need—hard enough to make me gasp, to push me onto my toes.

I'm still wet from his merciless teasing with the vibrator. I'm soaked. I'm ready.

He hisses as he pounds into me, muttering something between his teeth, and it takes me too long to figure out what he's saying: "*Is liomsa tú. Is liomsa tú. Is liomsa tú.*"

You are mine.

You are mine.

You are mine.

This is the man I need. This is the way I need to be fucked. This is all I desire in the world.

His fingers tear into my left hip, like he's going to carve me apart at the joint. His right hand shifts. It lands on the small of my back, covering up the black mark. He owns my *segno*. He takes it because it's a part of me, it's who I am, and who I'll always be.

"*Is liomsa tú!*" he shouts, and then he's coming hard, filling all the empty places inside me.

I come too then, but it's not like any orgasm I've ever had before. It's not in my pussy. It's not in my clit. It's in my entire body, in every nerve I possess. It's in my brain, and it's in my heart, and it's in the blackened flesh of my tattoo. It's everywhere, and it's everything, and I give myself over to it, and to Braiden, and to everything we are together.

I lose track of time and space and the limits of my body. Somewhere, sometime, somehow Braiden pulls me up beside him, against the pillows at the top of the bed. He works the clasp on my collar and sets the perfect emerald aside.

He wipes me clean with a warm, wet cloth, and he holds me close when I start to shiver. He puts a cool glass against my lips and helps me to drink. He places a square of chocolate on my tongue, and he covers me with a blanket while I let it dissolve.

He talks to me then. He tells me I'm his *piscín*. That I'm his good, good girl. He tells me that I'm strong and beautiful and brave and that he's never known another woman like me. He tells me he can't believe he almost lost me, and he'll never let me go again. As I drift off to sleep, he's saying he loves me, he loves me, he loves me.

43

SAMANTHA

I wake sometime after dawn. A mourning dove is outside the window; her soft flustered cooing sounds like a lullaby luring me back to sleep. Braiden lies beside me, his breaths deep and even.

When I stretch, my thighs ache. My arms are sore. I can count the tiny muscles between my ribs.

Staring at the ceiling, I think about an old joke—there's no such thing as bad sex or bad pizza. I don't know about the pizza part, but sex with Braiden is always fantastic. Plain vanilla fucking—the way we did it in the basement of the Hare construction site—is like making an argument in district court, having a judge rule from the bench in my favor. Wearing my collar, even when I top—or try to—is like winning in the court of appeals.

But surrendering to Braiden completely? Accepting the truth, that he's my Dom, and I'm his sub, that he's the one in complete control… The power he gives back to me, protecting both of us with my safeword... The trust I put in him... The absolute skill he has to draw out the strength in me...

All of that is like getting a unanimous decision from the Supreme Court.

Once I start thinking about being a lawyer, I can't forget the stack of papers we took from Russo last night. I can see the edge of the pile, on top of the dresser. Braiden left the documents there, next to my clothes, before we headed to the shower.

I need to know what's in those pages.

On the one hand, they don't matter at all. Russo is dead. I killed him. Those papers could include signed confessions to tax fraud, bribery, extortion, and murder, and Russo won't serve a single day in jail.

But on the other hand, I have to know what they say. I have to learn why Russo called me to his home in the middle of the night. I have to find out if I truly earned his trust after weeks of coddling him at the freeport.

Braiden stirs as I slip out of bed. His fingers trail over the warm sheets I've left behind, and his brow starts to furrow.

"Go back to sleep," I whisper, kissing his cheek.

He frowns for a moment, but then his breathing evens out.

Padding as quietly as I can, I retrieve the stack. While I'm at it, I pick up Braiden's T-shirt from the floor. I slip it over my head when I get to the armchair beside the window. Sitting, I start to read by the light that comes in at the side of the curtain.

The documents are damning.

I'm looking at shipping records, detailed invoices of goods going in and out of Russo's freeport gallery. There's a list of names and numbers, the payments he extorted from local businesses. I find another list, the bribes he paid to city and state officials.

But that's not all. When Braiden cleared off Russo's desk, he grabbed everything. There are half a dozen envelopes at the bottom of the stack.

I open the first one, and I bite back a gasp of surprise. It's filled with hundred-dollar bills.

There's a name scrawled in the upper left corner of the envelope: Mauricio. I look at the others. They all have names too: Bruno, Dario, Aurelio.

But the last one doesn't have a name. It's the heaviest one of all. I slip open the flap, and there's the money, wrapped inside a sheet of paper.

The page is covered by awkward printing, all caps. MIMI says the first line, and $1500. CIARAN $800. MIKEY $450.

This is the milk run. Braiden's milk run.

But it isn't. I've picked up something in the months I've spent working down the hall from Braiden. The amounts are too small, by at least a factor of ten.

And then I realize what I'm holding. Madden made the milk run. Madden paid his tithe. But he didn't pay his Captain. He wasn't working for the Fishtown Boys.

Madden paid his new boss. Madden paid Russo.

There's one last page, at the bottom of the pile. It's a partially completed tax return, as if Russo honestly believed I could assist him in declaring Madden's milk run tithe as income. Or maybe, somehow, in some twisted way, as a business deduction.

Was that Russo's intention? Was he finally ready to confide in me? To trust me as a lawyer?

Was he going to ask about Madden? About why his trained lap dog disappeared? Russo was never stupid. He had to suspect Braiden took out Madden, even if there was no proof.

Or maybe Russo only meant to taunt me. Show me one document in exchange for some perverted sexual favor, then hide away the others. Show me everything, then lock away the documents and say they never existed.

I need to preserve all this evidence now. I know too well how accidents happen, how a fire might destroy everything. The federal government will never use this information to prosecute Russo, but every page here is a goldmine for Braiden.

We'll make copies. Put some in the safe, here in the house. Put others in a bank vault. Secure them in Braiden's gallery at Diamond Freeport.

But for now, until we can do something official, I can take pictures.

I dig my phone out of the pocket of the jeans I wore last night. It's low on battery, but there's enough to run the camera.

But first, I thumb open my texts, drawn by the bright red badge that says I have a new message.

SONJA

Let's discuss.

She's attached a document with a terrifying title: Final Order.

Catching my lower lip between my teeth, I tap the screen.

There's a cover page: My name. The number of my proceeding. The date.

There's a summary finding: The Committee on Professional Ethics has unanimously concluded that Samantha Mott is unfit to practice law. Her license is hereby revoked, and she is ordered not to practice law within the state of Delaware.

There are five pages of reasoning. Five pages to sum up my entire legal career. Five pages to honor Gianni and Giorgia and the nameless man on the mountain.

It's not enough. It's more than I can bear.

I read through it again, every single word. Even though my stomach feels like it's being gnawed by bears, nothing in the opinion is a surprise. The panel despised what I did eight years ago. They were suspicious of my work at the freeport. They were revolted by my connections to organized crime.

Sonja's text invites me to discuss the opinion with her, but there's nothing to say. The decision is final. I cannot appeal.

It only takes a moment to forward the document to Trap Prince and Alix Key. I put their email addresses at the top of the form. Under *Subject*, I type: Resignation Letter. Under that, I type: Effectively immediately, I resign from my position as General Counsel for Diamond Freeport.

I think about adding more. I could say I'll talk to my successor, that I'll help transfer files and responsibility, but Trap and Alix know all that. I could tell them how much it means that they stood by me through the media storm, but they know that too. I could say I'm grateful that they've been there through everything that's happened with Braiden—from our wedding to our fights to…now—but there's no need.

So I read my single sentence one last time, and then I hit *Send*.

Almost as an afterthought, I forward the opinion to Teddy Newland. *FYI*, I type into the subject field. This time, it's easier to send the email.

The loss of a dream should be more dramatic. The end of an era should come with bright lights and trumpets. Instead, my legal career ends when I thumb off my phone and set it gently on top of Russo's papers.

Standing, I glance over to the bed. Braiden is watching me, propped up on one elbow, his hair mussed, his eyes sharp. He waits for me to speak, but when I stay silent he slips back the corner of the comforter.

"Come on, then," he says. "Come back to bed."

And I do.

44

BRAIDEN

"Ready?" I ask Samantha, staring hungrily at her reflection in the elevator door at Boston's Four Seasons hotel.

She's wearing the suit she wore when she took apart the Delaware Division of Revenue on my behalf. When we rode that elevator eight months ago, it took all my self-control not to wrap my fist around her hair and steal a kiss. I'm minding my manners this morning, too. The meeting we're about to attend is too important.

But I take a little comfort knowing I'm the only Captain in the Grand Irish Union who spent last night finding five new ways to make his Clan Chief come.

Because Samantha's my Clan Chief now.

I announced my decision to my Council in a meeting last week. Seamus, of course, already knew Madden was gone. The others understood as soon as I handed around Russo's papers. They agreed, to a man, that the Thornfield fire was too good a death for Madden. I didn't bother elaborating on the details of my brother's death.

Just as I didn't elaborate—much—on my logic for choosing Samantha to replace him. She's smart, I told them. She's fierce. I trust her with my life. I'm the Captain, I said, and she's my Clan Chief, and anyone who has a problem with that can leave the Fishtown Boys right now.

No one left.

"Let's go," Samantha says, meeting my gaze in the elevator door.

I laugh at the vicious determination on her face. She's perfect for her job.

When we get to the Four Seasons conference room, Samantha holds the door for me, an action that rasps against my lizard brain. But she's underscoring the fact that she's attending this meeting in an official capacity, as my second, and I can't argue with that.

I ignore surprised looks from the six other Captains and their Clan Chiefs. More than that, actually. The Boston family is still a holy show, no closer to settling their leadership this morning than they were the day after Kieran Ingram coughed himself to death.

Fiona's staking a claim because she's her father's only child. Aran Dowd says he's in charge because he was Ingram's Clan Chief for years. Keenan Rivers says the city's his because he paid his dues as Ingram's Warlord. All three of them crowd around one end of the table, their seconds shouldering each other for space.

Patrick Moran sits behind Fiona. Fair play to him—he phoned me first to say he'd be here. But he made it clear he wasn't asking my permission.

Precisely one hundred days have passed since Kieran Ingram coughed out his last order. By Grand Irish Union tradition, it's time to select our next General. We meet in Boston, because that's Union tradition too. Every Captain gets a vote—

Boston, New York, Philadelphia, Baltimore, Chicago, New Orleans, and San Francisco. Any one of us can stand for the job.

Fiona starts to call the meeting to order. Again, tradition. Boston leads.

I haven't seen Fiona since Madden worked her over, but she's at her best today. She's wearing a scarlet leather bustier and coal-black trousers. Those stilettos have to be four inches high. She could use one to take out Dowd and the other to take out Rivers, if she wanted to resolve her succession woes here and now. Her cheekbones are sharp enough to carve emeralds.

Rivers cuts her off like she's a child speaking out of turn. "Gentlemen——" he says.

Dowd interrupts: "As you know——"

Jockeying between the three of them goes on like that for a while, until Mickey Reardon pounds the table with his fist. "All right," he says in his broad Chicago accent. "We're all here for the same reason—to select our next General. So let's skip the greetings and the gossip and go straight to what matters. I'm stepping forward to serve."

To an outsider, what Reardon says might make sense. He's the oldest man at the table. Running Chicago, he's proven he can match wits with the Mafia, and with the Russian bratva that's made its way into the Windy City. His territory is huge, so he's got money to burn. The feds have been digging into his operations for years now, without finding enough to build a case.

But none of that keeps me from saying, "It's good of you to volunteer, Mickey. But I'm thinking I should be our next General instead."

Aran Dowd explodes beside Fiona. "You're the reason we're here today, boyo! You fucking murdered Kieran Ingram."

"I'll ignore that accusation," I say without raising my voice. "Seeing as you're under so much stress, Dowd. It must be exhausting, trying to convince your crew you're fit to lead them, instead of a girl."

"Ya knocked Ingram on his arse at Fenway!" That's from Rivers.

I study him coolly. "Has Boston ever chosen a Captain who's blind? I never set a finger on Ingram at the ballpark. Any man with one working eye will tell you the same."

He splutters, but it's too early in the day for us to come to blows. I surprise a tiny smile on Fiona's lips, before she lowers her eyes to her crimson fingernails. Patrick gives me one slow nod, as if he's keeping score in a high-stakes game of darts.

Truth be told, I could have kicked the shite out of Ingram in the middle of Boston Common, and half the men here would line up to shake my hand. Ingram made sure to take his tithe on legitimate income—whores, gambling, waste management contracts, and the lot. But all too often, he demanded a taste where he didn't have a right. He regularly hit me up for profits from Kelly Construction, and once the word was out about Boyle's green energy venture, Ingram developed a healthy appetite for that cash cow.

Plain and simple, the old man got greedy. So no one at this table is shedding too many tears that he's gone. Including, I suspect, Fiona, Dowd, and Rivers.

Reardon clears his throat, lumbering to his feet as he wrests back control of the meeting. "I hardly need to remind you, *dearthháireacha*, what I bring to the Union."

So now we're all his brothers. He spreads his meaty hands wide on the table, leaning forward like he's sharing the best way to butcher a hog. Because he's the most senior man present, and because he's charmed by the sound of his own voice, he proceeds to tell us—at near interminable length—why we should vote for him.

He outlines every deal he's made in the past twenty years. He catalogs every elected official he's got goods on in the state of Illinois. He points out the size of his territory, the number of small towns in the upper Midwest that already pay him tribute.

It takes him more than an hour to go over all the ways he'll serve us. I keep one hand on my wallet the entire time he talks because I'll be paying through the nose if he gets the Union's vote.

In the end, he stops just short of saying Jesus, Mary, and all the saints would vote for him, if we just gave them half a chance. When he finally takes his seat, his Clan Chief leans forward to whisper congratulations in his ear, nodding so hard I think he might concuss himself.

Fiona—God bless her—visibly swallows a yawn. "Braiden?" she asks.

I dive in before Rivers and Dowd start mewling that she has no right to run the meeting. "I've shared the Jameson with all of you over the years," I say to the table. "You know I've run a tight ship since I took over from my da. I've always paid heed to the Union, playing by its rules even when that's cost me dosh. I'll take a stand for the GIU against anyone who means us harm —Mafia or bratva, yakuza or the law. By now, you all know what happened to Antonio Russo. And I suspect you've heard what I did to my own brother when he turned traitor on us all. I respect the Union. I respect you. And I'll be your next General."

I'm aware of Samantha behind me, every molecule of my body tuned in to our unique frequency. Of course I know she's the one who executed Russo, and I'm not afraid to tell the truth to anyone who asks. But she and I agreed that it made *strategic sense* not to complicate the matter for the Union. Samantha can accept their believing I'm the one who blasted his bollocks through his brain.

Fiona realizes I've finished my pitch before anyone else does. "All right, then, Captains of the Grand Irish Union."

But before she can call a vote, Rivers interrupts. "Anyone else putting his hat in the ring?" He glares up and down the table, as if it's a personal insult that no one else is going for the title.

Fiona repeats herself, "All right, then, Captains of the Grand Irish Union." Before Dowd can figure out a reason to cut in, she says, "Following our tradition, Boston votes first. Then, we'll proceed in increasing order of seniority." Riding the wave of her own momentum, she announces, "Boston votes for Kelly."

Dowd and Rivers' protests can probably be heard all the way over in Dublin. Rivers is foolish enough to set his paw on Fiona's shoulder. That gets Patrick involved, which puts the other Boston seconds on their feet. Even though no one's carrying visible weapons, I've seen Patrick kill men with his bare hands, and it looks like he's ready to add to his total.

I'd let Fiona get out of the fix herself, but I have a point of my own to make. I'm fairly sure I'll regret the immediate fallout, but I'm playing a somewhat longer game. I wish I had the option of talking to Samantha, of seeing if she sees things the way I do. But ultimately, a Captain needs to take his own risks.

"Shut it." I don't try to make myself louder than the Boston scrum. Instead, I cut beneath the chaos—sharp enough and cold enough that every one of them feels the land collapse beneath his feet.

The sudden silence vibrates like a tuning fork.

"Today isn't about Boston," I say. "We aren't here to decide which of you has the better claim. That's a question for your own clan to debate, for your own men to manage. But none of us leaves this room until we've decided on a General. So each of you state your choice. Boston's vote is the majority, between the three of you."

I look around the table, measuring reactions. I hear Samantha behind me, tension tightening her breath. She's smart enough, though, to stay quiet. "Reardon?" I ask the Chicago boss. "Fair enough for you?"

He's done his own calculating. "Fair enough," he agrees with a slick smile that turns my stomach. And then, because he wants to look like the solution is his own idea, he says, "Dowd? Rivers? How do you vote?"

Dowd forgets to tailor his glare for me. He stares down the entire table before he says, "Reardon."

That puts Rivers in a bind. He doesn't want to agree with Dowd on anything. But as much as he hates his rival, he hates me more. Plus, he gets the added thrill of tweaking Fiona. "I vote for Reardon too."

Fiona may be fighting for her political life, but she's no idiot. She takes back control as if this had been her plan all along. "Boston votes for Reardon, then."

Her eyes are flint as she stares at me. I think of all the jousting we did when she was down in Philadelphia, all the ways she fought to show her strength. I'm glad Patrick stays standing behind her, even after all the others take their seats.

San Francisco votes next: Reardon. I'm losing, two to nothing.

New Orleans votes for me. I'll have to take Samantha to the Crescent City sometime. We can enjoy some blues and pay our respects to the clan. The vote sits at two to one.

Reardon's next. Three to one.

Baltimore hesitates. On the one hand, Reardon will reward him if he's the vote to end the battle. On the other hand, I've always played fair with my southern neighbor. When I've expanded territory for my Irish butter game, I've made a point of pushing west from Philadelphia, or north into New Jersey. I've left Baltimore room to grow.

Now, I watch his lips purse, ready for the *R* in Reardon. But in the end, he sinks back in his chair, saying, "Kelly."

That makes it three to two, and I vote for myself. Three to three.

There's one vote left: New York. Connor Boyle has watched the proceedings silently, his face settled in its usual unreadable calm. Boyle has seen me at dozens of Diamond Ring meetings. We've raced each other, bet against each other, and drunk beside each other. He saved the Book of Skreen from Russo. He sent Rider out to fight on my side at Fenway.

But Boyle's relatively new to running New York. He made his billions through green energy, not by managing a mob family. He's junior to everyone at this table except for the Boston scavengers.

The safe thing is for Boyle to vote for Reardon. Side with the senior man. Earn respect. Consolidate his own position for a future run at the title, once he's spent a few years managing his own clan.

Boyle's shoulders are as broad as the Brooklyn Bridge. He doesn't give a hint that he feels the weight of every eye in this room. His narrowed eyes look gold as he studies Reardon. They turn green when he looks at me.

Other men might give a speech. They might make it clear they're giving a gift, might hint at what they want in return. They might draw things out, reveling in their power over some of the most powerful criminal overlords in the country.

Boyle says, "I vote for Kelly."

Reardon takes his loss like a man. He shakes his head like we're all making the biggest mistake of our lives, and he sighs as if he's trying to knock Boyle over with the power of his breath alone. But he gets up from his seat and walks around the table to me. He holds out his hand, and we shake. And then he offers a conceding grip to Samantha, recognizing my Clan Chief as well.

I fetch the bottle we've all been ignoring on its table by the door, a small-batch Jameson that was twenty-two years old when Ingram was sworn in as General. I pour for all of them—Captains and Clan Chiefs alike—and Samantha carries the glasses around.

There'll be more tonight, centuries-old traditions that we'll honor. All the captains here will come to my suite upstairs. They'll bind their oaths with blood and fire. We'll all drink again, with a new bottle I'll track down this afternoon, one that will be held over for whatever man replaces me, may that be decades down the road.

I raise my glass to all of them, but I take extra care to catch Boyle's gaze. He looks back, as still as ever, and I wonder how I'll repay my debt.

For now, though, my Clan Chief leads the toast. Samantha's voice is steady and strong as she proclaims, "To Braiden Kelly, General of the Grand Irish Union!"

And with one voice, they all respond: "To Kelly!"

45

SAMANTHA

~

I hurry through the small cemetery behind the church of Santa Caterina, letting memory guide my feet. I haven't been in this Philadelphia graveyard for years, not since the funeral for my Zia Sara.

I was bitter then. Angry. I resented needing to upset my schedule, just so I could stand by a gaping hole and squeeze out a single blood-hot tear for Sara Canna.

Then, the only thing I could focus on was how she made me feel like an imposition. She barely tolerated my sitting at her table. She despised my sleeping under her roof. On her best days, she ignored me. On her worst, she told me I was stupid, greedy, ugly. She never passed up a chance to remind me that I should be grateful she took me in.

Now, I understand my poor aunt a little more. Zia Sara had already lost her husband to cancer. Then she lost her brother—my father—to Antonio Russo's mad plans. By granting me refuge, Zia Sara exposed herself to her don's wrath. Every time she looked at me, she saw danger to her own children.

Now, I find them all, not far from the stone wall that surrounds the cemetery. Zio Matteo. Zia Sara. Gianni. Giorgia.

My shudder is pure reflex when I see the date on those last two tombstones. That Night. A nightmare I've lived for so long, it's engraved on my blood.

I've brought flowers—five bouquets stolen from the stash for tomorrow. Aiofe had a hand in choosing all the flowers, insisting on tulips and peonies and chrysanthemums. I put one bunch on my uncle's grave and another on my aunt's.

I take more time placing the flowers on my cousins' graves. I feel like I should kneel between them. Like I should bow my head. But in the end, I stand by their feet and talk to them, holding the last bouquet in both hands as I try to keep my voice steady.

"I'm sorry," I say. "You both deserved so much more. You should have had time to grow up. To find jobs. Friends. Lovers. You should have had the chance to leave Philadelphia, if that's what you wanted. Or to stay. You should have been able to choose."

It's been almost twelve years since That Night. God, we were all so young.

"I don't know how you'd feel about my new job. If Braiden was Mafia, he'd make me consigliere. Put my law degree to use, defending him and all his clan. But the Fishtown Boys don't have that. At least, not yet. They call me their Clan Chief. Can you believe it?"

What would Gianni be doing now? Would he be trading stocks on Wall Street, the way he always said he would? Would Giorgia be putting the finishing touches on her first Fashion Week collection in New York?

"I've taken my own money," I tell them. "Savings, from what I earned at the freeport. I've hired Harry Asher, a private investigator. I've asked him to track down everything he can about the man on the mountain. It won't be easy, not after all this time. And there was never much to go on in the first place. But if anyone can find out who he was, Harry can."

I don't know what I'll do once Harry gives me a name, an address, a sketch of the man's life before he lost everything. If he has family, I'll try to make amends. If he was alone in the world, I'll try to support something that was important to him. That's all I can do—try.

I want to say more, but I'm running out of time. I have an appointment in downtown Philadelphia at three, and I still have one more stop before then.

Clutching my last bouquet, I kiss my fingertips and reach out, first to Gianni, then to Giorgia. "I love you," I say to my cousins. "Goodbye."

It's harder to turn away than I expected it to be. It's even more difficult to walk toward the oldest part of the cemetery. The gravestones are more elaborate here. There are carved angels and, over one site, an obelisk.

I make my way to a mausoleum in the shadows of the church. It looks like a miniature Roman temple made out of white marble, lined with columns. A name is carved over the door: Russo.

Huge floral displays sag beside the door and on the steps— crosses and hearts and one gaudy blanket shaped like a horseshoe. The flowers are dried out. Ribbons are bleached by the sun. Antonio Russo is already being forgotten.

I can't enter the locked mausoleum. I hesitate, not wanting to leave my flowers on the steps. I don't want anyone to see them and misunderstand.

But, in the end, it's more important that I kneel and leave them. I'll know the truth. That's what matters

"Eliza," I say, rising from my knees.

But I don't know what to say after that. *I'm sorry…* But her fate was set by others. *I miss you…* But wherever she is, she already knows that.

I forgive you, I think. But that's not right either. Eliza never meant to hurt me when she started the affair that led to her death. She wasn't thinking of me at all when Antonio Russo shoved a gun inside her body and pulled the trigger. She probably believed he'd never follow through on his threat; he'd never seek me out, never try to force me to take her place as his wife.

We were so young. So foolish. We never imagined evil like Antonio Russo existed. We never dreamed of what he could do.

So, in the end, I don't say anything. I bow my head, and I think about all the good times I shared with my cousin. All the times we laughed.

And then, I really do have to leave. I hesitate at the cemetery gates, looking back at my family one last time. Then I turn toward the street, automatically scanning for paparazzi.

But once news of my disbarment became public, the press finally lost all interest in me. I'd almost be insulted, if I wasn't so deeply grateful.

I hurry to the nearby parking lot. Liam Murphy waits there, standing beside the Bentley. He hurries to open my door as I approach, and I pick up my pace to meet him.

I can't be late to my appointment.

46

BRAIDEN

F airfax holds up three neckties for my approval. I choose the darkest green, so deep it almost looks black. He drapes it around my neck and starts to tie the knot, but his phone buzzes in his pocket.

After he reads the text, his sigh is more indulgence than exasperation. "Aiofe can't find her tights," he says.

"Go. I can manage this on my own."

The look he gives me drips with doubt, but he heads for the door. Pausing on the threshold, though, he looks back. "Your father would be proud of you," he says.

"Thank you," I say, knowing that's Fairfax's most effusive praise. "Now, go. The last thing we want is to keep the archbishop waiting because one little girl can't find her tights."

The door is almost closed when I hear Fairfax speaking to someone in the hallway. His voice is hushed, but I can't miss the urgency in his tone. Before alarm can spike my blood,

Samantha slips into the room, closing the door behind her. She turns the small button in the knob, locking us in.

I suspect my grin is somewhat ridiculous as I take a step forward. "You know it's bad luck for the groom to see the wedding dress before the ceremony."

"What? This old thing?" Samantha grins as I study her with blatant approval.

I offered to fly in any designer she wanted in the world. I said we could postpone the ceremony if her dress required hand-made lace and individually stitched seed pearls. I told her she could have a train as long as the church's nave.

But she insisted she didn't want a traditional white wedding gown. She had one for our first wedding, and we both know how that ended up. So Samantha's wearing an outfit she already owned.

The hem of the skirt brushes the floor. It's made out of yards and yards of black silk, covered with gigantic flowers. Fairfax is the floral expert in my household, but I recognize tulips. All the blossoms are in shades of gold and pink and purple, and they're gathered together by a wide purple belt. Like all of Samantha's favorite skirts, this one has pockets.

Her top is all black. The front is demure enough to satisfy the archbishop. But the sleeves and back might have him rethinking his priestly vows—they're made out of a fabric so sheer Samantha looks naked.

It's the outfit she wore to a party at Thornfield, back when she thought she had to compete with Fiona for my attention. Madden cornered her in those clothes. She almost left me, wearing that kit.

But she decided to stay.

"You're gorgeous," I tell her. And I'm not just talking about the sweep of her hair in some complicated knot, or the cosmetics that make her eyes look huge, or the shine of her lips. Everything about her is beautiful—her body and her brains and her bravery.

I love that I can make her blush with two simple words. I love that her laugh snags something deep inside my chest. I love that I have a wedding gift for her, something I meant to give her after the ceremony, but now is even better.

"Close your eyes," I say.

I watch her automatic refusal, her instinct to do what she wants, when she wants. And I watch her shut down that response. A patient smile quirks her lips, and she closes her eyes.

The box is on a chair, covered by the garment bag that held my tuxedo. I haven't wrapped it. Haven't shifted the contents from the bare-bones container my man delivered a few nights back.

I heft it onto the table, watching a line appear between Samantha's eyebrows as she processes the sound. She wants to peek. She wants to be in charge. But she waits until I say, "Go on, then. You can look."

The box is made of heavy corrugated cardboard. It's the width of a sheet of printer paper, the length of a legal-size one, the depth of a standard file folder. It's fitted with a lid, and a label covers one end: EVIDENCE. SIGN LOG BEFORE REMOVING.

No one signed the log. Not my man, who liberated the box from lock-up. Not the file clerk who accepted an especially heavy envelope to look the other way.

"Is that—" Samantha starts, her voice breaking with disbelief.

I don't answer. I only gesture for her to remove the lid.

There's not a lot to show for eleven years of investigation. Most of that time, though, was spent ignoring three deaths on a mountaintop, overlooking a crooked sheriff, forgetting a young woman's greatest mistake.

Philadelphia's Detective Tarrant came up with photographs of the crime scene. There are interviews with a handful of witnesses. Attempts to track down next of kin for a long-buried John Doe.

Samantha looks up from the debris, barely shaking her head from side to side. "I—" she starts. "I can't believe you—" And then, after swallowing hard: "Thank you."

I nod, because it's as much a gift to me as it is to her—a guarantee that no prosecutor will ever come after her for the horrible choice she made that night.

"But..." she says, staring at her clasped fingers as she trails off.

I have to touch her then, because she's sad, and because she's beautiful, and because she's mine. My finger curls beneath her chin, forcing her to look up at me. "But what?"

"Detective Tarrant..." she finally says. I can tell how much she hates what she's thinking. "He wouldn't just keep physical notes. He has electronic files that can be used against me. He has computer records."

"Had."

"Had?"

"He *had* electronic files. He *had* computer records."

Understanding widens her eyes. "You paid to delete them too? But there have to be backups, offsite storage, cloud—"

"You think Cole Wolf didn't think of all that when he volunteered to go fishing?"

"Cole..." She trails off, and I watch her test half a dozen questions about her former freeport client. She settles on the most surprising news I've given her about the hacker genius. "He *volunteered?*"

"When I told him it was a wedding present."

Her eyes are shiny, but she nods. Finally, she says, "It's a lovely gift."

"For the bride who has everything." She smiles at that, so I figure it's safe to go on. She's no longer in danger of ruining her makeup. "No prosecutor can build a case against you now. Everything that happened that night—you can put it behind you forever. We'll burn this all tonight. At home."

"Thank you," she says. "I..." And then she meets my gaze. I

capture a glimpse of something soft in her expression, something shy, but she settles on a wicked grin. "I have a gift for you too."

She shouldn't be giving me gifts. But I step back and wait to see what she has in mind.

"The last time I wore this skirt," she says. "I left some business unfinished."

That gives me a notion where she's going with this. Clever *piscín*. I settle my hands on my hips. "You did, did you?"

"I tried my hand at poetry, but I didn't quite match the high quality of rhyming from you and the others."

"It's a skill we Irish have," I boast, not quite hiding a grin.

"I'm not good at making things up on the spot, but with a chance to think a bit... I think you might like what I've come up with."

"Let's hear it," I say.

She squares her shoulders and raises her chin, the very image of pride. And then she recites:

> *"There was a young lawyer in Philly,*
> *Who fell for a man, willy-nilly.*
> *Her one need was blunt—*
> *His cock in her cunt,*
> *And that's why she screamed out so shrilly."*

I understand what it costs her to revisit that night, when she embarrassed herself in front of me. In front of Fiona. In front of all the Fishtown Boys.

And I know what is takes for her to use the word—cunt. She's always hated it. Always found it ugly.

It's the word I used against her, the sharpest weapon I could throw. But she's claiming it now. Making it hers. That's the same thing she's done with the Fishtown Boys, merging her life with mine.

So I don't laugh, even though I think she means me to.

Instead, I hold her gaze as if we're already upstairs, already standing in front of the altar. I say, "Not bad, for a first offense."

"Oh there's more," she assures me.

"Go on then."

She swallows hard and strikes another pose.

> *"Samantha's learned all of the rules now,*
> *End-of-day, wear a skirt, not her black trou.*
> *Her one need's still blunt,*
> *Your cock in her cunt,*
> *Till she loses her words, all but 'Wow, wow.'"*

I fight the curl of my lips. "I'm not sure about that last line. And the middle's a little repetitious, after your first effort."

"More personal, though. *Your* instead of *His.*"

"I noticed that," I say gravely.

She asks, "Want to hear one more?"

"Of course."

She stares directly in my eyes.

> *"After wife number one and your harsh rule,*
> *I moved from our room to the house-pool.*
> *My one need is blunt,*
> *Your cock in my cunt.*
> *Right now. Make me put on my sub jewel."*

"House-pool?" I ask.

"Poetic license."

"I sense a certain theme in your writing."

"Thank God," she says.

I step forward and settle my thumb against the seam of her lips. "You want me to add more rules to your life. Harsh ones."

She bites me.

I pull her close, doing my best not to ruin her hair. Her lips open under mine, and she's laughing as our tongues meet. She slips her hands under my jacket, easing her palms under my suspenders.

But I wasn't joking about rules—not entirely. She's my sub. I'm her Dom. I'm the one in charge, even here, even today, in these last few minutes before our wedding.

I force her arms to her sides and turn her around. Shoving her against the wooden table in the corner, I snap out an order: "Hands flat."

She obeys so quickly I'm forced to smother a laugh. I cover the sound of my smirk by sliding down my zipper. "Feet spread," I tell her, nudging her ankles apart.

Her fingers stiffen on the table. She starts to say something, but she stops. From the set of her jaw it was an objection, a clarification, a rule she wanted to superimpose over mine. But she swallowed it, remembering that I'm in charge.

She deserves a reward for that.

It takes both hands for me to gather her skirt, but I can hold the yards of fabric against her back with just one fist. Looking down between us, I realize she isn't wearing panties.

"In a church?" I ask, running my palm over her bare arse. "Aren't you afraid of attracting lightning bolts?"

She trembles as I slip a finger inside her. She's slick. Soaked. Looking over her shoulder at me, she says, "I won't tell if you don't."

I add another finger, and she gasps. "What do you want, *piscín?*"

She answers without hesitation. "Your cock in my cunt."

"Such a mouth on you," I tease, giving her another finger.

She moans, clenching tight around my hand.

"What do you need, *piscín?*"

Another immediate reply: "Your cock in my cunt."

I curl my fingers inside her. "I could make you come right now. Right here. Like this."

She closes her eyes. Bites her lip. But she doesn't tell me what to do.

I see what it costs her. I *feel* her determination in every muscle of her body. She wants to be fucked, but she knows not to ask.

So I tell her: "Or I can give you my cock in your cunt."

I shift the fabric of her skirt so I have room to maneuver. I pull my hand out of her soft, wet heat. I tease her opening with my cock, just enough to give her warning, and then I drive in, hard and fast and deep.

She cries out at the weight of me.

No. She cries out in pain.

I look down at the place where we're joined. Her skirt is bunched to the side. I'm staring at the gauze of her top, at the barely-there fabric ghosting across her back.

I'm ready to see the tattoo at the base of her spine. I'll never say I love it. But I love *her*, and Russo's ink is part of her. It will always be with us.

Except I'm wrong.

The tattoo is gone.

But that's not right either.

The tattoo has been *transformed*.

The medusa head in the center of her mark has been shaped into an intricate Celtic knot, each snake woven into the artwork. The bent legs have turned into shamrocks, three-leaf flowers arching around the knot. The outlines are in black, but the lines are filled with bright green ink.

"Samantha," I breathe.

I saw her back four nights ago, when we were at the Four Seasons for the Grand Irish Union. She hadn't covered up the old work then.

"Don't stop," she begs.

"I don't want to hurt you."

"You won't."

That's a lie. We both know it is.

But she's my sub. And she's armed with her safeword. And if she's giving me this gift, I'm not about to throw it away.

So I close my hands around her hips. I shift my weight, easing part-way out of her body. And then I give her what she asked for, what she needs, what we both need, until we're panting and grunting and groaning together, eyes closed, bodies merged, my cock in her cunt, exactly the way my queen deserves.

47

SAMANTHA

I t was never my plan to keep an archbishop waiting.

Better, though, for him to believe he's dealing with a nervous bride than that he discover the truth of how I've spent the past hour.

Re-doing my hair.

Fixing my lipstick.

Putting on panties.

Finally, Braiden and I stand in front of the altar at St. Columba's, just as we did eight months ago. The Fishtown Boys are here, and this time they've brought their wives and children. Trap and Alix sit in pews tonight, instead of being part of the ceremony. My assistant, Mary Rivers, and my roommates from Dover are here—Mary with a huge smile on her face.

Aiofe waits on the dais, my one attendant. When I come to stand beside her, holding a simple bouquet of tulips, she snuggles close and whispers, "You're so pretty!"

Fairfax stands beside Braiden. His bright eyes look out at the congregation, and I know he's reviewing how many bottles of champagne are on ice, how much food is ready at the reception.

Archbishop Morgan Killebrew is imposing in his full regalia. His voice fills the church in a way poor Father Brennan never could. The archbishop's stern certainty would be terrifying, under any other circumstances.

But he's here tonight so no one can ever question the validity of the vows Braiden and I are about to exchange. There's no possibility that the archbishop has been defrocked, that he's not a legal celebrant in the eyes of the church.

I can't imagine what donations Braiden made to bring the archbishop here tonight. More than replacing the roof at St. Columba's, I'm certain. More than he spent on obtaining the evidence from That Night. But he can afford it. He's General of the Grand Irish Union.

The ceremony moves faster than I remember from the first time. Everyone stands when they're supposed to, sits when they should, kneels when they must. Aiofe keeps her grip on my bouquet. Fairfax produces the rings at the right time.

And before I think it's possible, Archbishop Killebrew tells Braiden he can kiss the bride. I remember the first time we did this—the moment I realized I was marrying a man I'd never kissed before.

I've done so much more than kiss Braiden now. Yes, we've slept together. And we've fought together. And we've found the strength to reconcile, to find each other again, forever.

We've *lived* together. And now we'll rule over the Fishtown Boys together—forever.

This time, Braiden's kiss is sweet. This time, the archbishop tells us to go forth as man and wife. This time, Russo isn't here —there are no squawking phones, no alarms screaming out disaster.

This time Braiden takes my hand and we walk down the aisle, Aiofe and Fairfax following behind as all our family and friends smile and watch.

This time everything is perfect.

~

Thank you for reading *Irish Reign*!

With Samantha and Braiden's story all wrapped up, the next Diamond Ring dark romance is the true love story of Fiona Ingram and Patrick Moran.

Buy *Her Irish Savage* Now!
https://alixkey.com/PB7US

BONUS SCENE

∾

Samantha barely gave you a glimpse of the first time she and Braiden made love in their new Ardmore home. Want all the super-spicy details?

Get your bonus scene by typing:

https://alixkey.com/Bonus6

into your phone or computer browser.

MORE DIAMOND RING

∾

Or maybe you'd like to learn more about foul-mouthed Trap Prince, and how he came to create the Diamond Ring? (And, um, you're curious about my super-spicy, very dark, Cinderella-retelling romance with Trap, now available in a completed series!) Start the Kidnapped Series by typing:

https://alixkey.com/dring0

into your phone or computer browser.

∾

One last thing: If you want an absolutely free full-length, totally stand-alone Diamond Ring novel, featuring a gender-switch Jack and the Beanstalk retelling and starring Irish mobster Connor Boyle, I've got you covered! Just type:

https://alixkey.com/sins

into your phone or computer browser.

THANK YOU

I can't thank you enough for choosing *Irish Reign* from among all the dark Mafia romances out there! Without readers like you, I would never have my writing career.

You may not realize it, but *you* can be my hero. Study after study shows that the number one reason a person reads a book is because that book was recommended by a friend.

So will you tell one friend about *Irish Reign*?

Of course, if you're dead-set on reviewing my book on Amazon and Goodreads, I won't complain! Honest reviews are hugely helpful because many advertisers require me to have a certain number of reviews before I can buy ads.

Leave a review on Amazon
Leave a review on Goodreads

Whatever you do, don't be a stranger! I look forward to hearing from you soon!

www.alixkey.com
alix@alixkey.com

ABOUT THE AUTHOR

Alix Key was born in Potomac, Maryland, where she grew up making her twin brother and all her dolls act out her favorite fairytales. When an all-grown-up Alix discovered that very real dangers lurk in the woods, she figured out how to rescue herself. She now lives outside Dover, Delaware with her own Prince Charming. When not writing dark romance, Alix serves as the Chief Operations Officer of Diamond Freeport.

You can learn more about Alix at her website, www.alixkey.com.